# GRAYFOX
## MICHAEL PHILLIPS

# Books by the Phillips/Pella Writing Team

## The Journals of Corrie Belle Hollister

*My Father's World*
*Daughter of Grace*
*On the Trail of the Truth*
*A Place in the Sun*
*Sea to Shining Sea*
*Into the Long Dark Night*
*Land of the Brave and the Free*

*Grayfox*

## The Stonewycke Trilogy

*The Heather Hills of Stonewycke*
*Flight from Stonewycke*
*Lady of Stonewycke*

## The Stonewycke Legacy

*Stranger at Stonewycke*
*Shadows over Stonewycke*
*Treasure of Stonewycke*

## The Highland Collection

*Jamie MacLeod: Highland Lass*
*Robbie Taggart: Highland Sailor*

## The Russians

*The Crown and the Crucible*
*A House Divided*
*Travail and Triumph*
*Heirs of the Motherland*

A COMPANION READER TO
THE JOURNALS OF CORRIE BELLE HOLLISTER

# GRAYFOX

## MICHAEL PHILLIPS

BETHANY HOUSE PUBLISHERS
MINNEAPOLIS, MINNESOTA 55438

Published by Bethany House Publishers
A Ministry of Bethany Fellowship, Inc.
11300 Hampshire Avenue South
Minneapolis, Minnesota 55438

Printed in the United States of America

**Library of Congress Cataloging-in-Publication Data**

Phillips, Michael R., 1946–
   Grayfox / Michael Phillips.
      p.  cm.

   1. Frontier and pioneer life—West (U.S.)—Fiction.  I. Title
PS3566.H492G73   1993
813'.54—dc20                                 93–28750
ISBN 1–55661–368–7                                  CIP

To boys and men everywhere,
who are seeking the maturity of their own
personhood and being.

And to the women who will love and admire them for their
depth of character.

To *my* young men who are well-advanced on the
road to their manhood, Gregory, Patrick, and Robin Phillips.

It is my prayer that
you will each meet your own Hawks
as you progress along life's trail,
that you will learn to see the depths
of your Father's mystery and being and revelation,
and that you will, like Zack, discover character and strength
and the meaning of life within yourself,
and thus will come to know the depths of true manhood.

# ACKNOWLEDGMENTS

The following books were helpful in researching the history of the Paiute Indians and the 1860–61 period in the western portion of the Utah territory. I would like to acknowledge my appreciation for these authors and their research:

Gae Whitney Canfield, *Sarah Winnemucca of the Northern Paiutes* (Norman, Ok.: Univ. of Oklahoma Press, 1983).

Marion E. Gridley, *American Indian Women* (New York: Hawthorn Books, 1974).

Ferol Egan, *Sand in a Whirlwind, The Paiute Indian War of 1860* (New York: Doubleday, 1972).

Margaret M. Wheat, *Survival Arts of the Primitive Paiutes* (Reno, Nev.: Univ. of Nevada Press, 1967).

# CONTENTS

# A NOTE TO READERS

The story of *Grayfox* stands alone and may be read and enjoyed by itself. However, you will undoubtedly enjoy it more if you read it in conjunction with its companion volumes, each told by Zack's sister, Corrie, in the JOURNALS OF CORRIE BELLE HOLLISTER series. How Zack and his brother and sisters came to California is told in the book, *My Father's World*. The rest of the books in the series are listed at the end of *Grayfox*.

# PROLOGUE

Before my sister, Corrie Hollister, left for the East—that was in April of '63—she hounded me near every dad-burned day to get to writing down about the eight months I spent up in the mountains and deserts of Nevada with Hawk Trumbull.

"I ain't no writer, Corrie," I must've told her sixteen dozens of times.

"That doesn't matter, Zack," she told me back just as many. "You write it down, and I'll fix it up for you so folks can read it."

(She did help fix it up too, but I told her I wanted to write down this personal part all by myself. That's why it probably sounds a heap different than the rest.)

"Who'd wanta read it?" I asked her after a bit.

"I do, that's who. And I know Pa does, and Almeda. And don't forget your kid brother Tad. He's more'n just a mite proud of you, Zack, you gotta realize that."

I shrugged. Yeah, she was right. My little brother does look up to me some, I reckon.

"Lotta work just so my own kin can read it," I said after another minute. "Shoot, Corrie, I can just tell 'em all about it in a coupla hours—but it'd take me a month of Sundays to write it down! You recollect what a hard time Miss Stansberry—I mean Mrs. Rutledge—used to give me about my writin'!"

"You were a boy then, Zack, and you're a man now. Let's go visit her right now, and I'll wager she'll agree with me that you oughta write it down."

11

"I still don't understand why I hafta write it."

" 'Cause telling it's not the same, Zack. Then you got nothing to hold in your hand after you're done. But when it's written down, it's forever. Writing makes things more—more permanent." And mainly it's for *you*, Zack. For the rest of us, too, but mainly for what it'll mean to you someday. And to your family someday when you get married and have children."

"Shoot, Corrie, I just don't think I could do it."

" 'Course you could, Zack. Anybody can write down what's happened to them and what they're thinking. No big secret of how to do that. If I can, you can. Just write it down, that's all—just like it comes into your head."

"That's easy enough for you to say. You're a famous writer."

"But I wasn't when I started writing in my journal—that's what I'm trying to tell you. Besides, Zack, from how you told it to us, I think lots of folks would like reading about you and Hawk and what happened to you. No reason why it couldn't be just as interesting a book as anything I've written about. If they can make a book of my journals, there isn't no reason they can't do it from something you'd write too."

"A book!" I stared at her, thinking that she'd gone plumb crazy now. "Corrie, I can't write good enough for no book."

"You write down what happened to you, Zack, and I'll help you fix it up. And Mr. MacPherson—he'd help too because he likes to publish things like that. You know all the stories about the West by Ned Buntline and Edward Ellis and Prentiss Ingraham? Folks are keen to read *their* books, and they're all made up. I know Mr. MacPherson'd publish a story that was true about the Pony Express and the Paiute Indians and living with a mountain man and surviving out there where there's not much more than rattlesnakes. I know that folks'd want to read about that, Zack! You write down what happened, and I'll help you fix it up, and then we'll send it to Mr. MacPherson."

"I reckon I *could* write down what I did," I told her finally, "though it'd take me a coon's age. I don't write none too fast."

"Doesn't matter. You just work on it while I'm back East, and when I get back, then we'll see what's to be done next."

"Just tell what happened?" I asked her again.

"Yep," she told me. "Write it down just like you're talking. Pretend you're telling it to all of us. Writing is just talking on paper—nothing more to it than that."

Then she got a thoughtful look on her face.

"Actually, Zack," she added after a minute, "there is one other thing you oughta do while you're writing down what happened."

"What's that?" I asked her.

"I think you gotta tell about the *inside* of your story, not just the *outside*."

"I don't get you, Corrie."

"Outside is what you're doing. Inside is what you're thinking and feeling."

"What difference does it make what I was feeling? Ain't it supposed to be about what I done?"

"I reckon you're partly right, Zack," Corrie answered me. "But the minute you start writing, the folks reading what you did'll start wondering about who you are too. They'll like to know what was inside your head—what you were *thinking*—and what was inside your heart—what you were *feeling*—all at the same time as you're telling them what was *happening*. That's what most folks is interested in when they read—all of it put together. All about you."

I thought for a long spell on what she'd said. It sounded to me like a downright hard thing to do.

"It's just like talking, Zack," she said to me again. "Talking on paper. The only thing that's hard about it is that you menfolk aren't usually too practiced at talking about the feeling part. I reckon you feel things just as much as women do but you just don't know how to tell about it. But I reckon you can do it if you set your mind to it."

I thought a lot more about what she said, and in the end I figured my sister was right. I could give it a try, and if I didn't like it, I could always throw it away.

Besides, what Corrie'd told me made a heap of sense.

I did like the idea of having something to help me remember what had happened to me out in Nevada, even if it was just for me. I'd learned a lot of things from Hawk—a lot about life, a lot about myself. If I didn't write it down, maybe I'd forget most of it someday. I didn't want to forget any of it! If I ever did have a son of my own, I wanted to be able to give to him some of what Hawk had given me. And I reckon, too, I wanted to help him stay away from some of the fool mistakes I'd made.

So I decided to give it a try. I worked on writing everything down while my sister Corrie was in the East, which turned out to be longer than any of us figured it would be. Then when she got back to California and Miracle Springs, we worked on it some more together before sending it to Mr. MacPherson in Chicago.

What you got here's the result of all that.

I don't know how many of you're gonna care about reading it. I done it mainly for me, and for my son if ever I'm lucky enough to have me a son of my own someday. I reckon even if it's just for the two of us, it's worth it for that.

I left home to join the Pony Express in early July of 1860. I came back a little over a year later, in August of '61. So this is the story about my life during those thirteen months after I left home as a little kid, and came home pretty well started on the road to becoming a man.

# CHAPTER 1

# RIDING FROM HOME LIKE
THE WIND

*"You ain't got no right to call yourself my father no more!"*

The bitter words rang over and over through my brain. I urged my horse harder and harder, as if riding faster would take them away.

But they kept coming back, echoing in my mind . . . *no right . . . no right to call yourself my father!*

They'd been out of my mouth before I knew it, smashing against Pa harder and more cruelly than if I'd have actually hit him with my fist.

It was all I could do to force the tears to stay inside my eyes! A horrible knot grabbed at my stomach. How could I have said such an awful thing? But the words kept ringing through my head, like an iron gong crashing inside my skull from ear to ear. Above the pounding of hooves on the dirt, above the sounds of the wind on my face and the leather whip on the horse's rump—above it all the sound of my own voice kept yelling the cruel words at my own father.

On I rode.

I hadn't looked back yet, though my heart was sick over what I'd done.

But kids aren't usually able to calm themselves down and then go back and apologize for what they've done. And though I may have been twenty-one at the time, I was still a kid, as sure as my name was Zachary Hollister. And besides being a kid, I was full of all kinds of angry feelings toward my pa, though half my reasons for them didn't make much sense.

It was a mighty mixed-up way to feel—aching for what you've done and said . . . and guilty for hurting someone you half loved and half hated at the same time . . . and full of resentful and selfish thoughts that had got you believing all the accusations that had just erupted out of your mouth without you planning it. That's how I felt—angry, guilty, mixed up.

But I couldn't go back. I was too proud, too hurt, too mad, all rolled into one.

I reckon that's right common among young boys who figure they're old enough to be considered men but don't figure enough folks know it yet. They're too hardheaded to admit it when they go off and do something foolish that shows how much growing up they've still got to do. And then their pride gets them all the deeper into the hole they dug themselves into.

That's sure what happened to me! Angry and selfish and not so grown-up as I wanted to be . . . but too proud to admit any of it!

I'd told my father I was leaving home to join the Pony Express. I hadn't just told him, I'd yelled it at him—said he didn't have any right to call himself my father anymore. And though I was aching and crying inside, and feeling so alone in the middle of my hurt, another part of me had meant the words.

I'm ashamed to say it now, but it's true.

So I kept right on riding. I didn't turn back. And I forced back the tears. That was another thing that showed that I was still a boy. I thought it wasn't a manly thing to cry. And I kept riding from home as fast as my horse would carry me.

That was July of 1860.

# CHAPTER 2

## BELIEVING THE LIES

I was thirteen when we came to California.

Pa left when we were young, seven years before that, when we still lived in the East—New York State. I was seven or eight when Pa went west. Then the rest of us and Ma headed for California in a wagon train in 1852. Ma died on the way, and me and my older sister Corrie, with the help of the captain of the wagon train—Captain Dixon was his name—we got ourselves and our two younger sisters and younger brother out to California where we hooked up again with Pa. That was the five of us—Corrie and me, our sisters Emily and Becky, and little Tad. Corrie wrote about all that in her book, so I don't reckon I need to say much more about it.

After we got to California we lived with Pa at the claim he and Uncle Nick—that's our ma's brother who came west with Pa—had been mining outside the town of Miracle Springs, north of Sacramento. A couple of years later, Pa married a widow lady in town by the name of Almeda Parrish. That would have been in '54. Two years after that, our Pa became the mayor of Miracle Springs.

Maybe there's nothing wrong with all that. Nothing except that all those years, while I was growing from thirteen to sixteen and then eighteen, I didn't feel I had much of a claim on Pa's time or attention.

First, he was all tied up with the mine. Then it was Almeda and all kinds of trouble that seemed to happen to us. Becky got kidnapped once, and Pa had trouble from the past from being on the wrong side of the law a long time ago, back when he and Uncle Nick had been in the East. And after all that settled down, pretty soon he was getting himself elected mayor of Miracle Springs. Meanwhile I was growing up, and he didn't even seem to see it.

Don't get me wrong.

I ain't saying Pa actually done anything bad or mean to me. I reckon by most folks' standards he was a pretty decent pa to me, considering what he'd been through. It's just that I always felt kinda off to the side of things. I helped him and Uncle Nick with the mining for gold, and Pa was right good to me in a lot of ways. But to me, it always seemed like he had his mind on other things.

I reckon this is one of those times, like Corrie told me, when you gotta not just tell what happened, but tell how you were feeling too. So I was feeling like I didn't matter much to anyone—that nobody, least of all Pa, had much time or need of me. And I started to think that nobody really cared.

That's how all my trouble started—thinking those kinds of things. And now I see that they were lies. I ain't sure exactly where they came from—I guess from down inside that part of me where all I cared about was myself, and you take things to mean that everybody's against you. None of that's usually true. Most of the time people are nicer inside than you give them credit for, and probably think better thoughts toward you than you realize. But I reckon we all spend a heap more time thinking about ourselves than is good for us. And when we do, we start believing things that ain't true.

You don't have to believe those little voices that speak to you from out of your self, telling you untrue things about other folks.

But I did.

I believed the lies. And like they always do, they started right away poisoning my whole feelings and attitude toward Pa. But I didn't even realize what was happening until a lot later, when Hawk helped me see things clearer.

As I got older, I suppose I got quieter toward Pa, on account of how those lies had gone all through me. It was like my whole mind was poisoned toward him and everything and everybody.

By the time I was twenty or so, I was starting to think how I wanted to leave and get away from Miracle Springs. I never told anybody, not even my sister Corrie. I knew she loved me, and I'd always talked to her before. But I never even told her the hurt and anger and frustration I was feeling inside.

I just wanted to get away from home. I figured everything would be different and I'd be happy if I was free and taking care of no one but myself.

That's when I heard they were hiring boys for the Pony Express. I wanted to go and join up right away.

# CHAPTER 3

# THE EXPLOSION

I knew about the Pony Express, of course. Who in California didn't! Why, it was in the papers all through the early months of 1860 while they were getting it ready and building the stations. Then there were all kinds of celebrations that April when the first riders went out, both in San Francisco and Sacramento.

I'd loved horses and loved to ride for as long as I can remember. Little Wolf's father raised and trained horses, and Little Wolf and I had always talked about making our living with horses when we were grown. Little Wolf is an Indian, and we'd been best friends since almost right after we got to California.

But then one day the idea of *me* riding for the Pony Express hit me hard. It was while Pa and Corrie were in San Francisco at some political gathering. I met a fellow over in Marysville who said there were openings on the Express line and told me how I could get hired.

I practically jumped at the chance right then!

It would be a way to get away from Miracle. And the money they were paying riders was a lot—twenty-five dollars a week, plus your food and lodging!

I decided right then and there . . . I was gonna go!

But Pa and Almeda had other ideas.

I came home right away and told Almeda. She said I'd have to wait till Pa got home and talk it over with him. I don't know what got into me, but her words riled me, and I flared up at her. I'd never spoken so disrespectful to a woman in my life.

21

"When am I gonna be old enough to make up my own mind about anything?" I yelled at her. "You and Pa treat me like I'm no more'n about six!"

"Zack, I'm sorry. I just thought—"

But I was so upset I didn't even let her finish.

"Don't make no difference around here what I might think or what I might wanna do with myself!" I said back. "You all treat Corrie like she's a princess, but who cares about ol' Zack!"

I don't even remember what I said exactly, but it wasn't none too polite. I yelled and stormed some more and made poor Almeda cry. Then I turned around and left the house.

I went up in the mountains and camped alone by myself for a week or so, but that didn't resolve nothing in my mind. I was still all worked up and still determined in my own self to go ride for the Pony Express.

Finally I realized I'd have to go home eventually, even if it was just to get some of my things so I could go and take the job. So I rode down out of the hills. I knew Pa'd be back by then, and I knew it could get kinda ugly and tense between us. I wasn't planning to say nothing especially, just to get my things and go. But Pa's a headstrong man if you cross him. And after what I'd done and said, and how rude I'd been to his wife, I reckoned he'd be pretty riled when I got back.

I was sure right about that!

The minute I walked into the house, I could feel the air thick with all kinds of things nobody was saying.

# CHAPTER 4

## ME AND PA COME TO BLOWS

I don't suppose I looked too good—all sloppy and dirty, and with five days' worth of beard. I sure wasn't smiling.

I saw Corrie first when I walked in and gave her a little nod. I couldn't help wishing Pa wasn't there right at first. But he was, and there wasn't any way to pretend he wasn't.

"Where you been, son?" he asked me.

"Out riding," I said back.

"Where?"

"Just around." I was nervous, wondering what he was going to say. I moved over to the stove to see if there was anything left from breakfast to eat. I was famished.

"Surprised me some to find you gone," Pa went on. "When I'm away I expect you to look after the family."

I didn't say anything, just picked up a piece of bread and started chewing on it.

"You don't figure you owe no responsibility to the family, is that it?"

"It's your family, not mine," I said, half-mumbling.

"What's that you say?" asked Pa.

I repeated what I'd just said.

"What do you mean by that?" he growled back at me.

"What should you care what I do?" I said, not mumbling now but speaking out louder than I should have if I knew what was good for me. "You all got your own plans. Corrie's got her writing, and you all think she's pretty great at everything she does. And

23

you're busy being the town's important man. There ain't nothing Almeda can't do for herself. What do any of you need me for?"

"When I'm not here, I want you keeping a watch over things, that's what," said Pa, his voice getting more angry.

"Zack, please. I don't want—"

It was Almeda speaking now, but I cut her off.

"You don't need me, Almeda," I said. "Don't try to pretend."

"Zack, that's not true," she protested. She looked straight at me, and I could see the hurt and love in her eyes. But I was too stirred up and angry toward Pa to respond to her right then. "You know that I do need—"

"Almeda," I said, interrupting her again, "you don't have to try to make me feel good no more like you did when I was little."

"That's no way to talk to your mother, boy!" said Pa, and now he was good and mad.

"She ain't my mother!"

"She's my wife and a woman, and that means you better learn to talk to her with respect in your voice, unless you want my belt around that hind end of yours!"

"So you still think I'm a little boy too."

"You're still my son, and I'll whip you if I need to."

I turned away from him and laughed. It was all I could do to save face, but there wasn't any laughter in my heart. And even hearing my own voice was awful, for the laughter had a bitter, hollow ring to it.

Pa didn't like me laughing, either.

"You find something funny in that?" he asked.

"Yeah," I said, spinning around to face him again. "I'm twenty-one years old. I'm taller than you. I can ride a horse better than anyone for miles. But you still think of me like I was six years old. You don't even know what it's like for me. I got a life of my own to live, and you don't even know the kinds of things I'm thinking about. Everything's about Corrie and Almeda or your being mayor or the Mine and Freight. You got no time for me— you never had. What do you care what I do? You just expect me to be around to take care of things so you can leave whenever you want."

"What's that supposed to mean?" Pa challenged me.

"You figure out what it means," I answered him.

"None of that matters," he said. "You're not going to the Pony Express without my say-so. Whatever you may think, I'm still your pa. And I got a right to tell you what you can and can't do."

I was staring straight into Pa's face as he spoke, and I hardly knew what I was saying when I blurted out the rest of what I said. I didn't know all of what was inside me until suddenly the words started pouring out. I reckon they bit deeper into Pa's heart than an angry young fellow like me could realize at the time.

"You never knew what it was like for me," I accused him. "You never knew the times I cried myself to sleep back in New York, hoping you'd come home. I was frightened without a pa. I got teased and made fun of something awful 'cause I was little, and sometimes I came home with bruises and a black eye from trying to defend you when the other fellas said you was a low-down outlaw. I used to dream how good it would be to come home to feel the arms of a pa to hold me. I'd beg God to help us find you. But we never did, and I had to grow up alone like that. And it hurt Ma too. I'd see her crying sometimes when she didn't know I was watching. She kept on loving you and kept on praying for you—always asking God to protect you and watch over you. But I finally quit praying, because I was sick of being disappointed."

I couldn't talk anymore for a couple of seconds. I was almost shaking from all the mixed-up things I was feeling, and I'd never talked like this to Pa in all my life. And that's when the awful words came out of my lips that I had to keep hearing over and over and living with for the next year.

"So I don't reckon you got a right to call yourself my father no more," I said. "You may be my pa. But I figure I'm old enough to decide for myself what I want!"

Nobody else in the room knew what to do when I said that. They just all stood and stared at me in shock. Even Pa.

I knew I'd hurt him just as sure as if I'd stuck a knife into his gut. But when he finally did find his voice again, his words sounded harsh.

"However mixed up a job I done of it, I'm your pa—whether you like it or not!"

"I'm stuck here all the time with nothing but women and babies!" I shot back. "You can go off and do whatever you want, and you figure I got nothing of my own that matters?"

"You got no right to talk about your mother and sisters that way. You apologize to them, or you're gonna feel that belt like I told you!"

"Ha! Your belt ain't gonna come anywhere near my rump! And I ain't apologizing to nobody! It's true, everything I said. I told myself a long time ago I was getting out of here first chance I got. God knows I spent my muscles and blistered my hands working that mine for you all these years. You don't know how many days I sweated all day long, aching inside just for you to smile at me once and say I done a good day's work. But I might as well not even been there, for all you ever noticed! I don't reckon you'll figure you owe me anything for it. Well, that's fine with me. But it's all over with. I met a guy, and he's got a place arranged for me in the Pony Express. And I don't care if Little Wolf has changed his mind, I'm gonna take it. It's what I been waiting for—a chance to get out of this place!"

I couldn't look at anybody after I said that. I just turned and hurried toward the door. But Pa was closer to the door than me. He blocked my way and laid one of his big hands on my shoulder.

"No you're not, son," he said. "You ain't going nowhere without my leave. Now you get back in here, and we'll sit down and talk about it."

"I'm not talking about nothing," I retorted. "I've listened to all the rest of you long enough—and nobody seemed much interested in talking to me before. Now I'm going, whether you like it or not."

"And I'm telling you you're not."

"Too late. I signed the papers. I start my first run next week."

"Then I'll go talk to this fella and unsign them."

I couldn't help laughing again, not realizing how soon I would be regretting it.

"You're not leaving home, Zack! You hear me, son? You got duties to this family."

"Is that how it was when you left Ma?" I said. "Duties to the family!" I laughed again. "You talk to me about duty to the family? Where were *you* all those years when I needed a pa? Even after we'd come all the way across the country to find you, you didn't want us. You denied you even knew us!"

It was all so cruel to say, and even then I knew it wasn't true! But I was ranting like a crazy man by now, not even knowing what I was saying. I could tell how deep I'd cut into him because Pa's grip on my shoulder loosened. He stepped back, almost like my words had been a physical blow across his face.

"Well you can talk about duty all you want," I went on, "but I figure I've already about done as much in the way of duty as you ever did. You ran out on us, and even now you're always gone somewhere or other, but still you figure I'll do for you what you never did for me. Well, I tell you, I ain't gonna do it no more! If I go ride for the Pony Express, at least I ain't leaving a wife and five kids like you done!"

I had just wrested myself free of Pa's hand when I felt Almeda's gentle hand on my other shoulder.

"Oh, Zack," she said, pleading with me, her eyes full of tears, "if only we could make you see how much we all—"

But I was still backing my way clear of Pa, trying to make my way to the door, and I was in no mood to be restrained further. Without even thinking about it, and without hardly hearing her words, I reached up and threw her hand off my shoulder. Then I made for the door.

But seeing me rebuke Almeda so rudely was all Pa needed to jolt him out of his stunned silence. Grabbing at Almeda's hand was the worst thing I could have done.

Pa's eyes flamed with rage. He leaped forward and hit me hard across the jaw. I staggered and fell back onto the floor.

I don't know what my face looked like, but it was hot, and I was trembling from the blow. I crawled back up to my feet.

"It ain't no secret where your loyalties lie," I said. "Everything for the women, but you won't lift a finger unless it's *against* your own son!"

I turned again, tore open the door, and stalked off, slamming it behind me. I heard nothing more from inside the house.

My horse, Gray Thunder, was still saddled. I had my bedroll and what I needed for fire and cooking—plus the rifle Pa'd given me. So I didn't worry about food or money or the rest of my gear. I just mounted back up and galloped away.

# CHAPTER 5

# ON MY WAY

I planned to ride straight down to Sacramento, where I was supposed to see a man in the Express office. From there I would follow the trail east till I came to the Flat Bluff station, where I'd be trained by a fellow by the name of Hammerhead Jackson. He's the one who'd get me started with the job—or at least that's what the man who recruited me in Marysville had said.

As I set off to Sacramento, I rode up to Little Wolf's to say goodbye and to get something to eat. I asked him if he'd loan me three dollars and fix me up with a couple days' grub. He gave me five dollars, as much hardtack and apples as I could carry, and a few potatoes. Then I cantered off, only glancing back a time or two to see him still standing there, watching me go. I wished he was coming too.

By riding pretty hard, I got to Sacramento late the next afternoon. I was anxious to get to Nevada, so as soon as I got to town I hunted up the office of Russell, Majors, and Waddell, the company that ran the Pony Express.

I had a paper the guy in Marysville had given me when he'd been recruiting for riders. He said to show it to them at the office and they'd send me on my way. So I walked into the Express office as soon as I found it, and walked in holding the paper. The man looked at me kinda funny when I told him what I was doing and showed him the paper.

"What's your name, boy?" he asked.

"Hollister," I said. "Zack Hollister."

"What'd that other feller tell you about riding for the Express?"

"Not much, I don't reckon," I said.

"You know what you're getting in for?"

"He told me the hours is long and the work is hard, that your rump gets so sore you can't feel your legs no more, and that sometimes there's Indians."

"Well, he got it right . . . on all four counts," said the man, then looked me over up and down again. "And after what he said, you still aim to go?"

"Reckon so," I answered.

He just kinda stared back at me, then half shrugged, put a paper out on the desk, and licked his pencil.

"How old are you, boy . . . I mean, Hollister?"

"Twenty-one."

"Mite old for the Express."

He seemed to be thinking for a minute, then muttered something about not being able to be too particular. Then he wrote something down on the paper. It looked like he wrote down the number 18, but I was looking at it upside down.

"You got kin?"

"My pa," I said. "And my brothers and sisters and my step-mom."

"You got a whole family?" said the man.

I nodded.

"Didn't you know we want orphans?"

"Didn't figure it'd matter," I said.

He just shook his head. "How much you weigh?"

"Don't know."

"Well . . . you look to be about a hundred fifteen."

"I know it's more'n that, whatever it is."

"Don't matter. That's what we'll call it. He told you about the pay?"

"Twenty-five dollars a week?"

"That's it. They'll give you whatever else you need out at the station."

Again came that funny expression he kept looking at me with. "Your folks know you're here?"

"More or less," I said.

He hesitated a minute, then wrote something down, but even upside down I couldn't tell what it was.

He shoved the paper toward me. "Sign here, kid."

I did.

"Well, I reckon you're an Express rider now."

"What do I do now?" I asked.

"I reckon you ought to get yourself out to Jackson at Flat Bluff. He'll take care of you the rest of the way."

"Thanks, Mister," I said.

"Don't mention it, boy . . . good luck."

And that was that. Within an hour I was riding out of Sacramento on my way to the Nevada border.

# CHAPTER 6

## TO FLAT BLUFF

It took me five days of moderate riding to get to Flat Bluff. I stopped at all the other stations along the way, even met Warren Upson and several riders I'd heard about from the newspapers or from other folks. I heard plenty of stories about those I didn't meet, especially Pony Bob Haslam.

I rode up through the Sierras to the Sportsman's Hall station and then on to Friday's Station. It was pretty cold getting over the Sierras, with lots of snow everyplace. I was kinda surprised, it being as far into the summer as it was.

At Friday's Station, the stationman was gone and the only person around was a Mexican boy. I was anxious to get to the job, so I just got me something quick to eat and kept right on going, heading down into Nevada near Carson City and then cutting out across the high desert flatlands of what they called the Nevada part of the Utah territory toward Fort Churchill.

I didn't see a soul. There weren't no towns, no settlements, no farms, no ranches, no fences, no cows, no horses. There weren't nothing! Nothing but rocks, sand, scrubby plants, hills, lizards, and snakes . . . and the sun, which was cool and distant at first but then started to warm up the further east I went.

Across the high desert I rode, along long flat stretches that went on for likely ten or twenty miles, then up over a hill or small mountain, down the other side, and then out across the flat desert again. The ground was so flat between ridges that you didn't need a trail to ride on, you just needed it to keep track of your direction.

Over and over and over it went, just like that.

The only sign of life I saw was the Express riders I passed, and they weren't that many 'cause each stretch of the line was only run twice a week. But then everyone rode both directions out from his home station, and since I was going slower than the mail, I saw several of the riders twice.

As a rule, they didn't stop to do much talking, but once or twice they did. One fellow just whistled when I told him where I was bound and said I'd earn my pay for sure. I didn't like the sound of that, but didn't want to ask what he meant, either.

The only Indians I saw were from a distance, and I didn't know then how lucky I was! Later I found out that during that whole month of June, the Paiutes had been stirring up so much trouble it was a wonder the Express kept going at all. That's why they was looking for boys for the Nevada runs—all the regulars had quit! But I didn't know that, and I was riding right into the middle of it!

Only a few weeks before I'd come through, in fact, there'd been a big uprising near Carson City. The cavalry'd ridden out to stop it, but the Indians put up such a fight the cavalry'd had to retreat all the way back to the city. The Express was forced to shut down for three weeks. It'd only been operating again for about a week and a half when I come through.

I still saw patches of snow when I would ride up into one of the ridges, and I wondered at that. But at one of the stations they told me it was a snowstorm that finally helped the army under Major Ormsby force the Paiutes back up in the mountains so the line could be opened again. That was something—a snowstorm in the middle of June! Must've been the same one that put all that snow in the Sierras.

After the snowstorm, the Paiutes kept raiding further and further east, staying in the mountains. Some of the stories I heard were enough to make my hair stand on end. Nick Wilson at the Spring Valley relay station got a stone arrow-tip halfway into his skull. They got him to the Ruby Valley station, where a doctor tended him as best he could, but when I came through he was still in bed looking pretty bad. He'd been awake for about a week by then, and the only advice he had to give me was, "If you're heading east, Hollister, keep both your eyes open and a gun handy. That's just the direction the redskins are moving."

After talking with Nick, I found myself glancing around a lot more as I rode—and I made sure I got to a station every night. I wasn't about to bed down out in the middle of the desert after hearing all those stories about the Paiutes, especially when I heard about all that Pony Bob Haslam had been through at every station between Reese River and Dry Creek. As far as I could tell, he was just about the most famous rider of all.

I didn't ride too hard, though, because I didn't want to wear out my horse. I wasn't changing mounts every ten miles, like I would when I started carrying the mail, so I didn't want to gallop him too much. I reckon I could have used some of the Express ponies since I was an official rider.

I hoped I could keep Gray Thunder with me once I got on the job. Little Wolf and I'd found him two years before up in the Sierras. I'd broken him and trained him myself, and he was the best horse I'd ever had. I figured he'd be about as much of a friend as I'd have out here. I wouldn't ride him on the job, but I figured us two'd go scouting around the countryside when I was between rides.

The further east I rode, like I said, the warmer it got, until halfway across the flatlands it was downright hot. The weather sure could change in a hurry in this country! There wasn't no snow now, that was for sure!

And that was some desolate country, I can tell you—especially in the month of June! It was so dry that if you didn't have water with you, you'd die for sure trying to cross it.

I had a map the man at the Sacramento office had given me. It showed the Express trail and all the relay stations and home stations and the places where there was supposed to be water. But by the time I was halfway across Nevada, most of the rivers and creek beds were all dried up. I reckoned they'd have water in them during the winter, but you'd never know it now.

The ground itself was just rocks and sand, and the only plants was dried-up desert grasses and shrubs, looking like they wanted to be green but couldn't keep from being mostly gray and brown. There weren't no dirt to speak of, and it's a mystery to me how even those wiry, prickly things could grow at all.

I didn't see how much of anything could survive out there, but I would later learn about all the hundreds of kinds of critters that made the desert their home—not all of them too friendly neither, like snakes and scorpions. It was the driest, hottest, unfriendliest patch of country I'd ever laid eyes on!

Actually, I reckon I *had* laid eyes on it before, when we was coming across the other way in the wagon train on the way to California with Ma. But I reckon things look a mite different through twenty-one-year-old eyes than they do through thirteen-year-old eyes.

Now that I was riding it alone, it wasn't that hard to understand why this land had taken Ma's life. If a body was to take to ailing out here, why the sun could just drain the life right outta you—it was that hot!

I finally arrived at Flat Bluff on June 29. I rode up, tied up Gray Thunder, and went inside.

One look at the stationman, and I knew why they called him Hammerhead.

# CHAPTER 7

# HAMMERHEAD JACKSON

I never did learn Hammerhead Jackson's real first name. But after one look at him, there just didn't seem much else to call him.

He was a short, squatty man, easily five inches shorter than me, and built stocky and muscular, with big wide shoulders and legs that looked like tree trunks. I could have outrun him, but he sure wasn't the kind of fellow I'd want to tangle with! One look and you'd figure him for an ornery cuss. And listening to his gruff talk only made it worse. If he'd been hired to be hard on the Pony Express riders and toughen them up, they sure got the perfect man for the job!

Worst of all was the big scar—several inches wide—along the side of his head, running from one eyebrow back to his ear and then about halfway up toward the top of his head. It was such a grotesque deformity I could hardly take my eyes off it. On the one side his hair grew normally and was thick and black. But then on the other side, where his head was all dented in, it was mostly bald, with just a few scraggly hairs trying to grow, and the skin itself was ragged and scarred. It almost did look like somebody'd taken a hammer to the side of his head.

If it hadn't been for that, the rest of his face would have been pretty fearsome to meet up with, too, especially if he had his usual scowl on it. There was a scar over the eyebrow opposite the dented-in side, and his nose was bent just a little bit off to one direction. There were a few smaller scars and pockmarks on his face and cheeks, too, though the stubble of a beard covered most of them.

His jaw was square, settling down on a short, thick neck.

And as far as I could tell, Hammerhead Jackson was one of those kind of men who does everything to try to rile you. He always seemed intent on picking a fight, even though I couldn't imagine anyone wanting to tangle with him! Everything about his voice and his looks and his manner immediately told you this was a gruff old bull of a man who wouldn't take nothing from nobody.

"You don't look tough enough to ride out in this country, boy!" were his first words to me as he stood there in the doorway and scanned me up and down with his eyes.

"'Sides that, you're too blamed old!" His voice sounded like gravel slushing through Pa's sluice box.

"I can take care of myself," I shot back.

I don't reckon I was too convincing. He just let out with a big laugh, still looking me over. It wasn't a cheerful laugh, either, like Alkali Jones's.

"That's what all you young runts think!" he barked. "But toughness is in the eyes, and I can tell if it's there or not. And you ain't got it, boy!"

"Well, I can ride as well as anybody!" I was getting a little riled by now. "And whether you figure I can or not, I been taking care of myself longer than maybe some of your young riders. So you just give me a chance, and then you can get rid of me if you don't figure I'm tough enough for it!"

He didn't actually smile, but some of the gruffness seemed to relax out of his face.

"Well, maybe I was wrong about you, boy," I said. "You got grit, and you ain't gonna let an old coot like me bully you none. That's good . . . you might do after all. But I won't have to discharge you if you ain't up to the job—them Paiutes will take care of that. Come on in . . . what's your name?"

"Hollister," I said. "Zack Hollister."

"Well, Hollister," Hammerhead went on as he showed me where to put my stuff and where I'd bunk down, "I may have been testing you some, but I was speaking the truth when I said you gotta be tough to ride in this country. You musta heard about the Indian trouble?"

I nodded.

"Blamed Paiutes is the savagest brutes this side of the Comanches and Apaches. The run between Salt Lake and Carson's been on and off for months. If it ain't one of their kind, they'll kill it as soon as shoot a rattler. We ain't lost no boys yet, but we come close more times'n I like. And several stations been looted and burned—there's been some station people killed."

"Yeah, I heard," I said.

"You still wanted to come?"

"It's a job."

"Twenty-five a week . . . yeah, I know, it's good money. You figure it's worth getting shot at for, Hollister?"

"If I ride fast enough, maybe I won't have to worry about it."

"Paiutes has got fast ponies too. Half of 'em they stole from us! Takes more'n a fast horse. Takes guts and wits . . . and like I said before, you gotta be a tough son of a gun. You think you can do it, Hollister?"

"I aim to try," I said. "That's what I came for."

"Then I'll give you a chance to prove yourself. I gotta make sure what kinda stuff my riders is made of. That's my job, Hollister. I get paid to be tougher on you young bucks than the trail ever could. That's what the Express hired me for—to make men outta you! So you do what I say, you pay attention to what I teach you, or I'll box your ears. For your own good. Now, set yourself down. Rest of 'em will be in for grub in 'bout half an hour."

"Rest of who?" I asked, not exactly liking the sound of what might be in store for me.

"Smith, he's my station assistant, and the Barnes kid. They're both out at the stables tending the horses. Billy's been riding double stints. He's a tough little son of a gun, though I had to beat some sense into that lame skull of his when he first came. He's gonna be glad to see you! We been shorthanded out here ever since the Paiutes started causing all the trouble."

"When do I start?" I asked.

"Billy'll take you out tomorrow, show you the trail, take you partway, up over the ridge—that's the only tricky part. After that you got a clear ride all the way into the Stephens' Canyon station.

It's 'bout an eighteen-mile run east. You'll make your first ride day after that. Well, I gotta fix up this grub. Why don't you get your horse unsaddled and settled—they'll show you where out back."

I did like he said, but didn't see a trace of the other two men. There were plenty of empty stalls, so I picked one, threw two or three handfuls of grain into the feeding trough, and took care of my horse. He needed a good rubbing after all the heat and sweat and dust.

When I came back in a few minutes later, Hammerhead was busy in the kitchen area at the other end of the long rectangular room. I sat down against the far wall and watched him. He didn't look much like a cook, but then, Almeda probably wouldn't have called it a kitchen either! He seemed to be making biscuits, and I could smell beans bubbling slowly in a big pot on the stove. As far away as we were from anything resembling a town, I didn't figure there was much to be particular about. So I just sat there and looked at Hammerhead Jackson and wondered about what I'd got myself into.

It wasn't till some time later that I found out how the stationman had got so scarred up. Mason Walker, the rider who come in from the west two days later, told me about it once when we were alone. Hammerhead had been living further east, in Apache territory. A raiding war party had set fire to his house and massacred his wife and daughter. He took an arrow straight through the ribs on his right side and fell down unconscious, his pistol still in his hand.

Most of the Indians rode off, but one stayed behind, pulled out his knife, stooped down, and started to cut right into Hammerhead's head to scalp him. The unbelievable pain somehow brought him back into consciousness just long enough to tilt the pistol up and squeeze the trigger. The Indian died instantly, and Hammerhead blacked out again.

Any ordinary man would have been dead. But when a neighbor found him several hours later he was still breathing. How he survived, half scalped and with an arrow sticking into him, Mason couldn't say, except to add, "They don't make 'em tougher'n

Hammerhead Jackson, and that's a fact, Hollister. Don't cross him, or he'll put you out on the floor."

However it happened, he did survive, 'cause there he was in charge of the Flat Bluff Station.

The story was so gruesome it made me sick just to think of it. But if tough was what the Express wanted, I reckon they got it when they hired Hammerhead Jackson! I could tell that even before I knew what had happened to him.

"What are you running from, Hollister?" the gravelly voice said in the middle of my thoughts as I watched the stationman across the room.

"I don't know—don't figure I'm running from nothing."

"Everybody's running from something, Hollister. That's why they're out here, trying to prove they're men. What you got to prove, Hollister? You're older'n most of 'em. Why you trying to prove you're a man?"

"What makes you think I am?" I said. I didn't like his tone. I didn't know what business it was of his why I was here!

"Every boy's trying to prove he's a man. That's why you all do fool things like joining the Pony Express. Trying to prove they're as tough and as grown up as the next feller."

"I thought you wanted 'em tough."

"I do. But I like to know what demons is haunting 'em, too, so one of 'em doesn't pull a gun on me if I beat 'em around for turning sissy on me. Most of the time it's a feller's pa. What's your pa like, Hollister?"

I didn't answer. Hammerhead glanced over at me.

"That's it, ain't it? Yep, I figured as much. Always is."

"What makes you think you know so dang much about what I'm thinking?" I said angrily.

"Watch yourself, Hollister, or I'll tell Billy to give you a thrashing—or do it myself, for that matter!"

"Whoever this Billy is, I'd like to see him try!" I retorted.

For the first time since I'd got there I saw a slight grin break over the stationman's lips.

"You just might get your chance, Hollister," he said, "if you keep running your fool tongue off like that!"

I didn't say anything else.

"But to answer your question," Hammerhead went on, "I had a pa too. Every boy does, and that's why he's gotta prove he's a man—to get his own pa off his back. I hated my own pa's guts. But then I reckon hate made a man of me and saved my life a time or two.

"Hate's a good thing, Hollister, if it makes you tough. But just take one piece of advice—watch what you say around Billy. You step outta line, and he's like to pull a gun and shoot you dead. His pa ain't on *his* back no more. He's made a man of himself, and he's proved it more'n once."

# CHAPTER 8

# TAKING THE OATH

This was one of the main home stations, so it was bigger than most of the smaller swing stations I'd come through.

The house itself had three rooms. The big room where I sat now had kind of a kitchen at one end with a big wood stove, utensils and pans and cooking stuff hanging from hooks on the wall, and a big rough wood table for eating, with benches on both sides. Then over on the side closer to me there was a big fireplace, some stacks of wood, and a couple chairs, but mostly a lot of supplies scattered around in boxes or crates or on shelves. Nothing was very tidy.

This station was so far away from everywhere that when a wagon came to outfit it they had to bring enough to last a long time. So there were big barrels of molasses and borax and turpentine and things like that, burlap bags stacked all over the place full of wheat and ground flour and sugar and cornmeal and lots and lots of beans. All the meat was dried, and the fruit, too, on account of the heat—nothing would keep for long out there in the desert. Some slabs of smoked bacon hung on the walls, I found out the next day they had a smokehouse out back and had butchered a hog a couple weeks before. And the shelves held bags of coffee, some tea, honey, and lots of tin containers lining the shelves with other cooking odds and ends, medicines, rubbing alcohol, soap, dishes and pots, and all kinds of things.

The other two rooms off the main one were bunkrooms. One was Hammerhead's for himself. The other was bigger, with four or five wooden bunks built against the walls for the riders and Mr. Smith to sleep. That's where I'd put my things.

When Mr. Smith and Billy Barnes came in for supper, Hammerhead called me over and introduced me, then we sat down around the rough wood table. Neither of them said hardly a word to me.

Mr. Smith was maybe five or ten years older than Hammerhead, almost bald and a little fat. His eyes were mean and he never smiled. The few times he spoke, his voice sounded surly.

And even though Hammerhead told Billy I had come to relieve him of half the riding, Billy didn't seem any too happy about it. He just looked me up and down with an angry glint in his eye, as if he'd rather I hadn't come at all.

Everybody around here seemed angry. Any friendliness there was between them wouldn't have been enough even to match half a smile from Franklin Royce back home—and that wasn't much! They grabbed at the food, everyone trying to be first and take the most and the best. As far as pleasant supper conversation goes . . . there wasn't any!

When I was done, I excused myself and went out to the stable to see how Gray Thunder was getting on and make sure he had enough feed and water, and to brush and settle him for the night.

The next morning, like Hammerhead had told me, Billy took me out on the first four miles of my run, showed me the trail up to the top of the ridge east of the station, and pointed out the rest of the way to me, showing me everything on a map I'd be carrying with me.

He hardly said a word to me all the way out. I'd still not seen him smile once. His eyes had a faraway gaze in them that never went away. I found out later that he was an orphan, like a lot of the riders were. But I didn't find it out from him. Billy never said a word about himself. Most fellows like him never did. They kept everything inside, and you never had a notion what they was thinking.

Billy was shorter than me by a couple of inches and probably not a day over eighteen. But one look in his face, and anyone could tell he was a tough customer, just like the stationman had said. I don't know what he'd done or where he'd come from before the Express opened, but I sure wasn't about to ask!

That afternoon, back at the station, Hammerhead went over the map again two or three times with me. Then he issued me my blue dungarees and bright red shirt and handed me a light rifle and Colt revolver. He had me shoot both of them to make sure I knew how to use them. He seemed satisfied.

Hammerhead handed me a Bible, too, and told me to keep it with me when I rode. I was more than a mite surprised. Hammerhead didn't hardly seem the sort of man who had much religion to him, but I took it just the same.

Then we saddled up the pony I'd be riding and I took him out for a run so the two of us could get used to each other. He was smaller than Gray Thunder but just as fast, maybe even faster.

"They give you the oath when you signed on, Hollister?" Hammerhead asked me.

"No, I don't reckon so," I answered. "The man in Sacramento just had me sign a paper, that's all."

"All right, then you gotta take the oath before you can ride for Russell, Majors, and Waddell. Stick up your right hand."

I obeyed.

"Now say what I say after me," said Hammerhead. "You ready?"

I nodded.

"All right . . . I, Zack Hollister, do hereby swear before the Great and Living God—" He stopped. "Go on, say it," he told me.

"*I, Zack Hollister, do hereby swear before the Great and Living God,*" I said.

"—that during my engagement, and while I am an employee of Russell, Majors, and Waddell—"

"*—that during my engagement, and while—*" I stopped. I was a little nervous and had forgotten what he said.

"—while I am an employee of Russell, Majors, and Waddell—" repeated Hammerhead a little impatiently.

"Oh, yeah—*while I am an employee of Russell, Majors, and Waddell.*"

"—I will, under no circumstances—"

*"I will, under no circumstances,"* I said, and then went on to repeat after him everything he said: *"use profane language, that I will drink no intoxicating liquors, that I will not quarrel or fight with any other employee of the firm, and that in every respect I will conduct myself honestly, be faithful to my duties, and so direct all my acts as to win the confidence of my employers."*

"So help you God," added Hammerhead.

*"So help me God,"* I said.

"All right, Hollister, you can put your hand down. It's all official now. You'll be on the trail for the Express by tomorrow."

I couldn't help but wonder, after seeing what was in Billy's eyes and hearing Hammerhead talk about boxing my ears, how serious the two of them were about the Pony Express oath.

# CHAPTER 9

## MY FIRST RIDE

When I laid down that night on the hard bunk to go to sleep, I was thinking and wondering if I'd done the right thing. Everything I'd said to Pa came back into my mind again, along with everyone's talk about the Paiutes. I only half slept and half dreamed the whole night, turning over a lot, and listening to every sound outside. As much as I wanted to think of myself as a man and grown-up and not needing nobody else, down inside there was part of me that was scared. 'Course that part of you that is trying to act more grown up than you really are won't let you admit you're scared, and I wouldn't either.

Bright and early the next morning, everybody was up, and after breakfast they put me right to work. Mason Walker was due in about ten, and that's when I'd start my first ride east. Two or three hours after that, Billy'd be heading off west.

There was plenty to do to get ready, and Hammerhead wasn't one to let anyone be slack when there was work going on. He fixed me lunch to take with me, and we had to make sure my mount was good and fed. I had grain for him and water for us both in waterproof pouches slung across behind the saddle. There was a lot to getting ready, and Hammerhead had to show me everything that first time. Billy mostly did all his preparation by himself.

"Now, you got eighteen miles ahead of you this first stretch," Hammerhead told me. "Ain't no water between here and Stephens' Canyon. That's why you're carrying it, and that's why you can't ride flat out, neither. Let your horse tell you the pace he's comfortable with. Some of the runs are ten or twelve miles, and then you can fly. Eighteen or twenty, then you gotta pace it back just a bit. You got that, Hollister?"

"Yes, sir," I said.

"Well, looks to me like Walker's headed this way," he said, glancing off toward the west. There was no sound, but a tiny dust cloud on the horizon got gradually bigger as we watched it. "You know the route?"

"Think so," I said.

"Got the map?"

I nodded.

"Your gun?"

"Yes."

"Then I don't reckon there's more for it than for you to be off."

We stood there waiting, and within five minutes Mason Walker's dust cloud was billowing right into the station, with him and his horse right in the middle of it.

Walker reined in the foaming horse, jumped off, grabbed the leather *mochila* that carried the mail, and ran with it to me.

The exchange wasn't as fast as usual because I was new at it, but Hammerhead helped me sling the mochila over my saddle, then I jumped up and took off.

"Good luck, Hollister!" he yelled after me.

The next minute I was out of the station, galloping east up the ridge Billy and I had climbed the day before and then down across the flatland of central Nevada, riding hard but not what I'd call real fast.

There ain't much to do while you're riding except stare ahead to make sure you're on the trail . . . and think. That's one thing you can't help, 'cause your mind's about the only part of you that's free to leave the trail and go off someplace else.

Well, that first day I found my mind doing a lot of thinking all of a sudden about things I'd rather not thought of just then. But I couldn't help it!

First off, I started thinking about everyone back home. I reckon the first person to come into my mind was my brother,

Tad. Just seeing his face, smiling and maybe wanting to tell me something, sent such a stab of loneliness into my heart I couldn't stand it.

One day, not long before I'd left, when Pa wasn't home, he'd come to me all wet and muddy from up by the mine, with his face all lit up.

"Zack, Zack," he said excitedly as he ran up to me. "Come up to the mine with me."

"What for?" I said without much interest.

"I think I found a new vein of gold!"

"Aw, Tad, you didn't either."

"Just come and look—please, Zack. We could surprise Pa as soon as he gets home."

"Forget it, Tad," I snapped. "Let him find his own gold."

Tad's face had looked so disappointed I thought he was going to start crying. He walked off slowly, back toward the mine.

It was the last time I'd talked to him.

Remembering it made my eyes blurry, and I had to wipe them with my sleeve.

Then I thought of all the other times I hadn't been as helpful to him as I should have or hadn't had time for him when he'd wanted to play or show me something. Then pretty soon I was thinking the same way about Becky and Corrie and Emily.

That same day, I'd walked into the house after talking to Tad like that and had snapped rudely at Corrie too. That same look of hurt and confusion I'd seen on Tad's face came over hers too. And for the next couple of days I could tell she was avoiding me, probably afraid to talk to me, wondering if I'd get mad at her.

All kinds of little things came into my head, things I'd completely forgotten till right then. I couldn't get those two images of Tad and Corrie out of my mind—how they'd looked at me after I'd hurt them.

Seeing all their faces and remembering things we'd done together and hearing their voices in my head—it all made me realize how far away and alone I was.

There sure wasn't nothing I could do about it, though! There I was, riding in the middle of nowhere!

And I had to keep going!

Getting to Flat Bluff and getting started with my new job had kept me occupied, so I could mostly push my thoughts about my family and what I'd done to them down and away from me. The feelings were there, I reckon, because there was a kind of continual gnawing in the pit of my stomach. But I didn't open the door so my feelings could come up into my head and become actual thoughts that I'd have to look at.

I could already tell that the Pony Express was the kind of place where no one asked too many questions or got too personal. I always thought men and boys weren't supposed to get personal like women did, anyway, but it was even more like that in this kind of a place. Everyone out here was running away from something or someone, just like Hammerhead said, or else was trying to prove something—mostly, I reckon, to themselves. I figured that everyone here, just like me, had a story to tell about people they'd left and pains they were suffering inside without telling no one about it. Except maybe the orphans, and I reckon they were looking for something to belong to more than something to get away from.

Once I was out there on that first ride, it all began to come into my mind, kind of like water that finally rises up so high it breaks over the dam, and I couldn't stop the thoughts from coming anymore.

Especially I thought about Pa and what I'd said to him the day I left.

It wasn't easy to think about, and I kept doing my best to shove the memory of that day out of my mind.

By the time I rode into Stephens' Canyon station a couple of hours later, I was glad to have something to distract me from my thinking.

I met a few new people there, took a short rest, had some water and ate part of my lunch, and was off again on a fresh horse in less than fifteen minutes.

The next two stretches were fourteen and then twenty-three miles, and there was nothing to see along the way. It was the most boring land I could imagine. I don't think there was a single thing living out there. I couldn't imagine how the Indians survived in such country.

When I bedded down that night in the middle of the Utah-Nevada territory, I was plumb tuckered out!

# CHAPTER 10

# THOUGHTS ON THE TRAIL

For the rest of the summer and through the fall, I rode mostly on the same stretch I rode that first day—the fifty-five miles between Flat Bluff and the other stations, with two changes of horses along the way. But there were times when I'd ride on further east and times I had to ride west into what was usually Mason's territory too.

Things would come up, like somebody'd get sick or there'd be a change in schedule or one of the riders would quit—there were all kinds of things that happened that meant you'd have to ride a different run than you thought. That was part of what being an Express rider was all about!

The Pony Express wasn't exactly the kind of place you met people you'd call "good friends." You met interesting people, that's for sure, but they were all like Billy Barnes and Hammerhead Jackson—a tough breed, and not somebody you'd necessarily trust or talk to.

It made me think sometimes, when I was out alone on the trail, about how different men and girls were. Corrie and I talked about it later, but I noticed it out there too—how men like Hammerhead and Billy seemed to wear a thick crust all around themselves. That crust never cracked. They talked enough to go about the business of life, but they didn't ever show what they were thinking or feeling inside.

It made me think how I'd been around womenfolk a lot of my life—my mother and my sisters and then Almeda—and that maybe, just from watching them, I learned to think different and feel things more than some fellows like Billy Barnes.

All this started me wondering about myself and if I was the same as Hammerhead and Billy, with a crust growing around myself too. At the time I don't reckon I saw it as a weakness, though now, looking back, I can see that it's just about the biggest weakness there is about being a man.

In fact, I went through a time of trying to be that way myself, because it seemed that was the way men were supposed to be. I talked hard and tried to make the riders and the stationmen think I was just as tough as any of them. And I guess, too, I figured that was about the only way to get by out there. If those fellows started thinking you were soft, they'd make no end of trouble for you.

No matter what I started thinking about out on that trail, though, I always came back to Pa. At first I thought he was a little like Billy—tough and not talking too much. And then I began to realize that maybe I had some of that in me, too, and that part of why him and me hadn't talked much had to do with *me*, not him.

One day I was riding along—I think it must have been toward the middle of October, because it was cooler and I felt a bit of a chill in the air. I was thinking about Pa, like I did a lot, and about Hammerhead's saying that everybody out here was running away from something.

Suddenly the thought struck me: What if I *was* running away by joining the Pony Express—just like Pa and Uncle Nick did when they left Bridgeville? What if I was trying to avoid facing what I needed to, just like I always figured Pa'd done?

I didn't like thinking that way. But I *had* left my family behind, just like he did—a family that cared for me and was probably worried about me.

But no, I thought. My own case was totally different. I was a man now. I had a right to be out on my own. I wasn't running from anything. I was facing my life on my own. Pa had run away from the trouble facing him. I was not doing that. I wasn't afraid of danger.

Then I got to thinking about what it was like, as a kid, back in Bridgeville after Pa had left with Uncle Nick. Word got out that they'd been in a gang and got put in jail and then broke out. And not long after that I started having trouble at school, with other kids calling me names and making fun of me on account of Pa. Ma didn't believe the rumors, and she told us not to pay no attention to them, neither. But I couldn't help it.

And then I started thinking on one particular day back when I was about ten years old. No matter how hard I tried during the years after that, I could not erase the bitter memory of what happened that day. But I never told anyone about it, not even Ma. I kept it inside all these years, trying to make myself forget. But it still seemed as clear as yesterday as I remembered it that day on the Pony Express trail.

It happened just at the end of a school day. The big bell had just been sounding, and I was thinking of the plans I'd made to take little Tad fishing. He was just such a little tyke and looked up to me almost like I was a man, though I was just a little boy still. I can't remember why, but I was the last one to leave the classroom. Even the teacher had already left—I thought everyone had. But as I walked out and down the steps, suddenly somebody stuck out a leg and tripped me.

I tumbled down the last two or three steps, sprawling all over the ground. I wasn't really injured, though I spilled my slate on the ground and got my face and clothes all dirty. But what really hurt was that a group of three or four other boys were standing nearby, laughing at me, like they'd been waiting around to see it happen. They were several of the boys who were older than me and who caused me the most trouble. They laughed and mocked and swore at me and called me names.

I tried to pick up my slate and get up, but they shoved at me and pushed me back to the ground several times.

Finally I got back to my feet and tried to walk away.

"Not so fast," sneered the biggest of the group—he was thirteen. "I'm not finished with you yet."

I was afraid to say anything but afraid to keep going too.

"I want to know what it's like having a no-good jailbird for a pa. So before I let you go, you answer me what it's like being the son of an outlaw?"

"My pa's not an outlaw," I spat back, forgetting my fear for a second.

"You're a liar," the boy shot back. "Everybody knows what he did—and that he went to jail for it."

"He never done no such thing!" I shouted. Then like an idiot I dropped what was in my hand again and rushed at him.

It was only a second or two before he'd slugged me twice in the stomach and once in the face and had me pinned to the ground.

"Your pa busted out of jail!" he yelled in my ear. "You prob'ly don't even know that, but he's no good, I tell you."

"You let me go!" I cried. "Let me go, or I'll . . . I'll—"

"You'll what? Call your pa on me! Ha! When they catch your pa, you know what they're going to do? They'll hang him, and you'll have to watch!" He laughed with an ugly sound, then ground my face into the dirt. The others were standing around watching and laughing and taunting me too.

I tried to keep my eyes from shutting, but it hurt so bad where he'd hit me and now kept pushing and twisting at me. I tried to stifle my tears to show him I was tough, though I winced every time he'd jab at me or kick me with his knee.

Never in all my life had I felt so helpless, so alone. And nobody was there to help me. The bully had me totally at his mercy. I never felt so helpless before or since.

When the bully realized he couldn't have any more fun with me, he kicked me several times in the ribs, then got up and left with the others, laughing till they were out of earshot.

I laid there for another half an hour, crying both from the hurt and the humiliation. Finally I got up and staggered home as best I could. I met Tad, who was still expecting to go fishing. I said some things that weren't too friendly to him, then went up and hid in the hayloft. The last thing I remember about that day is crying again till I fell asleep.

I didn't have no one to comfort me. I didn't have nobody to tell me what to do next time. I couldn't tell Ma or Corrie. That's when I needed Pa more than ever—but I didn't have a father to tell what happened.

I suppose if I'd have told Pa all about it when I finally did see him again in California, he'd have felt just as bad, if not worse, than me about the incident. If we'd have talked about it, maybe the memory wouldn't have stung in the same way it still did.

But it was too late then. After we came west, I didn't need a father the same way as back when I was younger. I was becoming more like everybody does the older they grow. The older people get, I suppose, the more independent they become. Those early years were gone.

I was just about back to the station by then.

I tried to shake all the memories clear from my brain. That was a long time ago, I told myself. I had to be a man now, whatever had happened when I was a kid.

So a bully beat me up once. So Pa left. I couldn't worry about it now.

Besides, what would Hammerhead think of me if he knew what I was thinking about?

Or Billy Barnes?

# CHAPTER 11

# THE ACCIDENT

The Paiute war continued on and off through the summer and fall. And our territory, out in the middle of nowhere away from where the army was around, was about the worst. I don't know what it was about this lonely high desert that kept the Paiutes there—or how they could even survive in it. I couldn't see that there was any food or water or shelter or anything. How could anyone live for as long as a week out in that bare wilderness! But they were always out there in the hills someplace as a constant threat.

Most of the time, if you just rode fast enough and maybe fired a shot or two in the air over their heads, the Paiutes wouldn't come after you. And since the Express had the best ponies in the West, as long as you had an arrow's flight for a head start, there wasn't much they could do to harm you 'cause you could outrun 'em.

I only got chased two or three times those first few months, and then only from a distance. That didn't keep my heart from pounding in my chest! But I just rode as fast as I could and stuck my pistol over my shoulder and fired a few shots behind me as I went, and that seemed enough to frighten them away. And all it took was another five or ten minutes in the saddle and I was out of their sight.

What always worried me was what I'd do if suddenly a bunch of Paiutes appeared on the trail in front of me, too close for me to turn and hightail it out of there without getting an arrow in my back.

It happened to Pony Bob Haslam once. He was riding along full tilt and rounded a bend and suddenly found himself reining in his pony smack in front of thirty mean-looking Paiutes. When the dust and hooves and commotion all settled down after a few seconds, there he was, just one young white boy staring back at what looked to him like a couple of dozen bloodthirsty red savages!

I don't know if half the stories about Pony Bob are true or not. But the way Mason Walker told it was like this. After sitting there staring back at 'em for a minute or two, everything all quiet and still, Bob slowly drew out his Colt and started his pony off walking straight toward 'em. Holding his gun at his side, finger on the trigger ready to fire, he just rode up and kept going, right on through them, and nobody breathed a word. The Indians' horses edged aside and let him pass, and he rode off in the other direction, looking back as he went, till he judged he was out of arrow range, and then he flew into a gallop again.

I thought about that incident a lot, wondering if I'd have the guts to do the same thing if I ever got into the same situation. When it finally did, I don't know if it was because I wasn't as brave as Pony Bob or because the circumstances were different and the Indians weren't as close. But for whatever reason I didn't follow his example, even as much as I thought about it ahead of time.

It was the first week of December, and cold. There hadn't been any snow yet to speak of, but the sky was heavy and gray, and the wind cut right through. I was riding hard, not really thinking much about anything except how blamed cold it was.

All of a sudden I stopped dead in my tracks.

There they were, about a hundred yards in front of me. Twenty or twenty-five Paiutes, right in the middle of my path!

For a few seconds I just sat there, surprised, scared to death, my heart beating.

Then all kinds of possibilities started to run through my head.

I was far enough from them, I thought, that if I turned around and made a run for it back the way I'd come, I was *probably* out of arrow range. But then the mail wouldn't get through.

Then I thought maybe I could head out into the desert and try to get around them. But then all they'd have to do was ride back along the road wherever I tried to circle back. I could ride an extra twenty miles only to find them still there on the road once I got back to it!

Or I could do like Pony Bob and ride up straight through the middle of them and hope they didn't kill me. But they might!

All this went through my brain in a second or two. Then suddenly another thought came to me, but not something I was expecting. What I thought of was one of Rev. Rutledge's sermons from back at Miracle Springs.

"Everybody faces different kinds of problems in life," I could hear him say just as clearly as when we'd all been sitting in church listening to him. "For every one of you they'll be unique. I won't face the kinds of difficulties you will, nor will you face those that come to me."

*You're right there, Reverend*, I said to myself. *I doubt if you've ever been in a pickle quite like this!*

"There's never a solution that will work for every kind of trial that comes up in life," he'd gone on. "But there *are* three things you have to do to find whatever solution is right for your particular situation. Sometimes you have to face your problem head on. Other times, circumstances are such that you have to go around the problem to get to the other side. And finally, there are times when you need to just prayerfully and patiently wait for God to show you what to do. One of these three will succeed in surmounting all of life's difficulties. But the one thing you can never do is to just ignore your problem and do nothing and hope it goes away on its own. It hardly ever will."

I was riding White Eyes that day, a little roan mare with a white face. There I was, my pony's jittery feet prancing up and down on the rocky dirt underneath me, twenty or so unfriendly-looking Paiutes looking like they was about to let their arrows fly and charge me any second, and the words of an old sermon were going through my head!

Then all of a sudden I started laughing!

I couldn't help it. It just seemed like such a crazy thing to be thinking about at such a time.

*Shoot, Rev. Rutledge,* I thought, *that advice of yours don't do me a blame bit of good now! When you were talking about problems, you didn't have no Indians staring you in the face!*

Then I even tried to do what he said you couldn't!

I stopped laughing long enough to close my eyes and count to ten. It had come to me that maybe I was dreaming or that the Paiutes were some kind of winter mirage. Maybe they *would* go away!

*One . . . two . . . three . . . four . . .* I counted slowly in my mind, but fast enough so that if it didn't work, they wouldn't be on top of me by the time I reached ten! *. . . eight . . . nine . . . ten.*

I opened my eyes.

The Paiutes were still there! They hadn't moved an inch.

I wasn't laughing now. And the words of Rev. Rutledge's sermon began to make more and more sense. I found myself wishing I'd paid better attention that day, wondering if he'd said something *else* you could do about your problem besides going through them or around them like I remembered.

I probably could just keep sitting there, kinda combining the waiting and praying with hoping my problem would go away. But that didn't seem too likely to work. If I sat there long enough, they were sure to attack—that's just the way Paiutes were.

That left only the first two possibilities.

I didn't really think that Pony Bob's trick would work in this case. For all I knew this might be the same band of Paiutes he'd ridden through! Even if it wasn't, they'd probably heard about the incident just like I had, and weren't about to let themselves be outsmarted into letting another Pony Express rider ride through like that. If it did happen to be the same party, they probably thought I was Pony Bob and were sitting there figuring how to catch and kill and scalp me to get even!

No, I figured my chances were about zero in a thousand of coming out on the other side of them alive if I tried to tackle *this* problem head on.

*I'll have to say no thanks to solution number one, Rev. Rutledge,* I thought to myself. *And that leaves number two. This looks like a clear case of having to go around the problem!*

It was a pretty rugged area, almost mountainous, though off to my right was a pretty good-sized plain. The trail had been following the base of a steep ridge off to my left, the hillside was rocky and steep on that side of the path. On the top of the ridge— probably two, maybe three hundred feet higher than the trail—a flat plateau ran in the same direction as I'd been going. As I looked up I thought that if I could just get to it, I'd be able to ride along the plateau for quite a distance and still be going in the direction of the swing station about twenty-three miles away.

Now, the plain off to my right wasn't really all that flat at all, it just looked that way. Like so much of the Utah-Nevada territory, the ground was broken up by creek beds and gulches and little ravines. You couldn't see any of them because they were all sunk down below the ground level, so as you looked out across the area, your eyes fooled you into thinking it was a nice flatland you could just ride across.

Then an idea came to me.

Maybe I could fool the Indians the same way your eyes fooled you when you looked out across the plain.

If I hightailed it straight across to the right, making like I was going to ride way out into the plain and make a great big circle around them, I figured they'd bolt after me and try to angle them-selves so as to cut me off. Then, after they were headed away from the road, I would dip down into a wash, get out of their view, and double back, keeping low in the ravines and creek beds until I got back to the road. Then I'd scramble up the other side, lose myself in the huge boulders of the hillside, and gradually work my way up to the top of the ridge. I'd ride along the plateau for several miles until I could find my way back down to the trail, well past the Paiutes, and continue on.

It only took ten seconds to see the whole plan in my brain, and by the eleventh I was on my way!

I suddenly dug in my heels and headed my pony off to the right, and the Paiutes took off too, angling across the plain to head me off. My plan was working perfectly!

I rode for three or four hundred yards, then dipped down into a shallow, dry creek bed. I was glad there hadn't been any big storms yet. There'd only been a little rain, and the runoff hadn't started to make the ground wet and boggy in the hollows. I pulled my pony to a stop, jumped off, and waited for another ten or twenty seconds.

Crouching down, I crept up to the wall of the wash, climbed up on a rock, and carefully peered over the edge.

The Paiutes were riding furiously, expecting me to appear again any moment still riding in the same direction!

I crept back in the direction of the road, leading my pony along the creek bed until we were deep enough below the level of the plain that I could mount her without being seen. Slowly I doubled back, staying low in the ravines and washes.

Once I figured I was safe, I gave her my heels and lit out again, working my way through the maze of washes, ravines, and canyons, sometimes with rough walls of rock going straight up on both sides of me.

It took a while to pick my way back, but eventually I made my way almost to the trail. Then I climbed up and out of the ravine I was in, galloped quickly across the trail, and tore into the rocky terrain on the other side. Within another minute I was out of sight and safely behind the boulders and ridges of the hillside. Now I had to work my way up to the plateau on top.

The hill grew steeper and steeper the higher I climbed. From the trail, it had looked like a moderately easy ride, but now I found it was anything but. Small rocks and loose shale made the footing treacherous. There was no trail to follow. And I was still scared and pushing the poor horse too fast, which was a big mistake. The Express ponies were faster than anything on level ground, but they weren't made for this kind of slippery climbing.

We were probably safe from the Indians by now, and I know the pony was exhausted from not being used to the climbing. But by now I wasn't thinking too clearly. I'd been riding six hours that day already, and I had another three to go to the next station. Trust the Paiutes to show up right in the middle of the longest stretch I ever had to ride between fresh horses! Fool that I was, I should have turned around and gone back eight miles to where I'd just changed mounts.

I reckon I was three-quarters of the way to the top when I came to a little ledge that dropped off steep on one side but was fairly level along its surface. It was only about a foot or two wide— way too narrow with the cliff falling off below—and I could tell the pony was spooked.

It was a dumb thing for me to do. I knew enough about horses to know better. If Little Wolf'd been there he'd never have let me do it. But I was tired and still scared and anxious to get up to the top. So I leaned further and urged her into a trot instead of paying attention to her skittishness. She obeyed bravely and moved briskly along, but then all of a sudden the ridge gave way in front of us.

It wasn't much more than a jump of three or four feet to where the ledge picked up again. If we'd have been galloping on the trail below and come to a washed-out piece of ground twice that wide, she'd have leapt over it without even breaking stride, and I wouldn't even have felt a bump.

But this wasn't the trail, and she wasn't going fast enough for an easy leap. She hesitated, then reared!

Now, I've stuck tight to many a jumpy horse in my day, but by that point I was so tired I was barely hanging in the saddle, and she took me clean by surprise. I toppled straight off her back, landing hard and crooked on my leg.

I felt an immediate stinging pain. But there wasn't time to think about it because I'd rolled over the lip of the ledge.

It was steep, and I just kept falling! I rolled over and over, down across the hard ground, and slipping down along pieces of shale and bumping my head and arms and legs against rocks.

It wasn't exactly like falling over a cliff, but almost. I tumbled a long ways, flopping over and over, crunching and bouncing. The only thing I was conscious of was the sensation of falling—and pain all over.

Pretty soon, my brain started to go dark, like a bad dream was fading away. I was still tumbling and rolling, but everything in my senses drifted into a slow, quiet distant haze, and finally into blackness.

I don't know how I had enough of my wits left even to think it, but the last thing I remembered was the notion that this was what it must be like to die.

And I thought, *That must be what's happening to me.*

# CHAPTER 12

## A VOICE IN THE DARK

The next thing I knew, everything was still black.

I woke up real slow, and everything was fuzzy and faint. Nothing meant anything. I couldn't see because of the dark, but even inside my head it was all scrambled and blurry.

Then I became aware of a faint smell, real far away somewhere. I recognized it, but at first I couldn't remember where I knew it from. And there was a strange sound in the background too.

I tried to make myself remember. Then images and reminders of my fall started to come back to me—I could remember going down, down, straight down. . . .

Then all of a sudden I knew the smell! It was smoke. And the sound was the low crackling of a fire. That was it—a fire and smoke!

I was coming awake so slow that everything was all confused. Though my brain was trying to put together the puzzle of what had happened and where I was, it was having a hard time.

As soon as I recognized the sound and smell of the fire, the thought came to me, *I did die! I fell off the horse and died . . . and now I'm in hell!* Then from out of nowhere came a thought of Pa and the horrible things I'd said to him the day I left Miracle Springs. *That's the devil's own fire for sure*, I thought then. *I'm in hell on account of what I said to Pa!*

Suddenly I winced from a sharp throb in my leg.

My head must've been starting to wake up and work right then because right after that I thought, *But wait . . . I can't be in hell if my leg hurts. If I'd died, my body would still be lying out in the rocks of that ravine I fell into.*

Gradually my eyes were starting to work too. Some light was coming into focus from the flickering fire. Everything was black except the red-orange of the low-burning flames.

I struggled to sit up.

"Lay still, son," a voice said in the middle of the blackness.

My eyes shot open wide in terror at the sound. I had no idea who had spoken, and I couldn't see a thing. But my eyes must've been as big as a horse's!

It wasn't a voice you even thought about disobeying. It was strong, and not particularly gentle. Deep and almost gravelly. Again the thought went through my head that I'd died and gone to the fiery place. And if that was true, then I didn't want to stop and ask who the voice might belong to!

I did what the voice said and laid still a long time, wondering what would happen next. I was back to Rev. Rutledge's sermon. This time I didn't have any choice but to just wait!

"How you feeling, son?" asked the voice.

"Uh, all right . . . I reckon," I answered. I was glad to find out my voice still worked. I guessed I wasn't dead after all.

"Where am I?" I asked.

"You're safe, that's where. You had a bad fall back there."

It was all gradually coming back to me about the Paiutes, my plan to get up onto the plateau, the climb up the hill, the ride along the ledge, then the fall. Now I remembered why my leg hurt.

"Where's my horse . . . the mail?" I asked. "Gotta get the mail through. Is the horse safe?"

The voice laughed again, with the deep rumbling sound of boulders crashing down a hill after an earthquake. It was sure not anything like Alkali Jones's cackle! I'd never heard such a deep-sounding voice.

"That horse and whatever mail was on it is long gone, boy," he said. "We're miles and miles from where you fell, and your horse was likely miles away before I got to you anyway."

"The Indians . . . did the Paiutes get her?" I asked.

"Can't tell, son. Might be they did. I wasn't looking for your horse. I had my hands full just dragging you back up out of that crevice you got yourself into."

"Are we safe from the Indians?"

"The Paiutes know better than to bother me. Besides, I've saved enough of their lives to keep me in their good graces for fifty years."

"But . . . where am I?" I asked.

"Like I said, we're miles from where you fell. You're safe, that's all you need to know."

"But I gotta get back . . . back on the trail. They'll be worried about me. I gotta see about the mail."

The deep laughter rumbled out of the dark.

"Son," the man said, "you're not going anywhere. Your leg's broken in two places. You're miles from the Express line. And even if you had a horse and you were healthy, we're snowed in."

"Snowed in! Where in tarnation are we?"

"It'll all make sense in the morning."

"Why is it so warm if. . . ?"

"Just hold your questions till morning. You hungry? You oughta be—you been out for two days."

"Two days! What have I been doing, just lying here?"

"That's right, son. I dragged you up here, splinted your leg, made you as comfortable as I could, and then just waited. I could tell you were a strong little rascal and you'd wake up. So . . . you hungry?"

"Yeah, reckon I am," I admitted.

He handed me something in a bowl, a spoon sticking out from it. I could hardly see, even with the fire, but it smelled good. I picked out some chunks of meat in a kind of gravy and started munching on them. I didn't realize how hungry I was until the smell of that stew hit my nostrils and I tasted the meat. The bowl was empty inside a minute.

"More?" said the man.

"Yeah," I answered, handing him the bowl. "What is it?"

"Rattlesnake."

I gagged and turned away.

Again I heard the laugh from the other side of the fire. "What's the matter, son? You never eaten snake before?"

"No, and I got no intention of eating it again," I said.

"You'll die if you don't. It's about all I eat most winters up here, so you better get used to it."

"Where do you get them?" I asked. "There ain't no snakes in winter."

"Ah, you just have to know where to look. I do. I find them hibernating in their dens. They're sleepy and cold. I kill ten, maybe twenty of them if I spend a morning at it. Then I skin them and cut up the meat, stash it in the snow to freeze. Keeps me in meat all winter long. Then I just take out and cook whatever I need."

"That's all you eat, and you stay alive all winter?" I asked. "This is the high desert. No man can stay alive out here in summer or winter."

"You must figure I'm a ghost then," he said, "because I've been living off the hills here for eight years. There's food in the winter, water in the summer. Plenty for a man to live on—if the man knows how to find the provision the Maker put in the desert. No big secret to it. You just have to have the right kind of eyes to see what most folks can't."

"Which you got?"

"I'm alive, son," was all he answered.

Gradually I drifted back to sleep. I hadn't felt any hurting in my leg the whole time, not since that first stab went through it when I woke up. He'd said it was broke in two places, but it hadn't struck me yet to wonder why I wasn't screaming in pain from it.

# CHAPTER 13

# HAWK

When I woke up again, it wasn't so black anymore. But it wasn't light either. There was just an eerie glow coming from one direction and total blackness from the other.

I shook myself awake, more quickly this time. Now I could feel my leg, both hurting and cold, but on the whole I felt a lot better. The snake meat must've done me some good, as much as I hated the idea of eating it. I pulled myself up on my elbows and glanced around. Whoever my rescuer with the deep voice was, I didn't see him anywhere.

My mind hadn't been working altogether right before. I'd felt warm, but I hadn't paid much attention to where I might be. Now it was obvious that I was inside a huge cave. The fire was still burning, though my leg was freezing.

Then I heard footsteps and suddenly got scared. Whoever it was I'd been talking to in the middle of the night, I still hadn't seen him, and the tone of his laugh hadn't been all that pleasant. 'Course, if he'd wanted to kill and skin me to put in his rattlesnake stew, he'd already had two days to do it, so I don't reckon there was anything to worry about. But I couldn't help feeling nervous.

"Sleep good, son?" he said, coming toward me and sitting down on the opposite side of the fire.

The sound of his voice settled me down some. It didn't sound so bad in the light of day, if that's what the dusky half-light in the cave could be called. But when I actually set eyes on the man, my first impression did not make me feel too confident about my future safety. He *looked* like the kind who might cut me up and freeze my meat to go along with his chunks of snake!

His face was thin and long, and especially in the flickering light of the fire you could see its strong lines—sunken-in cheeks that you could see even behind the full beard, high cheekbones, a sharp jaw and chin. His whole frame was lean but not what I'd call skinny. That's how his face was too. There was no fat, just muscle and bone and hardiness. He looked strong and tough, like he'd been in a few tangles and probably given the other fellow the worst of it. He had lots of hair going all over the place, though it wasn't as gray or tangled as Alkali Jones's. The beard was black.

I couldn't tell a bit how old he might be. A beard always makes a man look older. And in the darkness of the cave, for all I could tell, the man might have been anywhere from thirty to fifty. He seemed to still have his teeth, every once in a while one of them would catch a shine from the flames.

He tossed a piece of wood on the fire, and sparks danced up from the disturbance.

"Where do you get wood around here?" I asked.

"Spend my summers gathering wood for winter, spend my winters storing away snow water down in the cave for summer. Everything you need's out here, son."

Now for the first time I looked in the other direction, toward the lightness. We were some thirty feet from the opening of the cave, but I couldn't see out.

"Why is the light so pale?" I asked. "Is the sun just coming up?"

The deep laughter came again. "Don't you know what you're looking at there, son?" he said. "That's snow—solid snow! Only lets in a bit of light."

"Snow . . ." I said. "But why is it there?"

"We're snowed in! I told you that last night. There's twenty feet of snow over the whole mouth of the cave. You're not looking at daylight, son, you're looking at a snowbank—from the inside!"

I lay quiet for a while, trying to take in this sudden new development, although I still didn't realize the full extent of what his words would mean. As it turned out, I didn't see the real light of day for two weeks, when we dug our way out after it had half melted down. And it wasn't the only time we got snowed in that winter, either!

"Is that why my leg's so cold?" I asked after a minute or two.

"In a manner of speaking, I suppose you'd say that."

"How do you mean?"

"I mean you're cold from the snow, all right—but not because it's out there."

"Where then?"

"Look down at your leg, son. I been packing that broken bone in snow on and off since the minute I got it splinted. That's the cold you're feeling, to keep it from swelling up, and that's why you'll keep the leg and be walking on it inside a month."

"So that's why it doesn't hurt . . . and it's all numb."

"Another day or two, and it'll be out of danger. It won't need the snow after that. Then we'll make you some kind of a crutch to go with the splint so you can hobble around some. Why, you'll be good as new come spring."

"Spring!" I protested. "I can't stay here till spring! I've got to get back."

"I told you before, you're not going anyplace anytime soon. Now, if we get a break in the weather and if you can get around on that leg—if you're of a mind to, then I'll take you down the mountain. But until then, you just better figure on getting used to this cave. It's going to be your home for a while, there's no getting around it."

Again I was quiet, thinking about what he'd said.

"What's your name, son?" the man asked.

"Zack . . . Zack Hollister," I answered.

"Well, Zack Hollister, I'm Hawk Trumbull."

"Why Hawk?" I asked.

"It's a name the Paiutes gave me. That was years ago."

"Are you . . . friendly with the Paiutes?" I asked.

The man called Hawk laughed again—I was starting to get used to him laughing. "No one is what you'd term *friendly* with them. They're not even friendly with themselves! Let's just say I know how to get along with them."

"That's more than the Pony Express does."

"I've got some advantages the Express doesn't have. I know some things the Paiutes need to know and where to find certain things they need. So they tolerate me, mostly for what I can do for them—you hungry?"

"Yeah . . . yeah, I reckon I am," I answered. "But don't you have anything besides rattlesnake to eat?"

Hawk chuckled. "The day'll come when you'll eat my stew and love every bite! But winter's not all the way here yet, so I've got a few things you might like better. I might even make you some biscuits one of these days. There's nothing like biscuits cooked on a stick over an open fire. How about some coffee?"

I suddenly realized the smell of fresh-boiled coffee was all around. I don't know how I didn't notice it before. It smelled just like home!

"Sure . . . do you have everything in here?" I added as he handed me a hot tin cup.

"Everything I need. No luxuries. But food and warmth and shelter, and lots and lots of room to myself. Hundreds of miles to call my own, and I learn something new from it every day. There's no life like it, son."

"Learn . . . learn what kind of stuff?" I said, taking a sip of the steaming black brew he'd made.

"About the world, about life, about myself. Mostly about the Creator."

"You mean God?"

"That's who I mean, son."

# CHAPTER 14

## BIGGER AND DEEPER

Laid up like I was, there wasn't much I could do except lay there and let Hawk take care of me.

He kept blankets and animal furs under me and over me, so I was plenty warm—almost cozy, if you could use that word about a cave. He gave me meals and checked on my broken leg every so often, packing it in snow again whenever it started to get red or swell up, and keeping the rest of me warm enough that the cold on my leg didn't bother me much.

We'd sit around the fire and talk a lot. But off and on he'd disappear deep into the cave to do some kind of work, he said he'd show me everything later.

Hawk spent considerable time shoveling snow away from the mouth of the cave and taking it down deep into the other end where he was building up his supply of snow and water for the following summer. He couldn't dig all the way out from the inside until some of it melted. But he got enough dug so that we could go outside, even surrounded by snow, and make ourselves a privy outside the cave, and feel like we were getting a little outside sunlight. Of course, he had to help me when we did, because I couldn't walk on my own for a long time.

He also worked at making me a crutch out of branches and pieces of wood he had in the cave. He had lots of tools—knives, axes, shovels, picks, pieces of wood, leather strapping . . . just about everything he needed, like he'd said.

Looking back on it now, I don't know how the time passed so

quick. There was nothing for me to do. Hawk kept busy, though I don't know how much of what he was doing he really needed to do.

We talked, but not all the time. Hawk knew how to be quiet, knew how to let silence say what it had to say. He didn't try to fill the air up every minute with words. That was one of the things he taught me—to be comfortable with silence. So during those first few days—though, like I said, we did talk—I spent a lot of time just watching him or staring into the fire. That was another thing he taught me in those early days—to watch and observe.

He never told me those things. He never sat me down and said, "Now, Zack, you gotta learn to appreciate the quiet, and you gotta watch and observe from what's going on around you and learn from it."

No, that wasn't Hawk's way. He let me learn what I was ready to learn. For instance, he just let me *feel* the silence and know that he was at peace with it and figure out for myself that silence was a good thing.

Later on, Hawk taught me a lot with words, too, but always the words followed. First came the silence and the watching—and sometimes that was enough. Sometimes words would come along afterward to add meaning and sense to it all. But they always came after I had already begun to figure out what the silence was saying or at least asking myself what it was supposed to be saying.

The things I learned from Hawk always had to do with such simple things. Yet he'd see huge meaning in them. He taught me to *see*, to find meaning . . . in everything.

Two of the first things I learned to look at different were the two things closest by during those first days—the fire and the pale light from the snow at the mouth of the cave.

Hawk would just start asking me a question now and then, maybe like, "Be pretty tough, wouldn't it, if there wasn't *any* light?"

Then we'd talk about light for a while, maybe going off in all kinds of directions in our conversation. At the end of it, I always knew he helped me understand the whole idea of light in a deeper way.

It was the same with the fire.

Fire's got a lure to it you can't help being drawn into. I'd find myself just staring into the orange and yellow flames, sometimes for hours. All it would take was a question or two from Hawk to set my mind going.

"Where does the smoke go?" I asked him.

"Little crack way up through the roof of the cave—twenty, thirty feet up there."

"Why doesn't the snow drip in and get us all wet?"

"Near as I can figure, the crack curves around and runs downhill for a spell, too, so whatever leaks down from outside doesn't get all the way down inside the cave. Smoke'll go up and down and all over the place long as there's an air draft pulling it. Water only goes downhill."

"It's so warm inside," I said. "I can't believe we're surrounded by snow everywhere."

"No better insulation than the earth, Zack," Hawk replied. "Once you get a good fire going, place like this'll stay warm enough to live in all winter."

Well, anyway, the days did pass quick. The snow outside melted down enough so that Hawk could finish shoveling his way through it. And gradually, using the crutch he'd made me, I was able to get up and about on my splinted leg. There was still a thick pack of snow everywhere when I finally did get out into the light of day, but breathing that fresh air sure felt good!

After that, there wasn't another big snowfall for quite a while, and we were able to start moving about outside. Already I'd almost forgotten my anxiousness to hurry back down to the valley and the Pony Express. I knew I couldn't ride yet, and Hawk Trumbull was starting to grow on me.

One day I woke up and Hawk was gone from the cave.

I crawled to my feet and hobbled outside. It took me an hour to find him, though he was only a hundred yards away, up on top of the hill behind the mouth of the cave.

I worked my way up to where he was sitting.

"Morning," I said.

He didn't reply. He just kept looking up at the sky. I was worn out from the climb, so I sat down a little ways off. Hawk just kept staring straight up into space. It was cold but bright and sunny, and the sky was a deep, deep blue.

We must have sat that way for twenty or thirty minutes, neither of us making a sound.

"Big, isn't it?" Hawk finally said after a long time, still staring straight up.

"You mean the sky?" I asked.

"Yep—the sky. It's the biggest thing there is."

That was a statement worth chewing on a while. And sure enough, Hawk didn't say anything else till he knew I was through chewing on it.

I'd always thought of things . . . well, as *things*—something you could touch or see. An object. If you're going to call something "big," I figured it ought to be something with *thing-ness* to it, something that's real . . . like a horse or a big tree or a mountain or the ocean. If he'd have asked me, I reckon I'd have said the earth, or maybe the sun, was the biggest thing there was. I'd have never thought of the sky, cause the sky *wasn't* a "thing." It was just . . . air—empty. It was a *nothing*, not an object. So I had to chew Hawk's statement all around for a while, and it still didn't seem quite right to me when he spoke up again.

"Yep," he said, "everything's bigger and deeper than you think, bigger and deeper than it looks at first. You've got to look past what you *think* is there."

"How?"

"You've got to look past the shells, past the outside, so you can see inside."

It wasn't that hard a statement to understand, but since I was still thinking about the sky, I was confused about what he meant.

"It's all about yolks and shells, son," Hawk went on. That was always his way—after he got me looking at something long enough to wonder about it, once he had my attention, then he would talk to me about what I'd been looking at. "That's it . . . yolks and shells. Everything's got a yolk and a shell. Trouble is, most folks can only see the shells 'cause that's what's visible to their eyes. So they figure that white, hard, oval thing *is* the egg. Tell me, Zack, is the shell the egg?"

"No, I don't reckon so," I answered, still not altogether sure what he was getting at.

"'Course not. The shell's just the shell. Ain't no good for a thing. Well . . . nothing, that is, except protecting the yolk, and that's mighty important in its own way. But what I'm trying to tell you is this: the life is in the yolk, not the shell. That's what I mean about looking inside—finding where the *life* is. Because, you see, everything's got a yolk—a place hidden away where the *life* is. Not just eggs. Everything! That's what life's about, learning to see past the shells and into the yolks."

He stopped. Again we sat there for a long time. He always gave me plenty of time to think about what he said.

"What does that have to do with the sky?" I said after a while.

"It's got everything to do with it," he answered. "I said it was bigger and deeper than it seems at first. But you've got to look long and hard to see it . . . to see *into* it . . . into its yolk, into its meaning, into the *why* of it."

He stopped and gazed straight up again.

"Look up at the sky," he said." Tell me, what do you see?"

"Just blue," I answered.

"That's all most folks see. You can't *see* the deepness. But it's the biggest thing in the universe. Though most folks see it every day, they can't see how big it is . . . or what it means, what it's supposed to be telling them. They look and look, but never see."

"What *is* it supposed to be telling them?"

"I can't tell you that, son," he laughed. "I can't make it too easy for you, or you won't learn to train your own eyes."

"Can you give me a hint what it's saying?"

He laughed again. "I reckon that's a fair request," he said. He was quiet a while, then said, "It's telling you something about whoever made it."

"You mean God?"

"Yep. Everything that is got made by somebody. Everything got made for a reason. If you look at that thing long enough and learn to look past what it looks like into the inside of what it *is* and what it *means*, it'll start to tell you about the person who made it, even if you never met him, and what it was made for."

He paused thoughtfully, then went on.

"A fellow could come into my cave and spend a week there," he said. "Even if he never laid eyes on me, he'd start to know a lot about me—that is, if he knew how to look. Lots of folks don't know *how* to look. But if you do, everything you set your eyes on has plenty to teach you."

"Like the sky?"

"You're getting it now, son," replied Hawk. "I won't tell you what the sky's saying. But for sure it's telling all who will listen about the One who made it. There's got to be a reason why it's so big, why it goes on forever, why it's over us and around us even when we're not aware of it or not thinking of it.

"You see what I mean, Zack? The sky's telling us about its Maker all the time. The only question is, who's listening?"

"I think I'm starting to see what you mean," I said.

"You keep on looking and trying to find out why the Maker made things like He did. You keep trying to see inside things to what they're supposed to mean, and you'll find out soon enough."

"Learn to *see*, Zack, my boy . . . learn to *see*."

# CHAPTER 15

## THE LAY OF THE LAND

Just about all of January and February we stayed inside. Hawk seemed to have most of what we needed, but every so often, when the weather let him, he'd go down to one of the trading posts for supplies, trading the skins we'd accumulated for what he needed. By the time my leg was well enough for me to walk normally, the winter was easing up and travel got easier.

At first Hawk only had one mule, that he kept in a cave lower down, complete with feed and straw when he'd be gone himself for a spell. So mostly we walked everywhere. But returning from the trading post in the first week of March, I saw him pulling along a second mule he'd bought for me to ride.

Nothing really changed too much after that, though. Riding that doggone stubborn mule was more work than walking! Every time I looked in its face I thought of Alkali Jones and his hard-headed beast! Leastwise, riding the mule, I was able to go out traveling with Hawk and find out more about this desert I'd ridden through so many times but never really seen.

Most of Nevada, Hawk told me, had once been under water back when the continents and land and mountains and lakes and rivers were all different than now.

All that came up one day when I asked him why there were so many caves around where we were, with such interesting twists and turns and pretty rock formations inside them. And why, too, you could still find so much water, even out in the desert, if you knew where the caves were, and why you even sometimes saw shells like Corrie'd brought back from San Francisco.

"You ever hear of John Fremont?" Hawk asked me.

"Sure," I answered. "My sister knows his wife and worked on his campaign for President back in '56."

"No foolin'!" exclaimed Hawk. "Your sister knows Jessie Fremont?"

"Yep."

"If that ain't something!"

"So what's John Fremont got to do with the caves?" I asked.

"He was the first white man through this region. He and Kit Carson came through here back in '43, looking for the Buenaventure."

"The what?"

"Buenaventure—a legendary river that was supposed to flow all the way from the Rockies to the Pacific. They never found it, of course, 'cause there ain't no such river. All they found was this."

Hawk stretched out his hand and swung it around in every direction.

"Nothing here but a few scraggly rivers and a hundred streams that flow for a while and then vanish under the ground. Fremont called it the Great Basin because all the water disappeared like it was draining out of the bottom of a sink.

"I don't suppose Fremont does have much to do with the caves," he added, chuckling. "I just thought of him exploring through here fifteen, twenty years ago. I read some of Fremont's work. I don't know about his politics, but the man was a first-rate explorer and cartographer."

"What's a cartographer?"

"Somebody who draws maps. Fremont's travels back in the '30s and '40s gave people in the East a more accurate picture of what the West was like than Lewis and Clark's stories did.

"The Indians say that thousands of years ago this all used to be a huge lake, called Lake Lahontan. Some folks figure it might have even been part of the ocean once, on account of it being such a salty lake, like the one over in Utah. Anyhow, it kept the land green, and there were fish and water birds, and water flowed into it from the mountains all around."

"What happened to it?"

"Everything changed. Gradually, of course. Seasons changed, it got hotter, quit raining as much, not so much snow in the mountains."

"When'd all that happen?"

"Who knows how long it took? But after a few thousand years passed, this whole place where Lake Lahontan had been turned into a great big high desert with chains of mountain ranges and valleys stretching north and south all the way across it."

"Any of the old lake left?" I asked.

"Only Pyramid Lake and Walker Lake—and a few little lakes scattered around. And the caves. Now I'm finally to the answer to your question, Zack."

"Yeah. This sure ain't the kind of place where I'd expect them. I never saw a single cave when I was riding."

"You don't see these kind. They were formed from the water of the lake going down. It found underground caverns to sink down into. The salt and minerals from the kind of lake it was, they were all left behind, making hard, crusty formations. That's what's kept these caverns from caving in like regular dirt would have. So that's why there's lots of caves around."

The longer I was with Hawk, the more of these caves I got to know. He used them for different purposes.

"Some of them are large, some small, Zack," Hawk told me after winter broke and we started our spring travels around the region. "Some've got plenty of water from underground springs, others are dry. In a couple of the higher ones—those that are dry— I bring in snow as long as it lasts to store in small hollows for summer. By the time you've been with me a while, son, there won't be anyplace you can't survive!"

As spring advanced we moved from cave to cave, depending on whether we might be tracking ground squirrels, sage grouse, deer, jack rabbits, marmot, antelope, coots, or sage hens. Sometimes we fished in one of the rivers or lakes.

"I don't hunt except for food," Hawk said, "though I'm always on the lookout for skins. That's what we use out here for clothes, shoes, tools, and all kinds of things. The Paiutes'll trade for them too. And pelts are how I trade for what supplies I might need down at the trading post at Desert Springs."

"What kind of skins?" I asked.

"Oh, coyote, deer, and mountain sheep up in the high country. I even know a place or two where once in a while I can trap a beaver—if the Indians don't beat me to it."

Traveling with Hawk as spring advanced to summer, I learned that water isn't as much of a problem in the desert as you might think.

"Springs are common, Zack," Hawk told me, "if you know what to look for."

"You'll show me?"

"'Course I will. Hot springs bubble up out from cracks in the ground at the base of most of the mountain ranges, and higher up, clear cold fresh water can be found most places too."

The reason the water was so hard to find, Hawk told me, was that the desert began only a few feet from every river, every lake, every stream, and every spring. Whatever water there was eventually dried up or sank into the sand and the hard-baked clay. So you might be walking along the sandy, dusty ground between dried-up grass and sagebrush and wiry shrubs of greasewood and never know you were within sight of a spring.

"You've got to learn the lay of the land," Hawk told me. "God's put everything you need right in front of you, you just have to learn how to see where it is. The Paiutes and Shoshone have survived in this land for generations, as barren as it looks."

Speaking of the Paiutes, Hawk gave me a real different picture of those Indians than I had gotten from the Pony Express. Hawk told me there were eight different bands of Indians who called themselves *Paiute*, which means "the People." Their specific name depended on what they ate, which depended on the regions they roamed.

"The Northern Paiutes—they're called the rock-chuck eaters, the jack-rabbit eaters, the cui-ui eaters, and the ground-squirrel eaters," Hawk explained.

"What's cui-ui?"

"Fish—big, ugly suckers they get out of Pyramid Lake."

"What about the others?"

"The Southern Paiutes are called the cattail eaters, the trout eaters, the grass-nut eaters, and the fish eaters."

"That everything they eat?"

"No. All of them'll eat whatever they can find. Around the lakes there're rabbits and ducks. Those that live out further from water eat insects, rats, grasses and roots and nuts—anything they can get. They can gather enough pine nuts in late summer to last them for most of the winter."

"Were the Paiutes always so vicious toward whites?" I asked.

"Not from how they tell it," he replied. "At first they just watched from a distance as strangers began to cross their land. Gradually, as more came, they got curious and crept closer. The first meetings were friendly enough. Chief Winnemucca told me once that he rescued an early party of explorers. By making signs back and forth he was able to learn that the party was lost."

"What happened?"

"The chief drew maps in the sand with a stick and pointed them in the direction they wanted to go. Same thing happened to Fremont later too. He wrote in his journal that the Paiutes treated him to a lavish feast of trout on the shore of Pyramid Lake. Then they gave him and his men directions they badly needed."

"How, if they couldn't speak to each other."

"Probably the same way that Winnemucca did with those other explorers—by making diagrams of mountains and lakes and using lots of sign language and pointing back and forth."

Hawk paused and let out a long sigh.

"No, son," he went on after a moment. "I'm afraid it was gold that brought the hatred and violence between the People and the white man. Thousands and thousands of white men came out West to find it. Many were friendly, but a lot others weren't. The Paiutes were treated cruelly and shamefully. So they tell me, at least, and I ain't sure I doubt it. I've seen enough with my own eyes to run my blood hot. The miners and the folks that followed after ruined hunting areas and spoiled rivers and took Indian women.

"Then, after silver was discovered over near Carson two years ago, the whites began moving into the land of the Paiutes by the thousands. I've run into a few I didn't like myself. They cut down the piñon pines so now you only find clumps of them here and there, and the Paiutes can't exist without them. They brought herds of cattle to graze on the rice grass, and the deer and sage hen and rabbit got a lot scarcer since then.

"That's why last year, all the Paiute bands assembled and made war—to protect their lands. I reckon the army sees it a mite different. But anyway, that's how it looks to me. That's why your Pony Express was attacked so often."

"So they're not really warlike," I asked, "like everyone says?"

"They used to be a very peaceful people. They only wanted to live at peace and be people, not warriors. But times change, and I'm afraid they can no longer be said to be a peaceful tribe.

"Yeah, they're warlike, Zack. But I don't think they want to be."

# CHAPTER 16

## LOOKING FOR WATER

It's almost impossible to describe just what Hawk did for me in the months we spent together out in the wilderness—what he taught me, how he changed me. It was all the small experiences that added up to new ways of looking at everything.

It wasn't just teaching me how to live, how to survive, in the wilderness, though that was a big part of it. Mostly he was showing me how to look for things, how to see things that most folks never do and that I sure never did before.

He was sure more than just a wilderness man. Sometimes I'd almost get to thinking of him, as crazy as it sounds to say it when I think of his appearance, like a preacher.

Our time together passed both slow and quick at the same time. As I look back, I can't remember everything that happened in the exact order. It all blends together in my memory.

Like once, when summer was approaching, we were riding along looking for water, following a dry creek bed. I was getting mighty thirsty . . . and a little worried. We were a long way from any of the caves.

Hawk just kept watching the ground like he could see water there, but it was plain to my eyes that the bed was dry as a bone.

Finally I couldn't stand it any longer.

"You really figure this creek bed's gonna lead us to water?" I asked.

"Sure as the sun's up there beating down on us," Hawk answered me.

"How can you tell?"

Hawk smiled one of his smiles that by then I'd learned meant, if not exactly that he'd been *waiting* for the question, at least that he was glad I'd asked it.

"Surely I've taught you enough by now about looking under the surface of things."

"Yeah, but you can look at that dry, sandy dirt all you want, and it ain't gonna make no water appear there on the surface."

"No, you're right about that. No water's going to appear right here. But there's water underneath."

"How can you tell?"

"Just can. When reading nature's signs is all you've got to keep you alive, you learn mighty quick what she's trying to say."

"So what's this dry creek bed saying?" I asked.

"It's telling us that up ahead somewhere there's water running in this same bed."

"Why ain't it here? What happened to it?"

"Disappeared into a sink. There's sinks all over this territory. There's one below us somewhere, and if we follow this stream far enough, we'll get to the water trickling down into it."

"But what if there just plain ain't no water, or if you never do find any?" I asked.

"There's always water," Hawk replied. "In an emergency you might have to get it out of a barrelhead cactus—like that one over there, though you don't see too many of these this far north."

He pulled up alongside one of the stumpy, barrel-shaped plants growing nearby, dismounted, and whacked off the top of the plant with his knife. The inside was full of a white pulp. He hacked away at it and finally pulled a big chunk out with his hands. Then he held it up in front of me, squeezing it in his fist.

"You see, if you work at it, drops of water'll start dripping out. It's slow work; they're not the wettest cactus in the desert. But if you can get past the thorns, there's life inside even these ornery looking things."

He got back on the mule, and we kept riding. All the time, Hawk was pointing out the little signs that told him water was around and that we wouldn't have to get our water from a barrelhead that day—things like the kind of plants and grasses, even the color and shape of the sand and its formations. And sure enough, about an hour later, all at once the stream bed was running with a decent flow of water, right to the hole where it disappeared straight down into the ground.

Hawk didn't say anything when we found the sinkhole. He knew I'd already learned one more lesson about looking past just what things seemed to be. We dismounted and all four of us—Hawk and me and the two mules—had a good long drink.

Then we sat on the ground and rested a spell and had something to eat out of our saddlebags, since we had water to go with it. Finally we filled our canteens and continued on our way.

As we went, Hawk started to chuckle to himself.

"What is it?" I asked.

"Oh, a funny picture just came into my mind."

"What?"

"Talking about water and rivers, the picture of a giant bear lying across a river popped into my head."

"Doing what?"

"Just lying there in the water, but so big that he caused a bend in the flow of the water."

We kept on silently a few minutes. I could tell Hawk was revolving the bear picture in his mind, trying to figure out what it meant.

"You see, Zack," he said at length, "God is all around us. The tiniest *and* the largest things, they all say something about him. This whole desert he holds on the tips of his fingers. Look up at the clouds."

I did.

"Just imagine the movement as God's way of breathing. Yet at the same time, he is so close that he lives inside us too."

"How did you get from the bear to the clouds?" I asked.

"I don't know," he replied with his rumbling laugh. "I was just following wherever my thoughts led. Sometimes interesting things come to you that way. But about the bear, I realized that if there was a bear lying there, causing the bend in the river, we would stand up and take notice! Yet God is so much bigger than any bear, and he is constantly doing things that are of far vaster importance, but we *don't* notice. The clouds moving over us right now are being blown by his breath. Even that rock we were just sitting on a few minutes ago is being held in place by his hand. Do you see what I'm saying?"

"That we could see the bear, but we can't see God?"

"Right, even though God is bigger. He is always holding every flower, every branch of every tree, every rock, every pebble. It is *his* hand that turns every bend in the river . . . but our eyes aren't used to seeing it. We grow too accustomed to our surroundings, and then we don't see that he is pouring life into everything—into every detail of existence, every rock and grain of sand in this desert."

"But if a bear was lying in the river, or if an even bigger bear was holding up that rock we were sitting on, we couldn't help but look twice at it!" I said. "The bear would be visible, but God's invisible, isn't he?"

"Yep," replied Hawk. "But not exactly invisible, because we have been looking at what God does all our lives. We *have* seen him, from the day you and I were each born, we just don't know it. We haven't trained our eyes to see the maker of bears and rivers and clouds and rocks all together . . . and what he's doing every day."

We rode on a little further. I think Hawk knew I had plenty to think about for the time being. But then he added one more twist to the conversation.

"Everybody has two eyes, Zack," he said. "But if you're really going to live, you need *four*."

"Four . . . how do you mean?"

"Two outside, two inside."

I didn't need him to tell me what he meant. I'd been with him long enough to understand.

"And the most important place to use your extra set of eyes isn't to look under the ground for disappearing creeks, is it, Zack? Or for bears lying in rivers."

"Nope. You've made your point, Hawk," I said, laughing.

"Where is it?"

"Inside your own self," I answered.

During our next stretch of silence, I thought about how Hawk himself was a just-about perfect example of all he was telling me. Nobody'd know by looking at him what was inside. Who'd be able to guess that a wild-looking mountain man like him would all the time be thinking about God? About the insides of things?

# CHAPTER 17

# LEGEND OF THE GRAY FOX

"I ever tell you the Paiute story of the gray fox?" Hawk asked me one day.

It was a dim, overcast day early in spring, still cold, and without any sign of new growth or greenery anywhere. It was even before the conversation we'd had about disappearing creeks and bears lying across rivers. On this particular day everything, from the flatland to the mountains and past the horizon up into the sky, everything looked gray and dreary. I suppose that's what reminded Hawk of the story.

"Nope," I replied to his question.

"Most foxes are red, right?" he said.

I nodded. "We got some brown and gray ones in California," I added.

"But out here in the high desert of the Utah territory there aren't hardly even any red foxes, much less grays. Almost none."

"So what do the Paiutes have to do with them?" I asked.

"Well the fox is a sly and crafty animal, and I reckon the Paiutes like to think the same is true of themselves. You know about the Paiute war last year?"

"Yeah. That was right before I came out, and everybody told me about it when I joined the Express. Keeping away from them was our main worry."

"With good reason," said Hawk. "War chief Numaga fought the cavalry almost to a standstill last year. There's been more white blood shed by the Paiutes hereabouts than in any other conflict since our kind landed several centuries ago. Man of peace that he was, once he was forced to it, Numaga was a brilliant warrior."

"What's that got to do with the fox?" I asked.

"Like I said, there aren't many foxes out here. Foxes want woods and trees. That's how they survive. They learn every nook and cranny of the terrain where they live—rivers, streams, caves, forests, hollowed logs—so that no other animal can catch them when they're in their own familiar surroundings. They can outrun and outmaneuver just about anything. They have bags of tricks to outwit their pursuers, even those who are bigger and stronger."

"I've run into their tricks trying to trap them."

"Right, like running in huge circles to tire out whatever's chasing them, especially dogs. They're fast enough that they can stop, get their breath, drink, even eat, and stay ahead of the dogs, and eventually wear them out. Or they might use their double-back technique, turning around and retracing their own steps right toward their enemy, then leaping off the trail to hide. The dogs chase past, and the fox then leaves in a new direction, while the dogs eventually arrive at a dead end. They'll do 'most anything to throw an enemy off their trail."

"Do you think the foxes actually think up all their tricks?" I asked, thinking more about some of my own past experiences.

"Who knows?" replied Hawk. "They're clever and cunning, that's all I know. I figure that's why rich folks in England and back East go on fox hunts, just to match wits with them."

"I still don't see what they have to do with the Paiutes."

Hawk laughed. "I'm just getting to it," he said. "The Paiutes like to think of themselves as foxlike. And I reckon they got a right to the claim if they can survive out in this wasteland like they have."

"Like you have, too," I said.

"Maybe you're right. But they been here longer, and there's more of them. And one thing's for sure—Numaga sure outfoxed Major Ormsby and the cavalry last year. Anyway, from a long time back the Paiutes have talked about, not a red fox, but a *gray* fox, maybe because of the color of the hills around here."

"What do they say?"

"They claim there's a gray fox that roams these hills, maybe wandered up from the White Mountains to the south where there's grays. They consider it kind of like an animal brother to the Paiutes. If they have a good hunt of deer or elk or antelope, they'll say the Gray Fox chased the animals to them. If they outwit an enemy, either the whites or maybe a certain tribe of the Shoshone they're not on too good of terms with, they'll say the Gray Fox ran through the enemy camp, spreading confusion. If they elude someone chasing them, they'll say the Gray Fox came between and spread false scents and confused the trail with markings and signs to throw them off. Any good thing they can't explain, they'll say the Gray Fox is responsible. It's a quick-witted, daring animal, not big and overpowering like a bear. It uses brains and craft and stealth to gain victory over its adversaries instead of brute strength."

"Is there such an animal around here?" I asked.

"You mean, has anyone actually seen it?"

"Yes."

"I don't know. The Paiutes claim to have caught glimpses of its eyes shining in the night, or of the tip of its furry tail. They believe in it and teach their children its ways. Young Paiute boys and girls grow up wanting to be the first to spot the animal. I heard that one of chief Winnemucca's daughters, Sarah, saw him last year, just before the worst of the outbreaks."

"I thought you said Numaga was chief."

"He was the war chief, Winnemucca was *the* chief. Actually his name was Poito, whites gave him the name Winnemucca. That was the old chief, who scouted for John Fremont back in the '40s. *Young* Winnemucca, the chief now, is Sarah's father."

"Sarah sounds like a funny name for an Indian."

"That's a white name too," answered Hawk. "Her Paiute name is Shell Flower. She lived with a white family for a year at the Mormon trading post, and converted to Christianity, though she still kept her Indian faith too. Always after that she has been known as Sarah to white folks. She and her sister later attended a Catholic convent school in San Jose for a short time too. Winnemucca's family knows the ways of the white man as well as any

Paiute. And now that the fighting from last year is over and most of them are on the reservation, things are peaceful most of the time and a lot of them are learning English."

"Is the reservation near here?"

"Not far. Just a few miles southwest."

"It sounds like you know the man Winnemucca as well as they know the way of the white man," I said.

"I've met his whole family, and believe me, there are more of them than Pony Express riders in this territory! In fact, one of Old Winnemucca's brothers they call Wahe, or the Fox."

"But not gray fox?"

"No, just Fox."

# CHAPTER 18

## IN SEARCH OF FOOD

We got on the trail of a small group of pronghorn antelope across the desert. It was early June sometime, and I'd been gone from home almost a year.

All we had was our two mules, and matching a pronghorn with a mule was like putting a snail up against a racehorse. So we had to use stealth and cunning, else we'd never catch it.

Finally we left the mules tied up by a watering hole and tracked the animal on foot.

It was about an hour later when suddenly Hawk stopped, looking straight up in the sky.

"What is it?" I said.

"I think there's Paiutes out," he said, shielding his eyes from the sun.

"How can you tell . . . you hear something?" I asked.

"No," he replied, "but you see those two eagles way up there?"

I looked but didn't see anything.

"No," I answered.

"Keep looking," said Hawk. "They're circling in a big lazy arc."

"That mean something?"

"Maybe not. But I have the feeling it means the Paiutes are out, and not too far away."

"How can you tell?"

"If you know how to read the eagles," he said, "they can tell you all kinds of things. Sometimes the eagles are looking down on something ten miles away. So all you gotta do is figure out from their movements what they're gazing at."

We kept on after the antelope, but I could tell that Hawk was being a little extra careful.

Twenty minutes later, after stalking up and down what seemed like a dozen rises and falls of the terrain, Hawk and I had managed to head the animal into a small box canyon. We were about a hundred yards apart and it had disappeared from our sight. Hawk signaled to me to rejoin him, and we inched our way to the top of a small ridge over which the animal had disappeared. Hawk shouldered his gun, ready to get off a shot before the animal saw us and bolted up the opposite side of the canyon and away.

But the moment we stuck our heads up over the top of the incline, what met our shocked eyes instead of the trapped antelope was a small hunting party of six or eight Paiute braves standing over a dead antelope, an arrow sticking out of its chest.

They saw us the moment we appeared, and the next instant four arrows were poised in their bows, the tips aimed straight toward us. My heart started pounding so loud I was sure Hawk knew I was frightened out of my wits.

I felt his hand on my shoulder.

"Nothing to worry about, son," he whispered. "These fellows have either strayed off the reservation, or else the antelope led us further west than I figured. You wait here."

Then, without a word, he stood up and walked straight toward the group of Indians. My heart pounded louder than ever.

I couldn't hear anything of what went on, but gradually the arrows came down, although the fierce expressions on the Paiute faces never changed. Hawk talked to them a minute or two in a language I couldn't understand, with an occasional wave of one of the Indians' hands adding expression to the interchange. I watched in silent fear that any second one of them might suddenly kill him and then come after me. But after a couple minutes Hawk turned and walked back in my direction. He came over the ridge and just kept walking away, signaling me where I was still crouching down to follow him. He never looked back, and never said a word until we were fifty or more yards away.

"Looks like they'll be enjoying that antelope in their camp tonight," he said finally, still walking. "I reckon you and me are going to be stuck with cattail pancakes."

"Again!" I groaned. "Didn't you tell them it was our antelope?"

"Sure," replied Hawk, "but they said they'd been following it all morning, and I didn't feel like fighting over it."

"I thought you said you were their friend?"

"*Friend* would not exactly be the right word," laughed Hawk. "They tolerate my presence is about as far as I'd say. I do them favors and show them things and they let me stay alive. But they wouldn't think twice of killing me, either. Don't worry. We'll have our antelope stew—just not today."

We made our way back to the watering hole and our mules. Out of the marshy bog we cut a bunch of pollen spikes off the cattail plants to take back with us—they were just coming out now that summer was approaching. It had been a long trek for nothing, and all the rest of the day we never saw a sign of another animal of any kind.

The day had tuckered me out and I was famished. The thought of cattail pancakes didn't exactly make my mouth water, but by then I would have been happy for anything going into my mouth.

Hawk ate the strangest things, but I reckon that anyone that wanted to stay alive out there had to eat what they could find. Besides the cattail pollen, earlier in the spring we'd eaten the inside shoots of new cattail growth. And Hawk had shown me where to find and how to eat all kinds of native desert plants—buckberries and rice grass, roots of many kinds, squaw cabbage (too bitter to even describe), red berries off the desert thorn, and mustard seeds. Hawk said the best food of all were the pine nuts, but they wouldn't be ripe until August.

When we got back to camp, we made a fire and mashed up the cattail pollen we'd gathered, making it into a paste with water, then mixing in a little cornmeal we still had from Hawk's last ride to Desert Springs for supplies.

Once the patties were made, we roasted them over the desert fire. It wasn't exactly antelope stew, but at least it was warm and kept the hunger away for another day.

# CHAPTER 19

## A TALK OVER CATTAIL PANCAKES

It hadn't taken long with Hawk for me to grow curious about why a fellow like him would be so religious. That's what I wondered at first.

After a while I found myself asking the question differently: How did a man like him get so *wise*?

It took me a long time to get around to asking him directly about it. It was one of those things I figured he'd tell me in his own time if he ever wanted to. But then all of a sudden, as we were sitting there roasting and eating our cattail pancakes, it just popped out without me even planning to say it.

"How come you know so much about God?" I asked.

Hawk thought a long time before he said anything.

"Pretty big question, son," he said finally.

"Too big?" I asked.

"No. No question's *too* big. There's no such thing as too big a question. Actually, it's a good question. Just took me by surprise, that's all."

"So what's the answer?"

Again Hawk thought for a long time. He wasn't the kind of man to start talking before he'd thought about something long enough to know what he wanted to say. If he didn't have something to say, he kept his mouth shut until he did.

Maybe right there was one of the things that made him wise.

But on this day, after a while, he did try to answer my question.

"Well, I reckon after I got out here in this wilderness all by myself, it started with watching nature and animals. It didn't take much to be able to see that there's an order and plan to the world of nature. And animals survive out here—and plants for that matter—because they fall in with the order of things. The world is the way it is for them, and they have no choice other than to fall into harmony with the order of things. You see what I mean?"

"I think so."

"I began to think about men, too," Hawk went on. "I've known lots of people in all kinds of situations in my life. It seemed to me, the more I thought about it, that there were only two kinds of people I'd known—those who were content with their lot in life and those who weren't. The first kind of people were happy, peaceful, and usually you enjoyed being around them. The second kind were discontent, struggling with everything that came along, at strife—both with themselves and with other folks. They were usually selfish, and weren't usually what you'd call nice. It made me stop to think and to ask myself which of the two kinds of people I wanted to be.

"When I thought of the animals again, I realized that men have a choice animals do not—whether to fall into harmony with the order of things in their world, just like the animals, or else not to. When they don't they will be discontent and at odds with everything around them, like the second kind of people I was talking about.

"I began to think further what that might mean. What did it mean to fall in with the natural order of how life was supposed to be? What *is* the natural order of our world?

"That's when I began to look into the hidden meanings of everything, and pretty soon I was thinking about who made it all and asking myself why. That's really the most important question in all the universe—*why*.

"Asking that question in a thousand different ways and about a thousand different things led me eventually into the discovery of who God is—what he's all about. You see, that's the answer to every *why* you can think of—that God made it or did it for a reason. The reason is nothing more than who God himself is.

"Well, if God made everything there is, and for a reason—I figured the *main* reason must be to show himself and what kind of a person he was. Who is God, and what is he like? That's got to be at the root of it all. That's the hidden meaning part, the yolk part.

"The second half of it must be for us to fall into the natural order of it all. He must have some reason why he made us, too. *We* mean something, just like the sky and everything."

"Now I'm afraid you lost me," I said. "What do you mean, people oughta *mean* something."

"What do we *mean*?" Hawk repeated. "What's our life supposed to be about? That's what I'm getting at."

I nodded slowly, understanding a little, but not completely.

"Then I remembered something I'd learned from when I was just a boy," Hawk went on, "about being created in the image of God. It isn't that I'd forgotten. I knew all about God. I was taught a lot about God when I was young. But then I found myself going down into the *inside* depths of the things I'd always known and asking myself what they *really* meant.

"That's how I found myself thinking about being created in the image of God. What did it really mean?"

"Did you figure it out?"

"The conclusion I came to was this—we're supposed to be pictures of God too, just like everything else. That's what we as people must *mean*. That's our purpose. *That* is the natural harmony that we have to fall in with—to be pictures, reflections, images of God. That's what we've got to accept, like the animals have to fall in with the way nature is. If we don't, we won't do any better than they. Life can't be a good thing for anybody unless they go along with that purpose.

"We're supposed to learn to be *like* God ourselves. We can't do that perfectly, of course. That's what sinning is all about. But that's still the purpose, the meaning of life—to be as much a small, little reflection of God as we can be in the midst of all the sin."

Hawk paused and took a deep breath.

"I reckon that's about the size of it," he said. "How's that for a long answer to your question? Never knew I was such a preacher, did you?" he added with a smile.

"But how did you get to be such a thinker and philosopher?"

He roared with laughter.

"I ain't no such thing."

"You sound like one to me."

"What—a thinker or philosopher?'

"Both," I said.

Again Hawk laughed.

"Most of the philosophers I've run into weren't what I'd call thinkers. The two ain't the same, if you ask me."

"I'm not sure I understand."

"Everybody's got the choice whether to be a thinker or not. Don't need to be a philosopher to be a thinker, Zack. You just need to put your brain to use. Being a thinker doesn't mean being a philosopher, just using the brain you've got."

"But a lot of folks don't."

"Everybody *is* a thinker. Some people just don't point their brains in directions that do them any good. They think about things that pass away, that are gone the next day, like the smoke from one of our fires."

"Yeah, I guess I see what you mean."

"For myself, I decided a long time ago that if I was going to spend so much time alone, and that if I was going to live out here like this, with no companion but myself and my own thoughts, then I ought to spend my time thinking about things that matter, and that would help me understand the order of things a man is supposed to fall in with. So I read a lot in the only book I got out here with me—that's the Bible—and I think about what's in it. Animals have their instinct to help them. Man doesn't have that. All he's got is his brain, which he's got to put to the best use he can, otherwise, life's going to be a pretty miserable affair. Anyhow, that's how I've come to see it."

"How come you're out here all by yourself anyway?" I asked.

Hawk got real quiet. I couldn't tell if he was angry at me for what I'd asked, or thinking how to answer. But I never got a chance to find out, because even as I found myself getting nervous for prying, we were interrupted.

It was while we were still sitting there around the fire that we heard the sound of a horse approaching.

# CHAPTER 20

# A VISITOR

Out in the middle of the high desert like we were, running into another human being, except for the Paiutes, of course, was an unusual enough occurrence to make us both stop what we were doing and look, first at each other in surprise, then toward the sound.

As soon as the rider was visible, coming around a big boulder forty or fifty yards away, Hawk got up and walked to meet him. The fellow pulled up.

"Howdy, stranger," said Hawk. "You're a long ways from the rest of the world."

The man didn't speak at first, just eyed Hawk, then looked over at me with no change in his expression. It wasn't a friendly expression either.

He was a rough-looking man, and his squinting eyes were full of suspicion and mistrust. He seemed looking for something that we were hiding from him. I immediately felt like he was angry with us, even though none of us knew each other. He wore a gun on his hip, and a long rifle stuck up behind him out of a saddle holster.

"We ain't got much to offer you," Hawk went on, "but you're welcome to it."

"Coffee smells good," the man said, speaking at last.

"Then come on down off there and join us. Zack, pour the man a cup of coffee."

The rider got down off his horse, tied it to a shrub, and followed Hawk over to the fire. I handed him the cup. He took a sip, then sat down.

"We've just been having some cattail cakes. Care for some?" said Hawk.

"Got anything else?"

"Nope, not here."

"What're you two doing way out here?" the man questioned.

"We live out here," answered Hawk. "But what are *you* doing out here all by yourself? We don't exactly get too many visitors passing through."

"You live where?" said the man, taking a drink of coffee and glancing around. "Here?"

"All around," said Hawk. "Not here exactly. We just happened to be here today and got hungry. We're mostly in those hills west of here." As he spoke he gave a nod with his head. "There's caves we use, and everything we need to make a life of it."

"Don't look like much of a life to me," said the stranger. "That all you eat—weeds?"

Hawk laughed. "We eat whatever we can. Almost had us an antelope earlier today."

"What happened?"

"Paiutes beat us to it."

"You let 'em take it from you? How many were there?"

"Only a half dozen. Yep, we let them take it. Having meat wasn't worth getting killed for."

"That's the kind of attitude what lets them Paiutes think they can do whatever they want," he grumbled.

Hawk said nothing.

"And you say you ain't seen no one else through here recently?" the man added, lifting the coffee cup to his lips but watching Hawk intently as he did.

"No," replied Hawk. "You're the first since this strapping young man here crossed my path last winter," he added, motioning toward me. "*Should* we have seen someone?"

"Maybe . . . maybe not."

"You looking for somebody?"

"I been tracking a half-breed."

"From where?"

"Out of Carson."

"That's a long ways."

"He's got three thousand on his head."

"What's his name?"

"Don't know what the Indians call him. In Carson he's only known as Redskin Tranter."

"Tranter his pa?"

"That's right."

"What did he do?"

"Stole some cattle, killed a rancher."

"What kind of half-breed?"

"Paiute or Shoshone."

"You figure he's coming this way?"

"I tracked him till yesterday, straight toward here."

"We ain't seen a soul, have we, Zack?"

I shook my head.

"Except those Indians a while ago," Hawk added. "But they were all from the Squirrel tribe. You a lawman?" Hawk asked.

The man shook his head.

"What, then?"

"Bounty hunter."

A brief silence followed.

"Well, we haven't seen the fellow you're after," said Hawk. "But you're welcome to share our fire and our coffee. If you need a rest, you can share our cave for the night. I'll make us up some stew when we get back there, and we can give you plenty of water. My name's Hawk Trumbull. My friend's Zack Hollister."

"Much obliged, I reckon I'll take you up on your offer," said the stranger.

"Name's Demming—Jack Demming."

# CHAPTER 21

# A GUEST AT THE CAMPFIRE

Hawk and I didn't have any time alone together the rest of that day. The man named Demming went back with us to the cave we were using, about an hour's ride away on our mules, and bunked down for the night with us. I knew Hawk well enough by then, however, to see that he wasn't altogether comfortable with the other man around, though he continued to be hospitable enough.

Demming spent a lot of time questioning Hawk about the Indians, the area, the trails and the water holes, trying to figure how to get back on the scent of the outlaw he was chasing. I think he could tell how much Hawk knew of the Utah-Nevada territory, and from the glint in his eye as he listened I think he realized that Hawk knew more than he was telling.

Whether he suspected Hawk of being friendly with the Paiutes I don't know. The more we found out about him as the evening wore on, the more I could see why Hawk wouldn't have wanted him to find out.

"This ain't bad, Trumbull," Demming said, taking a second helping of the stew Hawk had made. "Better'n that stuff looked you was eating out on the plain. What's in here, anyway?"

"Sage hen, little quail I had left over."

"It's the first fresh meat I've had since leaving Carson."

"I didn't say it was fresh," said Hawk. "The sage hen's been frozen down in our snow cellar. The quail was smoked and dried."

"I ain't particular," Demming snorted.

As he ate, every once in a while he'd throw me a look that

111

seemed inquisitive, like he'd seen me before or something.

"What'd you say your name was, kid?" he asked between bites.

"Hollister," I answered him, squirming a little.

"Where you from?"

"California."

The answer seemed to puzzle him. He thought about it a minute.

"Where in California?"

"North of Sacramento."

"Place got a name?"

"Yeah—Miracle Springs," I answered.

Again the puzzled look came over his face. "Hmm . . . I might have heard of it," he said after a pause. "What's your pa do?" he added.

I bristled slightly. "He's a miner."

"Yeah. What else would he be?"

He paused and sent his eyes scanning all over me again, again with that look that I didn't like.

"Where's your kin from, kid?" he asked.

"East."

"Where?"

"New York."

He seemed to take the information in with interest, though he hid his reaction well.

"What's your pa's name?" he asked.

At this point I was getting a little irritated by all his questions, and I suppose his bringing up Pa agitated me some.

"I don't see that my pa's name is any affair of yours," I answered, a little rudely, I'm afraid.

He said nothing, just eyed me carefully once more, then turned toward Hawk, who had been listening intently to every word but hadn't said anything.

"Where'd you learn to live out here like this? From the Indians?" Demming asked, now halfway glaring at Hawk with a look that wasn't any more friendly than the ones he had given me. Being around this man wasn't making me like him any more than

I had when he'd first ridden up earlier.

"I've been out here a long time," Hawk replied evasively.

"Around the Indians much?"

"Some."

"Get along with them, do you?"

"Don't have occasion to spend much time with them," said Hawk. "The Paiutes don't exactly welcome strangers, and the Shoshone aren't much better. But I've learned to live with them and keep myself alive, if that's what you mean."

"Ain't exactly what I meant, Mister," said Demming. "What I want to know is if you're one of the kind who thinks the Indians is as good as we are?"

"I don't know if I'm what you call one of those kind or not," Hawk said back to him. "The Indians are different than we are, that's for sure. And with the Paiutes you've got to be careful—they're a tough lot, and they don't look too kindly to white folks these days. But I figure they're human beings just like the rest of us."

"That's where you're wrong, Mister!" Demming shot back, and all of a sudden the fury in his voice was more than evident. "They ain't human! They're animals, and the sooner we're rid of 'em off our land, the safer it'll be for everyone."

"Ain't rightly our land," said Hawk, keeping his voice calm. "They were all here before I came, and they were here a while before that, I reckon."

"Don't matter. Their kind can't claim a right to nothing. They're animals, I tell you—don't even deserve to live."

The fierceness in Mr. Demming's voice by now was making me nervous. I was afraid he might jump up any second and clobber one of us, or pull out his gun if we said something he didn't like.

There was more than just anger in his tone. And more than that, a real mean streak too.

I don't figure I got a right to call any man ugly, so I won't use the word about Jack Demming. But if ever there was a man whose outside expression on his face matched the meanness and anger coming out of him, I figure he was the man. His face was dark from the sun, weathered and rough like the inside of a piece of leather, with a big scar from the lower part of one cheek down over his jawbone and onto the top of his neck. It didn't look like the kind of scar a decent man would get by minding his own business. A couple of his teeth were missing, and the rest were yellow, though he didn't show them much, 'cause he never smiled. His eyes were the worst of it, I suppose. They looked full of hate, that's all I can say about them.

He smelled too, real bad. I don't think he'd had a bath in months! Out there in the desert, I don't reckon a man can altogether help it sometimes. But even Hawk and me put together wouldn't have made a coyote stop and take a second sniff. Demming would have turned a whole herd of buffalo around!

As much as I couldn't keep from noticing his fearsome looks, Hawk kept calmly talking to him. And Hawk wasn't afraid to go straight into those deeper places inside the man's skin.

"You really hate the Indians, don't you, Demming?" Hawk said.

"Dad-blamed right I do—hate every one of the redskinned varmints!"

"Why do you hate them?"

"'Cause they're filthy, ignorant savage animals, and this country'll be a heap better off when they're gone."

"What's filled you with that kind of hate?"

"They killed my brother, for one thing."

"He do something to them to rile them?"

"How dare you, Mister!" spat Demming, half rising in a threatening movement. Hawk just sat there, watching him calmly. I don't know what Hawk would have done if Demming had drawn his gun. As gentle and as God-fearing a man as Hawk seemed at some times, he could also take care of himself. He'd never have survived out here otherwise. But Hawk just sat there, and gradually Demming eased back down onto the ground beside the fire.

"It's been my experience," Hawk said after a minute, "that the Indians don't generally go after someone for no reason."

"You're a fool, Trumbull," rejoined Demming. "You don't know the Paiutes!"

Hawk probably knew the Paiutes better than any white man

alive, but he didn't argue back. After another minute or so, Demming started telling what had happened with his brother. Hawk let him talk freely, and the story emerged.

Apparently Demming had come west in '58 and had settled up even further north than us in California, near Honey Lake Valley near Susanville.

"I built me a log cabin with my own hands, started me a herd of cattle, and sent off for my brother Dexter to join me."

It wasn't too hard to see that he figured on making himself a rich, landowning rancher.

Trouble was, Jack Demming was so full of hatred toward any and all kinds of Indians that he didn't care who knew it. He openly bragged about killing them whenever he happened to find one alone.

Early in 1860, Jack had walked through the snow from the ranch into Susanville for supplies. He spent the night in town, and when he arrived back home late the next afternoon, it was to find the ranch house plundered.

"Dexter was dead—murdered by the Paiutes," he said.

He told the story without any pain or grief or heartache in his voice, only hatred.

From that moment on Jack Demming had been bent on a vengeful vendetta against any and all Indians, wherever it led him, first with the army, and now on his own.

"You and your brother from around here, Demming?" Hawk asked at length.

"No, we come from back East."

"What kind of man was your pa?"

"What business is it of yours?" shot back Demming.

"None," replied Hawk. "Just interested."

"What's there to be interested in about Pa?"

"I just wondered if you got your hatred of Indians from him."

"Well, I didn't," said Demming in a surly voice. "My pa weren't never around. Dexter and me hardly knew him."

"Left your ma, did he?"

"No, I never said he left. He just didn't pay us no mind, except when he had a grudge to settle with someone else and we got in the way. As far as he was concerned, me and Dexter might as well not even have been there. Whenever he did come around, he was drunk and beat us to a pulp. We learned to take care of ourselves."

"That's why you gotta avenge Dexter's death, that it?"

"What's it to you, Trumbull? But yeah, maybe you're right."

"Your pa wouldn't care, even if he knew."

"You got it right there!"

"You ever write home?"

"Wrote my ma a few years back."

"They know Dexter's dead?"

"They might have heard."

"You didn't let them know?"

"My pa never gave us no never mind. Why should he care? What's it to you anyway, Trumbull? Mind your own affairs!"

# CHAPTER 22

# SURPRISE MORNING ATTACK

I awoke the next morning with a sharp pain in my back.

"Don't say a word, kid, or you're dead," growled an evil voice in my ear.

Demming had a knife at my back and was tying my hands as best he could with his free hand. It was early and cold, dew still in the air, light enough to see, but not yet sunup.

Still groggy from being awakened so rudely, I tried to say something.

"What do you want—?"

"Shut up!" retorted Demming angrily. His face was near mine, and his breath was foul.

He spun me over, throwing me on my belly, then jammed a knee in the small of my back instead of the knife. Then with both hands he tied my hands behind me so tight I could feel the leather thongs digging into my skin.

"What do you want with me?" I said, my face in the dirt. "I ain't done nothing—"

"I told you to shut up!" he repeated. He grabbed me and flipped me over onto my back. His arms were as strong as his breath, and he handled me like I was no more than a twig.

Demming glared down at me, then picked his knife back up and brought its sharp tip up to me and poked my neck with it.

"I asked you a question last night," he whispered. "Now I want an answer—that's what I want from you! Now, you tell me your pa's name here and now, or I'll slit that cowardly little white throat of yours so fast—"

"Drop the knife, Demming!" sounded Hawk's voice from ten feet away. I glanced over out of the corner of my eye. Hawk was standing with his rifle aimed straight at Demming's head. I'd never heard his voice sound so loud and commanding.

"Mind your own business, Trumbull," said Demming. "This is between me and the kid."

"The kid's business *is* my business. Now stand away."

"You won't shoot, Trumbull," said Demming, turning an evil glare toward Hawk. "I know your kind—yellow through and through."

The instant the words left his mouth, suddenly Demming lurched to his feet, yanking me up in the same motion. A second later he was standing behind me with one arm clutching me tight against his chest, the other stretched around my shoulders, his right hand still holding the knife against my throat.

"There, you see, Trumbull—you ain't gonna do nothing to me without shooting him first! Now, boy," he said, again to me, "I asked you a question. What's your pa's name!"

"Drummond," I said. "Drummond Hollister."

My voice sounded so small, like the croak of a tiny frog. I'm not ashamed to admit it—I was downright scared for my life! This man was mean, and I knew he *would* stick the knife into my throat if he got riled enough.

"Ha! I knew it," shouted Demming. "I saw it in your eyes and face. I knew you had to be Hollister's kid! Come on, now—you and me's gonna pay a little visit to your pa."

He began backing up, dragging me along and still shielding his own body from Hawk's gun, toward where his horse was tied.

"You're not taking him anywhere, Demming," said Hawk, still peering down the barrel of his rifle and following us slowly with his eyes. It looked like he was aiming straight for me.

"You might be able to take me out with a shot to the head, Trumbull," said Demming, still pulling me toward the horse. "But you won't pull that trigger, not in cold blood. You ain't got the guts for it!"

Hawk said nothing, just kept watching down the sight of his carbine.

"What'd my pa ever do to you?" I asked.

"Me and your pa rode together. Long time ago, kid, but I ain't forgotten. He and that brother-in-law of his made off with all the loot."

"He never took a penny," I said.

"Ha! That what he told you?—then he's a liar as well as a thief. He and Nick took it all right, stashed it, then busted out of jail and headed west with it. Me and Dexter vowed we'd find 'em someday, and that day's now. I knew following Krebbs' trail would pay off someday."

"Buck Krebbs!" I exclaimed.

"Yeah, you know Krebbs?"

"Yeah, and my pa killed him."

"Krebbs was an idiot."

"You'll get the same if you tangle with my pa!" I shouted, hardly realizing I was defending him.

"Don't count on it, boy. I got more brains in my little finger than Krebbs had in his whole head. You and me's gonna go have a talk with your pa! I figure he's worth a whole lot more'n some half-Paiute renegade."

"I won't take you to him."

"You won't have to. I know the place, remember? Miracle Springs! I'll tie you up somewhere, then ride in alone. That's gonna be one reunion I'm gonna enjoy—seeing the look on ol' Drum's face when I tell him I got his boy, and it's gonna cost him fifty thousand to ever see him alive again. Ha, ha, ha!"

Demming's laugh sounded more wicked than his voice. I didn't have any doubts that he meant what he said."

We'd gotten to the horse by now.

Demming stopped.

"Get up there, Hollister," he said, steadying me with his left hand.

I hesitated. The next moment I felt the knife blade scratch the skin on the back of my neck.

"Get up there!" he shouted.

This time I did my best to get my foot into the stirrup and

struggle up onto the horse's back. It was hard to do it with my hands tied.

Suddenly a shot rang out from Hawk's gun.

The horse jumped, and I fell off backward onto the ground. Another shot echoed, this time accompanied by the metallic sound of the bullet against Demming's knife, which flew from his hand and hit some rocks several yards away.

It only took the second or two for Hawk to be on top of Demming.

Even as I hit the ground with a thud, I heard the two men's bodies crash down beside me.

Neither was using a weapon now, other than their fists. Grunting and struggling for position, they rolled over each other several times.

Suddenly they were apart.

Hawk climbed to one knee, but almost the same instant Demming's boot crashed into his chest and he fell over backward. The bounty hunter threw himself on top of Hawk, pelting him with blows to his face and stomach.

I struggled out of the way, managed to get myself to a sitting position, and worked at my hands furiously to loosen the knots. But it was no use. If only I could find Demming's knife! I glanced all about while working to get my feet back under me.

Meanwhile, Hawk had thrown Demming off him and was again struggling to his feet. This time Demming came at him with his whole body, trying to knock into him with hands and head and shoulders all at once. But Hawk had regained his footing enough to sidestep the attack, throwing Demming to the ground as he passed.

Demming fell, but instantly spun around, cursing violently.

As the two men fought, I got back onto my feet and managed to locate Demming's knife where Hawk had shot it out of his hand. I sat down, hands still behind me, and fished about with my fingers as best I could to slit the dried pieces of leather. I gradually felt the cords beginning to loosen, but from the wetness and sharp stinging I knew I had drawn some of my own blood in the process.

Hawk and Demming were both on their feet by now, exchanging blows. Dust was flying all about their feet, and both their faces were pouring sweat and covered with red, bloody gashes. Hawk was cool, though his eyes contained an intensity I had never seen. Demming was seething, hatred evident in every fiber of his frame.

Frantically I kept working at the leather around my wrists!

A sharp fist landed on the side of Hawk's ear, sending him reeling sideways. Demming followed it with a flurry of jabs to his stomach and midsection.

Grunts and blows and the scuffling of boots filled the air. I was afraid Hawk was getting the worst of it!

But then all at once, as Demming rushed at him to deliver a huge punch with his fist, Hawk ducked and lurched to one side. Demming's momentum threw him off balance, and he stumbled. Hawk grabbed him by the scruff of the neck and spun him back around to face him.

"Why, you good for nothing, filthy—" Demming swore viciously between pants for breath.

But the rest of the words never left his lips.

Hawk's fist smashed directly into Demming's nose and lips. He staggered back stunned, eyes watering and blood flowing from his nostrils.

The blow had been the hardest Demming had received. I thought he was going to wobble back and fall to the ground.

But he was a strong man. Getting separated from Hawk gave him the chance he needed. He continued to back up, wiping at his nose with his left sleeve and drawing his pistol from his holster with his right.

"You'll regret that, Trumbull!" he growled. "Now I'll have to kill you, and I'm going to take the boy all the same."

"I'm not going anywhere," I said. "Drop the gun."

Demming turned and saw me holding Hawk's rifle on him, my wrists red and bloody, still with a few leather strands hanging loose but at least untied and free.

"Ha, ha!" laughed Demming. "Don't make me laugh, boy!" he said. "You ain't got the guts, either. Even if you did shoot me, your fool friend here would be dead before—"

*Crack!*

The morning air exploded with another shot from the rifle. But I hadn't been trying to miss like Hawk had on his first shot. I was sure glad right then for all the times Little Wolf and I had gone up in the mountains after rabbits and wood rats, seeing who could shoot the most in an hour. It had made dead shots of us both.

The pistol flew from Demming's hand as he cried out in pain.

The next second, Hawk was picking up the pistol off the ground. He looked it over to see if it could still be used, then turned it upside down and emptied the chamber of its bullets.

He walked over to Demming's horse and took the rifle from its holster.

"I'll just be keeping this," he said, then threw the empty pistol back at the bounty hunter.

"I can't leave a man out here in the desert without some kind of a gun," he said. "Now, get out of here, Demming," he added. "Don't let either of us see you again."

"You'll regret this, Trumbull!" Demming seethed.

"I already do."

"I'll kill you for this! And Jack Demming pays his debts."

"Revenge only kills those who seek it, Demming."

"Aw, don't preach to me, you blathering old fool!" spat Demming. "I'll get even with you both."

"Get out of here, Demming."

Demming mounted his horse. I still had the carbine pointed at him. He looked over at me, his furious eyes staring out of a bloody and dirty face.

"I won't forget you, Hollister," he said, glaring at me. "And you can tell that pa of yours that I haven't forgotten him neither."

I didn't say anything, but just kept staring at him from behind the rifle.

"Now it looks like I got a score to settle with the both of you," he added, then dug his heels into his horse's flanks and galloped away.

# CHAPTER 23

# WHERE DO YOU FIGURE WE'D GET TO?

Two days after he left us, while we were riding along, Hawk brought up Jack Demming again, though at first I didn't realize he was talking about him.

"Where do you figure we'd get to if we kept riding straight ahead there?" he said, pointing with his finger in the direction we were going.

"How far?" I asked.

"All the way."

"*All* the way?"

"Yep."

I thought a minute. "I reckon all the way up to the top of that peak there," I answered finally.

"What if you kept going past that?"

"Past it . . . I don't know, down the other side of the mountain, I guess."

"Then what?"

"Further across the desert," I suggested, uncertainty creeping into my tone.

"Come on, Zack, my boy. Haven't I taught you anything yet?"

"Up the next range and down into the next valley, and up the next ridge?"

"You're thinking small. I said *all the way*."

I thought again.

"All the way across the desert," I said finally. "Up and down and past the whole chain of ranges."

"Further."

"Clear across the Utah territory."

"Further."

"To the Rockies . . . past the Rockies," I said.

"Think bigger," said Hawk.

"Clear to the end of the country, to the Atlantic Ocean."

"Bigger!"

"Across the Atlantic."

"Bigger, Zack. *All* the way . . . all the way to the end!"

"Around the whole world!" I said finally.

"Now you got it, son!" Hawk exclaimed. "If we set our mules moving straight in that direction, and they could swim, and we had food and lived through it all, eventually we'd go all the way around the world."

"But no one really *could* do that," I said.

Hawk laughed. "Yeah, you're right. I was just trying to make a point, and it's this: if you're going to set yourself to go in a direction, you gotta be prepared for where it'll take you. You gotta think about the consequences of where you're pointing yourself ahead of time."

"I'm not sure I follow what you mean," I said.

"Well, let's say a young feller decides to join the Pony Express," said Hawk with a poker face. "If he knows what he's about, he'd better think through all the implications of what that decision might mean. What'll become of him when the smoke clears, that's what he needs to ask himself ahead of time. If he goes off half cocked, why, he's liable to run into all kinds of things he never anticipated."

By now the twinkle of fun was showing through in Hawk's eyes.

"Like I didn't, huh?" I said.

"I said no such thing. All I'm saying is that it behooves a body to think about where the road they're on is leading if they keep on following it."

"I think I get what you're driving at."

We rode on slowly for a while, maybe five minutes, without another word. Hawk always gave the words a chance to sink in.

"Let me give you another example," Hawk finally added after a while. "This time I'm not talking about you, but about that feller Demming. Tell me, what did you think of him anyway?"

"Can't say as I thought much," I replied. The truth was, Demming had scared me more than just a little, and ever since then I'd been thinking about Pa, getting worried and confused all together. I didn't know what to think, or what I oughta do about warning Pa.

"Yep, the poor feller's a sad example of what a man can sink to if he doesn't pay attention to which direction he points his horse in."

"Huh?"

"He pointed himself in some direction when he was young, and now he's the kind of man he is because of it. Everything leads somewhere, Zack, like I said."

"You mean riding with the gang, the robbing, and all that?" I asked.

"Oh, I reckon that's a part of it," Hawk answered. "But that's not what I meant exactly about which direction he pointed his horse. Everything follows from something, from which direction you point your horse. The smoke always clears eventually, and you find out what you're left with. I'm talking about character, Zack, about the kind of person you are. You get me?"

"Not exactly."

"Demming's angry, he's bitter, full of resentments and hatred. How'd he get that way? Not from the robbing, though I ain't saying that's a good thing either. But bitterness and hatred come from choices you make inside about what to do with feelings you have that maybe you'd be better off getting rid of. Demming held on to a lot of feelings he should have thrown away and gotten rid of.

"Tell me, Zack," Hawk added. "Is your pa as full of hatred as Jack Demming?"

That was a hard question to face. I hadn't been finding thoughts about Pa too pleasant.

"No, I don't reckon he is," I said finally.

"You see, it ain't only what you do, though you gotta pay attention to that too. It's what you do with those feelings inside that go along with what you're doing on the surface—that's what's gonna decide which way your horse is headed. Once it's pointed, if you don't change it, it's gonna keep going. Eventually it'll lead a man like Jack Demming to become the sort of fellow he is. So you gotta pay close attention to where you point those feelings inside you."

# CHAPTER 24

## COOKING UP A CHARACTER STEW

"Ideas are like that too," Hawk said after we'd ridden along for a while in silence. "Ideas, and especially choices."

"Like what?" I questioned.

"Like what I was saying before—pointing a horse, or one of these slowpoke mules of ours, in a direction and thinking about where that direction will lead.

"Everything you think, everything you do—it all has consequences. One idea or choice always leads to another, and another after that . . . and another after that. Just like heading that direction will lead to the Rockies, then to the Atlantic, and eventually around the world."

I didn't reply. I wanted to hear what he'd say next.

"If you say or do something, then what follows from it? I don't mean just down the road a little ways, but if you follow it all the way, clear to the end . . . all the way around the world? You get me, Zack?"

"I'm not sure."

"Every idea always leads to something else. Every choice you make moves you one step closer to something else. Every idea and choice has implications. They're like footprints. They line up in a direction, and that's the direction you're going in. Lotta folks never think of outcomes and repercussions. But me, I'm *always* trying to think of them. I'm uncomfortable and nervous if I'm not two or three steps ahead of myself."

"I've noticed that," I said. "Your eyes are always roving around, peering about, looking down the trail, up the mountain, ahead of us, behind us—all over."

Hawk laughed.

"I don't suppose I even notice anymore," he said.

"You do it every second."

"I reckon you're right," he said. "Mostly I'm trying to keep a few steps ahead of myself in my thoughts and my choices. If I say something or do something, I want to know what it's likely to lead me into tomorrow. See what I mean?"

"I think so."

"Let's say I was heading out for two days across the desert, where I knew there was no water—now, if I drank all the water I was carrying the first day, that would have definite results. Do you know what that result would be?"

"You wouldn't have any water left!"

"Right," Hawk laughed. "Everything's like that, though maybe not so easy to see. Tell me, Zack, do you believe God is good or God is evil?"

"How could he be anything but good?"

"All right, then let's say you get caught out in a terrible thunderstorm, and lightning's flashing down nearby—you think you might be scared?"

"Likely so."

"If God is good, why would you be scared? Won't he take care of you?"

"Yeah, I reckon so."

"Who made the lightning and the thunderstorm?"

"God."

"And you say he's good?"

"Yeah."

"If he's good, won't he take care of you?"

"I reckon. But people still get killed in storms, and in lots of other ways too," I said.

"Does that mean God *isn't* good?"

"No, I reckon he still must be."

"Even if people are dying?"

"People have to die."

"And God is still good?"

"Yeah."

"Do you see what I'm aiming at, Zack? If you say God is good, then it must mean something to you. It seems to me that one of the things it means is that you ought not to be afraid. If you say God is good, then you've got to follow out and see where that statement leads you. All the way up the mountains and down the other side . . . clear across the country. Not much sense believing something if you don't know what the results are going to be."

"Yeah, that seems true enough."

"Lots of folks only follow what they say as far as is convenient for them. Like when they get up high into the mountains or come to a wide river or even the ocean, instead of keeping going to see where their direction leads, they stop their horse, get out of the saddle, and quit. That's why I kept pushing you a while back until you said around the world. You gotta learn to follow your ideas and what you believe all the way to the end like that too."

"You're always doing that with me, trying to make me look past where I'd get off the horse if I was by myself."

"I try to, son. It's the only way to be an honest thinker. It's the only way to see things like they really are."

"What were you going to say about God being good?" I asked.

"The way I look at it is that saying God is good leads to the conclusion that he's gonna take care of you, no matter what happens. Even if you die, God's still good. Even if you get struck by one of those bolts of lightning, he's still taking care of you, 'cause he's still good. You see—saying you believe something, well, that's got consequences. Thinking it through till the smoke clears, that's what I call it."

"So are you never afraid?" I asked.

"Heck, yes. I'm a man just like every other man. I ain't saying I'm never afraid, 'cause sometimes I am. Plenty of times, in fact. I was afraid when I was fighting Demming. A man full of hate fights to kill—they're the hardest to whip, the angry ones. I'm just trying to help you see how you've got to follow ideas out to the end and see what comes of them."

"What about choices?" I said. "You said your choices and what you do leads places and has results too."

"Yeah, and in some ways I reckon the choices a feller makes are even more important than the ideas he holds, 'cause your choices go into making you who you are. That's how your character gets put together—by all the choices you made all your life."

"How do they do that?"

Hawk thought for a minute.

"Let me see if I can say it like this. Imagine your stepma fixing your family a big pot of stew. She might put in some meat and some carrots and potatoes and celery, maybe some onions and peppers, a little salt, maybe some wheat or barley. A stew can have most anything in it, can't it?"

"You're making my mouth water just talking about it," I said.

"Mine too!" said Hawk. "Well, anyway, the fact is that she could make just about any kind of stew she wanted—a beef stew, a chicken stew, a ham stew. It could be thick or thin. It could be mostly vegetables or mostly meat. And what would decide what kind of stew it turned out to be?"

"What she put in the pot?"

"That's it exactly! That's why every stew's likely just a tad different from every other stew."

"And that's just like people, right?"

"Now you're getting it, Zack, my boy! Exactly like people. We're all different, too, depending on what *we* put in our *own* pots."

"You're saying I'm like a stew."

Hawk laughed.

"Did I say that?"

"You *implied* it," I said.

"You got me there! Thinking it through till the smoke clears—you're a quick learner!"

"So am I like a stew?"

"I reckon you are. So am I. So is every man or woman alive. We're cooking it up ourselves, all our lives, throwing in new ingredients all the time. The more kindness we throw into the pot, the more kindness there is in the stew. The more unselfishness we put in, the more unselfish our character will become. But a man like Demming, who's been tossing in anger and bitterness and hatred and selfishness all his life, why, by this time his is a pretty foul-smelling batch of stuff I sure wouldn't want to come near."

"But does what you did when you were a kid matter that much?" I asked.

"You bet it does. Everything goes into the pot."

"But half the time you don't know no better."

"It ain't so much that every tiny thing has that big an effect. But every bit of bitterness or anger or selfishness you throw in your stew makes it easier to add more the next time. So what you do when you're young matters a lot if it means you get headed in a certain direction and you keep going that way and never turn your head toward someplace else. The anger and selfishness gets all the more natural the more of it you put in the stew, till before long you're just an angry, selfish person. You just kept putting those kinds of choices into your stew until that's all it tastes like."

"Sounds kinda hopeless if you're a brat when you're little."

"Nah, nothing's hopeless. All you gotta do is point your horse in a new direction . . . make a new, better-tasting stew. It's just that most folks don't take the energy to go someplace else than where their horse is already going. Too much work for them."

"But how does somebody make a new kind of stew if it's already full of bad-tasting vittles?"

"It might take a little time, but you just gotta start putting better-tasting things into it. And there ain't no law against sticking a spoon in the pot and taking something out, either. What would your stepma do if she threw a big onion into her stew and then realized it was rotten and was gonna spoil the whole thing? Likely she'd fish it out pronto, right?"

"I reckon."

"Character stews ain't no different. They taste like what they got in them. So folks who put in good-tasting stuff like kindness and generosity and patience and love, folks who take out the rotten onions—those are the kind of folks you like to be around. They're pleasant. Their characters *taste* good to the soul."

"I do see what you mean," I said.

"Anybody can make a pleasing stew that folks'll want to partake of. It just depends on what kind of ingredients you put into it. That's your choices."

# CHAPTER 25

## A SECOND STRANGER

Three or four days after Demming left us, Hawk said to me from out of nowhere, "What are you angry about, Zack?"

"I ain't angry," I said.

"Sure you are," laughed Hawk, treating it in a matter-of-fact way, even though after we got to talking about it, the conversation grew more and more serious.

"Why do you think I'm angry?"

"It's written all over you," replied Hawk. "I don't mean angry at me, or angry about some certain thing that happened. I mean that you're just generally angry down deep inside. It's not all that hard to see if you know what you're looking for. In your own way, you're carrying grudges from the past just like Demming."

"You can see it in me, huh?" I said, more like a grunt than anything else. I wasn't sure I liked what Hawk was saying.

"I'm practiced at seeing what's going on down underneath the surface, remember? People's got more things going on down under the surface than creek beds and hillsides, that's for certain."

"What makes you such an expert on it?" I said, the tone of my voice probably confirming exactly what he'd said. "What makes you think you know what's going on inside other people so well when you're just out here all alone by yourself?"

"Because I been spending all these years doing the best kind of learning a fellow can do."

"What's that?"

"Getting to know what's going on inside *me*," Hawk replied.

"So what do you figure I'm angry at?" I said, still with a cocky, halfway defiant tone.

It wasn't usually Hawk's way to say something to me that I didn't ask for or that he didn't figure I wanted to hear. But for some reason, on this particular day, even though it was obvious my attitude wasn't the best, he kept boring right on toward me. I guess he knew I needed to hear what he had to say, and I'm glad he told me, though it wasn't too pleasant at the time.

"Most anger comes from folks figuring life's just not going like they'd like it to. From all you told me about your pa and your family, it sounds to me that you think you've had a pretty tough time all these years, not having your pa around and all."

I was glad enough that I never had a chance to reply.

Later on, when I was looking back on those days, I asked myself why it never seemed to occur to me to go back and warn Pa about Demming. I don't even know how to answer my own question, except that I suppose I didn't really think Pa was in any immediate danger because Demming was still after the half-breed. If I'm really honest, I guess I was still trying so hard not to think about Pa that I couldn't let myself admit the danger was real. You get so accustomed to thinking your folks can take care of themselves and don't need anyone's help that it hardly crosses your mind that they might *need* your help.

Our conversation was interrupted when suddenly we happened upon the half-Paiute Tranter that Demming was tracking.

If I thought the bounty hunter had a mean streak, this young fella had a temper that was a whole lot worse. He carried a look in his eye that made me sure he would have killed us for three cents. When we stumbled across him, though, he was in no condition to kill anybody, being half dead himself. Even though we did our best to help him, he had a malicious look in his eye that seemed to hate us even more for trying to help him.

We found him laying alone on the ground, no sign of a horse, unconscious, with a bloody gash along one side of his chest. It was obvious from one look at him that he was part Indian. His hair was black, his skin dark and tanned from the sun but somehow pale and lifeless at the same time. He wore a big knife at his side but didn't seem to have anything else with him.

"Oh no!" exclaimed Hawk the instant we saw him. "What have we got here?"

Hawk ran to him and knelt down. For all I could tell he was dead. Hawk put his ear to the man's chest.

"He's still alive," said Hawk, "though barely."

"You think he's the guy Demming's after?" I asked.

"No doubt about it."

"Looks like he already found him," I said.

"No," said Hawk, standing up. "The way I read our friend Demming is that if he found him, this poor fellow would be either dead or on his way back to Carson City in chains by now—probably both."

"But it looks like he's been wounded pretty bad."

"That blood's been dried a while. He and Demming probably tangled sometime earlier. Looks like a knife wound. The sun and loss of blood probably got too much for him. He's pale. Come on, help me get him onto the back of my mule."

"Is it safe to move him?" I asked as I stooped down to pick up the man's feet.

"We got no choice. He'll be dead inside of two hours out here. If the sun don't see to it, the vultures will."

Unconsciously I glanced up into the sky. The big, ugly birds were already starting to gather.

"Why don't we take him to the Paiutes? He'd be safe there, and they could worry about him."

"If we could find them, they'd probably kill us before letting us explain that we didn't do this to him. Who knows if they'd even want him in the first place? Indians aren't much more fond of half-breeds than whites. I think I'd rather take my chances with just one wounded half-Indian than with the whole tribe of healthy full-bloods."

Hawk took off his shirt, washed the man's face and chest and the wound with cold water from his canteen, doused some whiskey over the wound, and tried to get him—even though he was still unconscious—to sip some whiskey and water mixed together.

Then we managed to hoist him onto the back of the mule, and

within a couple of hours we had him in the shade inside the cave we were nearest to.

Eventually he began to come around a little, though when he did he was none too pleased to find us staring at him. Almost the same instant that his eyes opened into two thin slits, one of his hands reached straight toward his knife.

He didn't find it. We'd learned our lesson with Demming.

Besides, if there was one thing Hawk knew as well as the desert, it was Paiutes, so he'd taken the knife out of the man's belt and hid it.

# CHAPTER 26

## HAWK THE MEDICINE MAN

We didn't need to have worried about Tranter, though.

He was in bad shape and was back asleep again in less than five minutes. He'd lost a lot of water and a fair amount of blood. Luckily for him, Hawk managed to get him to drink two or three gulps of water before he lost consciousness again.

Hawk made some stuff out of weeds and water and the inside pulp from a desert cactus bush, and he put the salve on the man's wounds. Then he sat up with him most of the night so that any time he so much as stirred, Hawk lifted up the Paiute's head gently, put a cup of water to his lips, and tried to get him to drink.

A sip or two at a time, he managed to get enough water into Tranter to start bringing color back to his cheeks.

Hawk mashed up some other plants and herbs with some cattail pollen to mix with the water so that as he took to drinking a little more he got some nourishment along with it.

I don't know where Hawk learned so much about medicine, but not much he did surprised me by now. I don't think the half-breed would have been any better tended to in a regular Eastern hospital.

Tranter was with us several days. I don't know how badly infected the wound was, but whatever Hawk put on it seemed to make the swelling and redness start to go down by the second day.

That first night, Tranter was delirious on and off, saying some of the most dreadful things, sometimes calling out, sometimes shouting angrily, sometimes almost weeping like a child.

"He's done some bad things, Zack," Hawk said. "Been some places no man oughta go. Near as I can tell, his father was one of the first whites in these parts, probably from Fremont's time or even earlier. Took an Indian woman—might have raped her for all I know—and had this son that he wound up hating because he was half Indian. No wonder this poor feller's so filled with venom toward both red and white."

"That don't make sense," I said, "if he's half white."

"Nothing about bitterness holds up to reason, Zack," said Hawk sadly. "One of his kind is never accepted in either world, so he winds up hating both—and deep down, hating himself most of all."

"But why would his own father hate him?"

"Hate's got no more reason than bitterness. Nothing about it'll make sense if you try to analyze it. Fathers and sons been in the business of hating each other ever since sin came into the world. It must be about the most terrible grief to God there is."

We were both quiet a few minutes. It was dark and late. The fire was burning low, and I didn't want to keep talking in that direction for fear the talk would get too close to my own situation again.

"Must be a terrible thing to hate yourself," I said after a spell.

"Most awful thing in the world," replied Hawk. "If a feller's in a fix like that and he doesn't know that God's his father, then there ain't nothing for him to do but lash out in hatred toward everybody else."

A cry suddenly went up from where our injured guest was laying.

" . . . kill you, Tranter . . . if I get my hands on you . . . never be no good. . . . vile blood in you . . ."

He breathed in and out several times, laboring, head moving back and forth like he was trying to wake up, the muscles of his face contorting into grotesque shapes.

Then he shouted out again, this time almost in the pleading voice of a child.

" . . . please . . . let me stay. . . . Get out. . . . You disgrace to Weeping Feather. . . . No longer your tribe. . . . Please . . .

cause no more trouble . . . mother, please help . . . try to be good . . ."

More labored breathing, more moaning. Then suddenly a deep and angry voice of hostility broke from his lips.

" . . . never get away . . . get my clutches on you . . . ain't never acted like a pa . . ."

I shivered just to hear the words. They were too much like the words I had said to Pa when I left home a year earlier.


On the third day Tranter woke up, clearly much improved in body, if not in temper.

Looking Hawk and me over as if seeing us for the first time, he took Hawk's offer of food and water. But when Hawk tried to talk he said nothing.

Tranter lay still for another several minutes, then all of a sudden he rose, turned his back on us, and wandered off into the desert without a word. Hawk sprang after him, tried to get him to take some food or at least some water.

He kept going without a word, refusing Hawk's offer.

Finally Hawk hurried back to where I was standing, got the man's knife that he'd kept hidden, then ran back and handed it to him.

Tranter took it, almost looked like he was thinking about using it on Hawk right then, but turned and continued on until he was out of sight.

He was too weak to get far. I don't know where he was figuring to go. Hawk walked back slowly. I knew he was worried about him.

But there wasn't much more we could do.

# CHAPTER 27

## WHERE DO THE ROOTS GO?

A day or two later we were walking along a particularly desolate stretch of ground. There was scrub brush growing and some desert grasses. Here and there some scraggly kind of tree was trying to survive.

"What do you figure is under the ground here, Zack?" Hawk asked me.

"Nothing much," I replied. "Just rocks and dirt."

Hawk stopped, knelt down, stuck his fist into the ground, and dug down with his fingers, scooping out the dirt to make a little hole.

"Get down on your knees and look in here," he said. "Tell me what you see."

I did like he said.

"You mean the little roots?" I asked.

"Yes, that's what I mean. I can't believe after all this time I'd ask you what's under the surface and you'd say *nothing much*!"

I laughed. One thing I *had* learned by now was to feel the fun in Hawk's voice, even when he kidded me by pretending to be gruff.

"Sorry," I said. "I'm still learning to see under and inside things, like you're showing me. But half the time my eyes still see the old way. It's just going to take more practice, I reckon."

"Well, you reckon right, Hollister," groused Hawk, still pretending to be sore, but just giving me a bad time. "Practice is exactly what it takes. *Training's* more what I call it—training your eyes to see, just like if you was training your eye and arm and finger to shoot a rifle or training your legs to stick tight to a horse or training your muscles for some kind of contest. *Training*—that's what it is. Inner-eyesight training, the most important kind of self-training a man can do."

"So were you going to tell me about the roots?" I reminded him.

Hawk reached down again, and this time he wrapped his big hand around a medium-sized desert shrub about a foot high. He yanked it up and pulled it out of the ground. Hanging down all around it were more strands of roots than you could count.

"You see, Zack, there's more of the plant *under* the ground and hidden from view than there is on top. That's where the life is. All around out here—"

As he spoke, Hawk swung his hand wide all about him.

"—everywhere, if you dug under the surface, you would find this big, huge system of roots all tangled and twisted about each other. Everywhere—under every foot, maybe even every inch of the desert. Do you know what that means?"

I shook my head.

"It means there's hidden life and meaning and growth going on under *everything*, no matter how desolate it might look on top."

He paused a moment.

"People are just like all these plants," he added. "You pull them up, and you scratch and dig around the ground under them, and you'll find their roots too. Nothing can live without roots. *All* living things get their life from their roots. If you want to know why some plants grow tall and straight and others grow low and crooked, you got to look at the roots. If you want to find out why some plants produce pretty blooms and others make thorns instead, you got to look at the roots of the kind of plants they are. If you want to find out why some plants are pleasant and pleasing and others are poison, you got to look at the roots. If you want to find out why some plants produce food that gives a body energy and others don't seem to make anything that's any good for anybody, you got to look at the roots.

"The roots are everything. The roots are what make a plant

what it is—where the roots go, where they come from, what kind of soil they go down into, and what they do with that soil. And it's all underground. Your eyes can't see it, but it's happening all the time regardless, even in what looks like a desert like this. Now do you see what I mean?"

"Some, I reckon," I said. "But you seem mighty interested in plants and roots. Why are they so important?"

"It's not the plants themselves. They're just pictures of how people are. You look down underneath men and women, and they got just as many roots growing down and out as plants. That's one of the reasons why folks all turn out so different, on account of their roots going in different directions and getting different kinds of nourishment out of the ground."

"I should have known that's what you were getting at," I smiled.

"Everything in life is not what it looks," Hawk added. "Everything's upside down in importance from how most folks see them. The way to get ahead is to put other people ahead of you. Backwards. There's more than just looking inside. You gotta learn to see the upside-downness of everything too. You have to train your eyes not just to look inside, down, under, and at roots, but to turn everything over from the world's way of looking at it.

"Is something highly thought of in the world? Chances are it's of low importance in God's way of looking at it.

"Is something despised in the world's eyes, like trying to be a servant to someone else or help people like we did Tranter? That kind of thing's nothing in his eyes or a man like Demming's. But it's of great importance in God's sight."

I nodded, taking it all in.

"It's just like the roots," Hawk went on. "Everything in life is upside down from what it seems. Life is hidden. A tree looks like it's above ground, but it draws its nourishment from the dirt which is invisible."

Hawk paused.

"There's one big difference between plant roots and people roots, though," he added.

"What's that?"

"People roots can go in any direction they want."

"How so?"

"Doesn't matter if you compare people to a stew or to a growing plant. Either way it's the same. We put the ingredients into our own stew and it winds up tasting like how we made it. If you're talking about people plants, we decide ourselves where our roots are going to go and what kind of soil we're gonna let them draw nourishment from."

"Aren't a person's roots his own folks?" I asked.

"Yep. Everybody's got roots from their own kin and past, and you can't change that. But everybody sends his own roots out too. Those you decide for yourself how they're going to grow and in which directions. You can't really change what comes into you, but you can choose what to do with it once it's there.

"Those two fellers we just met had some pretty nasty roots coming into them, but they could have found some good soil if they'd wanted. There's good soil around for anybody to grow in. But instead, those two've let their roots grow down into bitterness and hatred and vengeance. It's not hard to see that the plants they've grown into aren't too pleasant."

"I see what you mean. Not a good-tasting stew."

Hawk smiled kind of sadly.

"Not too good," he repeated.

The conversation fell silent.

I wasn't sure I understood all of what Hawk had been saying and hinting at. But I had the feeling there was more to it than I realized right at that moment.

# CHAPTER 28

## CRISIS!

The day after our talk about roots, we again heard hoofbeats approaching. After so many days alone out under the sky, we seemed to be running into people everywhere!

We were out in the open, and even if we'd wanted to hide, we'd never been able to. They were galloping straight toward us. Before we even had the chance to think about what to do, suddenly we found ourselves surrounded by half a dozen Paiutes on their pinto ponies, arrow tips pointed straight toward us.

Hawk remained calm. At least on the outside. I was scared to death!

One of them yelled something at him. It sounded like a command.

Hawk looked over at me. "He says we're to come with them," It was late in the day, only an hour or two before dusk.

"What for?" I asked.

"He didn't say. But I have the feeling we'd better do what he says or those arrows may not feel too good."

"How did they know where to find us?"

"That's the part that worries me," said Hawk, beginning to move slowly toward our mules, and motioning me to follow. "I didn't know they had me so kept track of. They rode up like they knew exactly where we'd be."

"That's not such a pleasant thought," I said.

"Downright unpleasant," answered Hawk. "I thought I was the one keeping track of *their* movements. Makes me wonder why

145

they've kept me alive all this time."

"Maybe they're not as dangerous as people think."

Hawk nodded his head with a solemn expression. I couldn't read his thoughts.

We mounted our horses, and the next minute we were heading off across the plain amid the Paiutes, some ahead, some behind us. All I could think of was that they were going to kill us or boil us alive or skin us and eat us or something! Why hadn't they just put arrows through us and been done with it!

After a rapid ride of fifteen or twenty minutes we slowed, and for the rest of the way, climbing up into some rugged hills, we went at a slower pace. They didn't seem to mind us talking, and as we went side by side, Hawk and I had a long conversation. Probably the thought of dying made both of us wonder what we were about to face.

As we rode along, I sure wasn't thinking about anything more than whether I was going to live through the night.

"Let me ask you a question, Zack," said Hawk as we rode. "What do you figure makes a fellow a man?"

I thought a long time.

"That's a mighty big question," I answered finally.

"You and I been together a good long while," said Hawk. "I figure you're about ready for me to ask it."

"Why, you been waiting to ask me that all this time?"

"Not directly. Watching'd be more like it."

"Watching for what?"

"To see how you was absorbing everything, to see how you was learning to see the inside of things. Especially to see how you was learning to see inside yourself."

"And you figure I'm learning to see that way?"

"Yeah, I do, Zack. I figure you're seeing a heap of things different than you maybe once did. You're a good learner. That's why I figure you're about ready to ask yourself that important question. So what *do* you figure makes a fellow a man?"

I was quiet for a while, thinking to myself.

"Courage, I reckon," I said after a long quiet spell. "That'd be one thing."

"Courage—that's good," replied Hawk thoughtfully. "I reckon that's part of it. But what do you mean by courage—never being afraid, doing brave things, being tougher than the next guy? What do you think courage is?"

"I guess maybe a little of all those things," I said. "Though I reckon a man's got a right to be afraid once in a while, just so long as he can be brave in the middle of it."

The instant the words were out of my mouth I remembered Pa telling me something like that when Buck Krebbs took Becky and we had to go after him. It surprised me to think of Pa and Hawk telling me the same thing.

"Yep, I think you're right there," Hawk continued. "So you figure it's all right to be afraid, as long as it doesn't keep you from being courageous?"

"I reckon that's something like it, as long as you're not afraid too much. You ever afraid, Hawk?"

"'Course I'm afraid—I've told you that. Maybe even more'n you figure a man oughta be. Only a fool's never afraid. Sometimes it takes a man with good sense to know when he *ought* to be afraid!"

"I guess I never thought about that part of it."

"What else about courage? You think it means doing brave things?"

"Seems like it would."

"What kind of brave things?"

"You know, the kind of things that most folks'd be afraid to do."

"Daring exploits, eh, Zack? Fighting the dragon to save the village and the princess!"

We both laughed, but I knew Hawk was still waiting for an answer.

"Something like that," I said, "but not dragons."

"What, then? Facing a charging Indian who's trying to kill you, shooting a rattlesnake, saving someone in danger, going up with your fists against a bully, riding across a desert to help a stranded settler, fighting in a war?"

"Yeah, all that kind of stuff."

"Going up against something bigger than yourself?"

"Yeah."

"Fighting it, conquering it, braving the fearsome enemy and winning the battle—that's what courage is?"

"Hmm . . . now that you mention it, I don't suppose you'd necessarily have to win. Lot of brave men have done lots of courageous things and died in the trying."

"So it's just having the courage to face the enemy . . . being brave, being strong, whatever the outcome?"

"Yeah, maybe that's it. Not being a coward no matter what the odds."

"All right. So having courage and being brave to face danger, even if you're afraid, is part of what it takes to be a man—what else?"

Again I thought for a while. I knew Hawk was content to wait as long as it took.

"Being able to take care of yourself, maybe," I ventured after a couple of minutes. "Not necessarily when there's any big danger around, but the rest of the time."

"Being able to be independent?"

"I reckon something like that."

"Not needing anybody's help?"

I nodded.

"Not needing anyone else?"

"I'm not saying you gotta be a hermit—"

"A loner like me," Hawk put in with a wink.

"Yeah. I ain't saying there's anything wrong with how you live, but a man doesn't *have* to do that to be a man. But still he ought to be able to take care of himself."

"Self-reliant?"

"That's something like it. A man oughta be able to get along with people, but he shouldn't have to depend on them for everything. That's part of what growing up is, ain't it—learning to stand on your own two feet and fend for yourself?"

"I'm asking you," said Hawk with a smile.

"Okay, then I'm saying it—a man ought to be able to take care of himself."

"So, courageous and self-reliant—what else? What kind of

*person* does it take to be a man—down inside?"

"I don't get your meaning."

"Okay, let me say it like this." Hawk looked away a minute, thinking, then turned back to me. "Should a man be a *thinker,*" he said, "to be a full-fledged *man?*"

"A thinker?" I repeated.

"Yep, a thinker. Should a man use his head to prove what he's made of—or his hands?"

"Well . . . both," I said.

"He ought to be able to use his head?"

I nodded. "Nobody wants to be a fool. You gotta know how to use your brains."

"All right, let's say I put two men in front of you. Jake's a tough hombre who can ride any horse alive, broken or not. He's quick on the draw and can shoot a jack rabbit from a hundred yards from the back of a horse at a full gallop. Cross him, and you'll wind up with a fist in your mouth. Jake's killed several men, and's not afraid of any man or beast alive. He's as tough a customer as they come.

"Talk about taking care of himself—Jake's been on his own since he was eleven. And courage? Why, he's as brave as they come. He's no thinker. He never reads books. He can barely read at all. Ideas and thoughts and all the kind of stuff you and I talk about, none of that would interest Jake in the least. He proves what kind of stuff he's made of with his hands and fists and muscles every day, but his head never really gets involved—at least not the *inside* of his head. He's a good hard worker too, and there's nobody you'd want on a ranch more'n Jake if you could get him."

"Sounds like Demming. Is it him you're talking about?"

Hawk paused, looked away again, and took in a deep breath.

"Nope, they're a lot alike, but that's not who I mean."

"You said two," I prompted.

"Yep," said Hawk, glancing quickly back toward me. "The other feller is completely different—night and day different than Jake. His name's Mr. Fenwick. He's a music professor and makes his living teaching his students about the history of music and about how to play musical instruments. He's kind to everyone he meets, and he really cares about his students. He's a short man who wears glasses, and he *is* a thinker. He reads all the time and thinks about things other than music. He's especially interested in spiritual things and thinks about God a lot. That's why he loves music—because he believes that God made music. But except for playing musical instruments, Mr. Fenwick can't do a thing with his hands. He shows what kind of stuff he's made of with what's *inside* his head. He's never been in a fight in his life, has never held a gun, and hasn't ever faced the kind of danger that comes across Jake's path nearly every day.

"Now, Zack, which of these two would you say is the most thoroughly a *man?*"

Hawk eyed me intently.

"I see what you mean," I said. "It's not easy to say without knowing them both. It *could* be that the fellow called Fenwick is brave and courageous too."

"Right you are, Zack. But you wouldn't think that about him right off. And it could be that all Jake's toughness is just to hide the fact that deep inside he's timid and afraid."

"I never thought of that."

"Happens all the time," said Hawk. "Folks aren't always what they appear on the surface. That's why I keep telling you always to look to the *inside*—with people most of all."

We rode along a while further without saying anything.

"After all this, ain't you gonna tell me what you think it takes to make a man?" I asked finally.

"No, I figure you got plenty to think about for one day. Besides, we got enough problems staring us in the face to keep us busy with other things. I have the feeling we're about to find out which of the two kinds the men in this pack are."

I looked up. There was a camp up ahead.

"Will you tell me sometime?"

"I don't know. If you want me to."

"I do."

"Then maybe I'll tell you . . . if we live long enough!"

# CHAPTER 29

# IN THE CAMP OF *The People*

It was getting dark by the time we arrived in the Paiute camp. One of the first people we saw was the half-breed. The hateful look on his face as we rode up made me shiver clean through, even more than the thoughts I'd been having the whole ride about getting skinned alive by the Paiutes.

He glared at us like *we* was the ones that had wounded him. I suppose I should have been glad he was recovered, because he sure did look strong again, but that wasn't really the first thing that came into my mind when he looked at us.

I wondered how long he'd been here and if Demming was still after him now that he was in the company of the whole tribe—if Demming even knew where he was.

But I didn't have too much time to think about what the man called Tranter might do to us, because the next minute we were being yanked off the mules and half dragged along through the camp. Then we were standing in front of a powerful-looking Paiute, clearly a chief of some sort. Hawk told me he was the young Winnemucca.

He was dark and weathered, just like the half-breed, and dressed mostly with cloth attire, but with some small skins and feathers about him too. I couldn't tell his age. The main thing I noticed was his stern expression. It didn't put my mind at ease about our prospects for seeing the sun rise the next day!

It didn't take long to find out what they wanted.

It seemed that the chief's oldest daughter was missing.

The chief's second daughter, Sarah, who Hawk had told me about earlier, acted as translator, telling us in perfect English all that had happened.

Laughing Waters had been missing for two days. At first the Paiutes figured she was just off by herself, but by nightfall her mother and the chief had got worried. No one had seen her. Several parties had ridden out into the surrounding hills, but none found a trace of her. All the next day they kept on getting more anxious, until halfway through the afternoon a lone rider was spotted approaching the camp. By the time he arrived, every one of the Paiutes—men, women, and children—had gathered around, hoping for some news about the daughter of Chief Winnemucca.

There was news all right, but not the kind they'd been hoping for.

The rider was Jack Demming.

He rode straight into the Paiute camp, all cocky and full of bravado—almost with a grin on his face, to hear Sarah tell it, almost daring them to lay a finger on him.

He had the girl, he told them, looking the chief straight in the eye as if he weren't afraid of a thing. She was in a cave ten miles away, tied and gagged. They could kill him, but then she'd be dead from the snakes and scorpions a long time before they ever got to her—if they ever did find her. More likely she'd die right where she was, and no one would ever lay eyes on her again. Even if she managed to get away on her own, there weren't no water for miles, and she'd be so twisted and confused by the time she got back on the plain that she would never know the direction back to the camp. The only way they would ever see the chief's daughter again, the bounty hunter said, was to agree to his conditions.

The terms Demming laid down were simple enough: the half-breed, unarmed, and bound with hands behind his back, in exchange for the girl. There wouldn't be no negotiations. That was the deal. The Indians were supposed to send the half-breed out several miles from camp to a spot Demming named, and he would release the girl at the same place several hours later. He'd said he would be back the next morning for their answer.

With that he turned and galloped away.

That had all taken place several hours ago. Within a short time the party had been sent to fetch Hawk and me, and now we stood there listening to Sarah telling us all that went on.

She didn't seem like all the other Indian women around the camp. There was a gentleness about her—a look in her eyes that was somehow different than what you'd expect out there in the desert. Maybe it was the result of the time she'd spent with white people. Or, I wondered, could the look be the result of her being Christian?

Finally Sarah finished and everything fell silent. She looked at her father. He nodded to her, and she went to sit down with the other women. The chief looked across to Hawk where he and I were standing.

"So I make you, Hawk, responsible to bring daughter to me," he said, his own English broken but understandable. "You white like evil man Demming. You find, you make listen, you bring daughter."

"Demming's no friend of mine," said Hawk.

"He white."

"That doesn't make him a friend. I don't even know the man."

"That's a lie!" Tranter burst out, standing a few feet from the chief. "I saw him in your camp, eating your food, sharing your fire."

"You shared that fire and food yourself a day or two later," Hawk reminded him.

"If I hadn't been out of my head at the time, I would have killed you both."

"If it hadn't been for Hawk, you'd be dead!" I said angrily. "He kept that wound in your side from getting more infected."

"Shut up, Zack!" Hawk growled at me, jabbing me in the ribs. "Leave this to me."

"Silence!" sounded the voice of the chief. "Daughter must be found. Other things put aside. You, Hawk—you white man Paiutes trust. You not bad like other white man. You know desert, desert lets you live. You know Paiute, Paiute let you live. You know white man. You find Laughing Waters."

"Bah, you can't trust 'em!" spat Tranter. "Let me kill 'em both right here, and then I'll go find the—"

My knees quivered just to hear him talk like he did. I had no doubt that, given the chance, he'd pull out that huge knife of his and stick it into both our hearts in a second. But the chief interrupted him.

"Silence, son of Weeping Feather!" said the chief, turning and glaring at Tranter. It was the first time I'd heard what the Paiutes called him. "You cause of trouble. Kill and steal and make white man angry, then come here, only bring trouble. You no true Paiute. You nothing—evil mixed blood. You one I should kill. Only give you refuge to honor your mother. Weeping Feather brave woman. But you evil."

"Let me go after Demming," said the son of Weeping Feather. "You're right. I'm the reason he has come and has taken your daughter. I'll find Laughing Waters and kill Demming."

"Fool!" spat the chief back to him. "You weak. Wound still bad. Man called Demming kill you and Laughing Waters."

I was thinking to myself that Demming and Tranter were so much alike, bitter enemies though they were, that they deserved each other. What more fitting end to all this than for them to kill each other and die together in their hate? I don't suppose those were very honorable thoughts, but when you think you're about to die, you don't have much control over the directions your brain takes.

In the meantime, the chief was talking to Hawk again.

"You find, Hawk. You bring Laughing Waters."

"What about Demming?" said Hawk.

"You kill. We kill. No matter to me."

"But I know nothing about Demming—no idea where he might be."

"We give you name of Hawk. You always see what even Paiute not see. You have hawk eyes. You find."

"And if I can't find her in time?"

"Then we kill boy."

My eyes opened wide, and my heart began pounding even harder than before as the chief nodded toward me. While I struggled to keep from collapsing in fear, the chief went on, and what he said next was even worse.

"We keep boy. Man Demming has Laughing Waters. You bring daughter, we give you boy. Harm come to girl, boy die. Maybe you die too, Hawk. You not bad . . . but you white."

The chief gave a nod with his head, and two dozen Paiute braves scurried forward. Within a minute Hawk and I were tied up and being shoved toward a tentlike enclosure made of willow branches and cattail mats with brush and skins thrown over it.

There was a small fire in the camp, but it didn't offer much light as we were being pushed along. The moon hadn't come up yet. I couldn't see Hawk's face, but I could almost feel him thinking.

"You leave camp daybreak," the chief said to Hawk. "You hide in hills. Demming come, we say we agree. You follow. Get daughter. Kill Demming. Bring daughter, we give you boy."

Nothing more was said, and in another minute we were shoved to the ground inside the little shelter. Several of the Indians stayed behind, standing guard around the outside of it.

# CHAPTER 30

# A TALK BEFORE FALLING ASLEEP

After a while they came in and built a fire for us to sleep next to. I didn't understand why they cared about our comfort if they were going to kill us anyway, but the fire felt good. The desert got cold at night!

Neither of us were sleepy, though—that's for sure.

So we lay there on the ground, still tied up, staring into the fire, and talking. Two or three Paiutes at a time hung around, but whether they could understand us as well as the chief, Sarah, or Tranter could, I don't know. They didn't seem to pay much attention to our conversation, but it was sure a conversation I would never forget.

We found ourselves picking back up on what we had talked about riding toward the Paiute camp.

"Well, son," Hawk said after neither of us had said anything in quite a while, "I reckon now's the time."

I glanced up, a look of question on my face.

"Time for what?" I asked.

"Time for us to find out what kind of stuff we're made of. Time for you—and maybe me, too—to figure out what being a man means," he answered.

Everything about courage and bravery and all the rest of what we had talked about earlier in the day came back into my brain.

"Looks like we got ourselves into a fine pickle. So tell me,

157

Zack, you remember the two fellows we were talking about earlier?"

"Yeah."

"Which of them two'd you like to have to help us out right now?"

"You mean Jake and the other man?"

"Mr. Fenwick—right. Which of those two do you figure would stand the best chance of getting us out of this alive?"

"I don't know—I reckon Jake."

"Why?"

"He'd be tougher and braver, I reckon—more likely to fight off the Paiutes or capture Demming or something."

"He's more like Demming himself?"

"Yeah. Demming could *be* Jake, the way you describe him."

Hawk chuckled, but without humor.

"Yep, they're cut out of the same cloth all right."

It was getting late, but we kept talking. How can you sleep when you're scared and you know it might be your last night alive on the earth! So we wound up talking about all kinds of things. It was probably halfway through the night before we finally dozed off.

"I asked you before whether you figured a man ought to be a thinker," Hawk said. "I don't recollect you answering me."

"Maybe I didn't."

"What do you figure? What's your answer about whether a man ought to be a thinker?"

"I don't know. Seems like he oughta be."

"Jake's a pretty manly sort, but only with his brawn, not his brains."

"Yeah, I guess I don't know what to say. Maybe there's gotta be both."

"I'll tell you what, Zack—I ain't at all sure Jake could get us out of this fix we're in. Figuring he was tough enough to take on anything just by being mean and ornery and waving his gun around, he'd likely get himself killed, and us along with him."

"I see what you mean."

Again it was silent a while.

The fire was almost out, and the one Indian left guarding us was asleep. But Hawk kept talking. I think he was talking to keep our minds off our predicament.

"All right, then, I'll ask you about something else," he said. "What about feelings?"

"How do you mean?"

"Should a man be tender and sensitive?"

"That sounds more like a woman than a man," I said. "The man you call Jake would laugh in your face. Demming too."

"I'm sure they would. But I ain't at all sure Demming's the sort of feller I want to be like. So . . . should a man have feelings?"

"Yeah, but a *man's* kind of feelings."

"What are a man's feelings?"

"The same kind of thing we were talking about before—bravery and courage and that kind of thing."

"And anger and revenge—those kinds of hard manly feelings?" I nodded. "But what about gentler feelings? I mean real deep things like love and sympathy and compassion. Should a man feel them?"

"Hmm . . ." I said. "I don't know. Sounds more womanly than manly."

"You don't figure feeling those soft kinds of things would help us find Demming and rescue the chief's daughter?"

"Don't seem very likely."

"Yeah, well I ain't so sure. The way things are looking, seems to me Fenwick might do us more good about now than Jake."

"But he wouldn't have any experience at these kinds of things."

"But we need ideas, Zack, not muscles. And maybe we need a little compassion too. Takes more than bravery to make you risk your life for somebody. You gotta *feel* something to go along with the bravery."

"Hmm . . . I reckon maybe you're right."

"Let me ask it another way then, Zack. I said Jake used his hands and Mr. Fenwick used his head. I think we were getting around to figuring that maybe a man ought to be able to use both. 'Course Jake had feelings too. But hard kinds of feelings. And what about the heart? Should a man use his heart too? If your hands are where you *do* things and your head is where you *think*, then your heart is where you *feel*.

"Let me put my first question to you like this. Is it *doing* or *thinking* or *feeling* that makes a man?"

"I don't know. Now you're putting all kinds of new things into it—more than stuff like being brave and taking care of yourself."

Hawk laughed, almost like he'd forgotten where we were. "I'm just trying to get you to look at the question from all the way around it," said Hawk. "You'll never find the answers to things if you only look at the question from one angle. You've got to walk all the way around something, looking at it every different way you can, before any kind of a complete answer will come to you. So should a man have feelings?"

"I reckon," I answered. "Just not too much. Not like a woman."

"How much is too much?"

"I don't know."

"Well then, I'll leave that for you to figure out later too. Here's another question for you, looking at it from still another angle. Should a man talk?"

"Talk. What do you mean? 'Course he oughta talk."

"I mean, should a man talk about what he's thinking and feeling? I reckon all men do think and feel—but should they talk about it?"

"I see. You mean how women are always talking about what they're feeling?"

"Yeah. You figure maybe a man ought to keep it inside?"

"Like the fella Jake probably would?"

"Right. You and I been doing lots of talking about what we think. Does that make us more or less a man? But we ain't talked a whole lot about what we're feeling."

"Men don't, do they?" I said.

"I don't know. What do you think, Zack? Does your pa?"

"No, I don't reckon he does much," I answered.

It was quiet a long time. I was finally getting sleepy, and I could feel myself drifting off.

"So what are you feeling right now, Zack?" Hawk said.

"I'm scared," I said.

"I'm glad to see you aren't afraid to admit it."

"What about you?"

"I'm scared, too. A man'd be a fool not to be. Besides, sometimes fear makes a body more wise and careful."

"You think Jake would be scared?" I asked.

"Down deeper than he'd want to face, 'course he'd be scared, unless he's an even bigger fool than I think," said Hawk real thoughtfully.

I was so sleepy by then that I didn't even notice how real he made Jake sound.

"But then Jake'd probably find himself dead tomorrow, and I don't plan to let that happen to either of us," Hawk added.

"What you gonna do?" I mumbled groggily.

"I ain't sure. But we're not getting out of this alive unless we *do* use our heads—and maybe our hearts too. I ain't at all sure Jake could do us much good. We're gonna have to use everything we've got—our courage and our brains and our feelings—or we're done for."

# CHAPTER 31

# WAITING

When I woke up, Hawk was gone.

It was daylight, though still early. The Indian guarding me was awake and eating something, but he paid no attention to me when I woke up. He didn't offer me anything to eat, either.

I was too nervous to eat, but was hungry nevertheless. And I was some kind of sore to have slept—or tried to!—all night with my hands and feet tied.

I figured they'd already let Hawk go to find the girl. All I could think of was the words I'd heard last night. Pieces of the conversation kept running back and forth through my mind.

*If I can't find her in time?*

*Then we kill boy . . . we keep boy . . . you bring daughter . . . harm come to girl, boy die. Maybe you die too, Hawk . . . you leave camp daybreak . . . bring daughter, we give you boy.*

I laid there a few minutes, afraid to move. I was pretty stiff and cramped, and so eventually I rolled over. The Indian glanced over at me, then got up and left the tent. A few minutes later he came back, followed by Tranter.

He bent down over me, then smiled a wicked smile.

"Today's the day you will die, little white boy," he hissed. "I will kill you all—you and that foul dog called Demming! Yes, and your sentimentalist Trumbull. Old fool! He will curse the day he saved my life. Ha!"

"You may kill me," I said back at him like an idiot. "But Hawk's too smart to let you hurt him. You'll never—"

163

*Wham!* went his foot across the side of my head. I should have known better than to open my stupid mouth. Hawk had said fear sometimes made you wise and careful. It didn't seem to be helping me much!

"You are as big a fool as he is!" Tranter shouted—or he would have been shouting if he hadn't been trying to keep his voice low. It was obvious he didn't want the rest of the camp to hear his threats. There seemed to be some kind of code of honor between men like Chief Winnemucca and Hawk Trumbull, and I had no doubt if Hawk produced Laughing Waters I would be as safe in the chief's hands as anywhere. But the son of Weeping Feather clearly had another plan to end this crisis—one that didn't involve Hawk and me living to tell about it!

He pulled out his knife and knelt down beside me, flashing its blade right up to my eyes, then sliding it slowly across my cheek, grinning as he did, and watching me squirm.

Then he rose and left the tent without another word, leaving the other man standing watch. Slowly the guard sat down and resumed eating whatever he had been munching on before.

I sat up the best I could with my hands and feet tied and looked around the tent. There wasn't much to see. Nobody lived in it. They must have just used it to put things in they didn't want to get rained on. There were a few skins and tools, pieces of wood, what looked like crude fishing poles and a fishing net, and a nice-looking bow, although the quiver beside it was empty. I knew how to use a bow and arrow well enough from all the time me and Little Wolf spent together. But even if I could get my hands on it, a bow by itself wouldn't do me much good.

What was I thinking anyway? There was a whole tribe of Indians outside! *Paiute* Indians—as ornery and mean as they come, if you listened to anybody except Hawk tell about them!

It wasn't much longer before I realized there was something *else* that needed tending to besides staying alive! Slowly I got to my feet and did my best to tell the brave I needed to go outside and be alone for a minute. He must have gotten my message, because he untied my feet, took me outside, led me a little ways from the camp, and left me to do my business, though he watched me the whole time.

It felt good to walk, and I looked around as best I could to take stock of my surroundings. The tent where they had me wasn't too far from the roped-off corral of ponies off in the direction of the rising sun, but other than that there wasn't too much to notice.

I asked myself what kinds of things Hawk would notice, but I couldn't think of anything. I guess I had a long ways to go before I would be able to really *see* like he'd been teaching me. Everything was quiet. I figured they were waiting for Demming to make his appearance again. Hawk was probably out there somewhere waiting too, hiding out of sight. For all I knew he was watching me right then.

The next hour or two went by so slow that I almost began to forget my danger. After we were back in the tent my guard didn't retie my feet, which made it a little more comfortable.

I signaled the man about something to drink and he called outside. Another Indian brought me water. After that I lay down again, wondering if there was anything I could do to help Hawk. One thing was certain—I couldn't help him laying there in the Paiute camp with my hands tied in front of me! We would sure have a better chance of tracking Demming with both of us than with just one of us!

Vaguely revolving half a dozen ideas in my brain about how I might escape—all of them ridiculous as long as the Indian, a strong brave twice my size, was watching me, I drifted off to sleep once again.

# CHAPTER 32

## MAKING A RUN FOR IT

Sounds woke me!

I don't know how much time had passed. I might have slept for five minutes or an hour.

All I was aware of at first was commotion, shouts, running and scurrying in the camp.

I opened my eyes just as a second brave poked his head into the tent and said something to the man who was watching me. He jumped up, I guess figuring I was still asleep, and ran outside.

I didn't know what the commotion was about. All I knew was that suddenly I was alone!

Instantly I was wide awake and on my feet!

I crept to the opening and peeked out through the skins. The two Indians were running away from the shelter. It looked like the whole camp was moving in that direction.

Then I saw the reason why.

Demming had returned. The chief was walking out to meet him, and most of his camp was following not far behind. I supposed they were just curious, plus they also wanted to keep an eye out in case Demming tried anything.

Without pausing long enough to really think about what I was doing—'cause if I had I'd have realized how crazy it was!—I grabbed the bow, snuck outside the enclosure, crept to another one that was close by, and peeked inside.

Nothing there!

Using precious seconds going from shelter to shelter would

have been foolish had it gone on much longer. But lucky for me, in the second tent I found what I was looking for—a quiver with six or seven arrows in it. I would rather have found a knife or a gun, but it was better than nothing.

I threw the string of the bow over my head, grabbed the rabbit-skin quiver, and bolted down the slight hill toward the ponies. It was a good thing my hands were tied in front of me instead of behind!

No Indians were around. They were all watching the chief as he walked toward Demming on the opposite side of the camp!

If I'd have thought of it, I'd have taken out one of the arrows and used the tip to cut through the leather thongs around my wrists. But I was so frantic that I wasn't thinking of anything except getting away. I scooted under the rope of the makeshift corral and found a pony that still had a rope halter around its nose. I fumbled hurriedly to take off its hobbles, then did my best to lead it under the surrounding rope and out of the corral, then struggled to mount.

I nearly fell several times, with my tied hands and trying to hang onto a bow and quiver, and with no stirrup to use. The commotion had gotten the ponies restless, too, and they were starting to whinny and move about. My own pony seemed uneasy about this stranger trying to mount—I'm sure I didn't smell the same as its Indian masters.

I knew someone would spot me any second!

Finally I managed to struggle and pull myself up onto the pony's back.

I kicked its sides with my heels, and the next second we were galloping away from the Paiute camp, down a little hill, and then out across the plain.

Almost immediately I heard shouts behind me.

Clinging tight with my knees, hanging onto the rope halter and the quiver for dear life while the bow bounced around across my back, struggling to keep my balance with hands tied, I don't know how I managed to stay on that pony's back! I do remember feeling a flash of thankfulness for all the time I'd spent riding bareback with Little Wolf.

I glanced back. Several braves were already mounting to chase me. I don't know what had become of Demming. I'd completely forgotten him by now!

I kicked and shouted at the pony. Now that they were after me there wasn't much need to keep quiet! If only I could get my hands loose!

Everything came back to me from months earlier.

Suddenly no time had passed, and I was riding for the Pony Express once more! Here I was out on the plain, trying to get away from the Indians again. So many thoughts flashed through my brain—the conversation I'd had in my mind with Rev. Rutledge, riding through the rocky ravines, struggling up the mountainside, the fall, my first meeting with Hawk, and a hundred things that had happened since.

I'd thought I was going to die on that day. Had the moment finally come on this day instead?

I could feel the wind whistling through my hair as I rode, yet inside my brain the thoughts slowed down to a different pace. Thoughts of Miracle Springs came to me—thoughts of home, memories and images of faces and happy times from the past. I hadn't thought of home for a long time. I thought of Pa pretty often, but I hadn't let myself remember how good it had sometimes been at Miracle Springs. Maybe the more time that goes by, the more you remember the good things that happened.

Probably only a minute or two passed while I was thinking those things, yet when I came to myself it seemed like waking up after a long sleep.

All at once I was aware again of the wind, of the sound of the galloping hooves beneath me. Then I remembered that I was fleeing from the Paiute camp . . . running for my life!

Again I looked back, expecting to see a war party of angry Indians twenty or thirty yards behind me and closing rapidly.

I was alone!

No other human being was in sight.

Still I continued to urge the pony on at top speed, not believing what my eyes had seen.

A minute or two went by. I was breathing hard and starting to feel lightheaded.

Again I glanced back, still at a full gallop.

Still there seemed to be no one pursuing me.

I eased the pony back to a trot, then finally stopped completely. I turned halfway around, squinting into the distance and listening carefully. I saw nothing and heard nothing. Once the dust from my own tracks had floated off in the wind, there was still no sign anywhere of other riders.

I didn't know what had happened.

But there could be no mistake now—I was alone in the desert, with no one to keep me company but the hard-panting Paiute pony.

# CHAPTER 33

# TRYING TO SEE WHAT THE BIRDS SAW

I got down and tied up the pony.

The first thing I had to do was get my hands untied. That wasn't too hard, using the arrow tips.

Then I had to try to figure out where I was, find some water, and decide what to do.

Hawk had taught me a lot about surviving in the high mountain desert. Now I was going to have to see how well I'd learned!

I reckon there are times of learning and times when you've got to put into practice what you learned, and now was one of the second. Like Hawk had said when the Indians were taking us into their camp—it was time to find out what kind of stuff I was made of.

I looked around and tried to figure out where I was. I'd been riding low on a sort of valley floor. It was a fairly flat area, without as many washes and gulches and invisible canyons as where I'd escaped from the Indian band chasing me last winter.

I climbed back up on the pony and rode slowly to the top of the nearest ridge, then stopped again and looked all around.

I knew where I was, all right. I'd come just about due east from the Paiute camp. I hadn't realized it, but in making my escape I'd come up through a pass across one of the many little ranges of hills that crisscross all through the high basin. The camp wasn't visible, but I was pretty sure where it was. Hawk and I had come from the other side of it, further to the west.

If I had left the camp and ridden straight east—now that I thought of it, the sun had been in my eyes the whole time—then Demming had approached the camp from the opposite side. I'd escaped by riding the other way from where all the Indians were busy with Demming.

Come to think of it, maybe that's why I'd outrun the Indians that had chased me—maybe they'd lost sight of me in the morning sun. It didn't seem too likely, but it was the only thing that made even a little bit of sense.

I dismounted again and sat down on a rock, trying to think what I ought to do next.

If Demming had come into the Paiute camp from the west, it stood to reason that he'd tied Laughing Waters up somewhere that direction too. *But* . . . he would know that the Paiutes would think exactly that.

I tried to put myself in Jack Demming's shoes.

What would he do to trick the Paiutes and throw them off track?

He *wouldn't* ride into their camp from the same direction where he'd stashed the girl.

Therefore, that probably meant she was out *here* somewhere— east of the camp, and that I might be closer to her at that moment than Demming himself!

If I was right, I could expect Demming to leave the Paiute camp, head west, and then circle wide around east after he was out of sight. At least that's what I would do if I were trying to keep my movements and directions secret.

Anyway, it was the only idea I had!

The question was: Did Demming know about me and Hawk being around?

Probably not. Why would he?

If he didn't, and if I was right, then I could expect to see him coming this way before too much longer . . . with Hawk somewhere back out of sight tracking him.

And neither of them knew I was here!

What should I do!

How could I find the chief's daughter before Demming got back?

I racked my brain to remember what Sarah had said were Demming's exact words.

He said she was in a cave ten miles away, tied and gagged. *They'd never find the girl alive . . . she'd be dead from the snakes and scorpions—likely right where she was . . . no water for miles . . . if she managed to get away she'd be so mixed up by the time she got back on the plain, she'd never know the direction to get back to the camp.*

Ten miles . . . that could mean anything! Demming could have been trying to mislead them about the distance . . . it could be ten miles as the crow flies . . . or ten miles as he rode it by horse, including circling around.

That clue wasn't much help!

*Snakes and scorpions* . . . what had Hawk told me one time? We'd been riding along and he'd casually said something like, *There's a place you never want to go near if you can help it, boy— there's more rattlers and scorpions up there than in all the Utah-Nevada territory.*

Come to think of it—we *had been* out near here someplace! I remembered now.

Hawk had pointed up toward a range of rocky, arid hills. He'd said there were more canyons and dead ends up there than any-where. What had he called them? *The badland hills.*

Demming had said she'd be twisted and confused before she got back down *onto the plain.* There was *no water for miles!*

So Demming may have thought, I said to myself. But Hawk would know where to find water. Besides, snakes need water too— that was another thing he had taught me. *Watch yourself when you find a watering hole, Zack,* he said.

In any case, that had to be it!

Demming had Chief Winnemucca's daughter in the badland hills!

Now all I had to do was remember where they were!

*Oh, God,* I prayed, hardly even realizing that I'd started talking back and forth to God, *help me remember. Help me find her! Give me, like Hawk says, eyes to really see. Hawk's not here, God, so help me to be able to see and do what he'd do to find the chief's daughter before Demming hurts her. I want to see like Hawk sees and understand deep into things like Hawk does. Help me see, God . . . help me see what you want me to see.*

I wasn't even through praying when suddenly some words of Hawk's popped into my mind.

*Keep your eyes looking up, Zack,* he liked to say, *always up. Whether you're looking at the sky or praying to God or looking on the up side of a situation instead of the down side of it . . . you're always better off setting your sights high than low. That is, if you want to get the high and the best things out of life. Watch the eagles, son, and the hawks. They got eyes like no human. They see things, they know things. You can learn a lot from them, more than folks realize. If you learn to see with an eagle's eyes, they can tell you a lot about what's going on down on the earth, even far away where you can't see with your own eyes.*

Suddenly I shot my eyes upward and spun my head around in all directions, squinting toward the horizon all the way around.

Yes, there were some birds flying and circling about—way off there toward the southeast from where I stood! They looked to be three or four miles away.

*If only Hawk were here,* I thought. He would be able to tell what they were doing. He would be able to make sense of it all.

I squinted to try to see the birds more carefully.

I recognized the motion, the wingspan, the circular flight patterns. Hawk was real interested in birds and was always teaching me of their ways. He was proud of the name the Paiutes had given him and he took it seriously.

I continued to gaze.

Those weren't eagles or hawks.

They were vultures!

Almost the same instant that the dreadful thought dawned on me, suddenly my eyes beheld the range of hills they were flying around. I hadn't stopped to look at them before because I'd been concentrating my attention more straight eastward.

But suddenly I knew I'd seen them before when riding with Hawk.

The vultures were circling around one small area of the *badland hills*!

The next instant I was on the pony and flying down the slope toward the flat plain that lay between the ridge I had climbed and the hills Hawk had warned me never to go near.

# CHAPTER 34

## REMEMBERING TO LOOK UP

I reached the foothills in twelve or fifteen minutes.

Immediately the footing was treacherous and steep, so I dismounted and continued on foot.

Glancing back, I couldn't believe it—there was a small dust cloud in the distance, and it was moving toward me!

I had been right! Demming was circling back!

He had probably seen the dust from my pony's hooves too, though I might have made it across the flat before he'd reached the other side of it.

I glanced up.

The vultures were directly above me, but I couldn't see any other sign of life. If Laughing Waters was here, she was out of sight . . . but somewhere close.

How could they know? I wondered. I thought to myself again about Hawk always talking about being able to see what wasn't plainly visible, being able to see what most eyes couldn't. I guess vultures had that gift too.

Now I had to find what they saw . . . and fast. Demming would be here in five or ten minutes!

I struggled up the rocky slope, pulling the pony along behind me, glancing frantically all around for any sign of a cave or any other place where Demming might have tied up the girl.

*Give me eyes, God*, I prayed once more. *Help me see what those vultures up there see. Help me find her!*

There were caves all around as I got higher up into the hills, some of them deep, some not more than an indentation in the stone walls. There were small canyons and gorges too, and within minutes I found myself surrounded by such a maze of twisting and turning paths and ravines and possible directions to go that my heart began to fail me.

I would never find her! Especially not before Demming got back! Also, I was so thirsty, and there was no water up here.

I dropped the pony's rope and ran into a cave that appeared to my right.

It was dark inside. I stepped forward slowly, calling out as I went. I hardly stopped to consider that if the chief's daughter were here, probably the *last* thing she would do would be to say anything. How would she know I wasn't Demming? Besides, Demming said she was tied and gagged anyway, so she *couldn't* answer my calls!

Suddenly a sound froze me in my tracks.

I would know it anywhere!

Slowly I began inching my way backward—very slowly!—while the rattles from some unseen snake's tail continued to sound in the darkness.

Inch by inch, in mortal terror of fangs I couldn't see, I crept back toward the cave's mouth.

The instant I knew I was out of reach from a coiled spring, I turned and dashed into the open light, breathing hard and sweating freely.

That had been close!

I looked down into the valley. I could see the figure of Demming on his horse now. He had covered half the distance since I saw him.

*Is Hawk on his trail?* I thought, *back there somewhere out of sight?* If he was, I couldn't do anything that would mess up his plan.

But if Hawk wasn't behind Demming, then I couldn't delay. There wasn't much time left! I had to act quickly.

I looked up again at the vultures.

*Keep looking up, Zack . . . always up. Watch the eagles, son, and the hawks. They got eyes like no human. They see things, they know things. You can learn a lot from them, more than folks realize. Keep your eyes up . . . learn to see with an eagle's eyes.*

Right then I hoped his words applied to vultures too!

Sometimes the hardest thing to do is slow down long enough to think. That was another thing Hawk said. *You gotta think before you do,* he said. *The brain part's got to come before the hands part. It may seem like a waste of time, but it saves time in the end.*

His words flashed through my mind in an instant as I stood gazing up into the blue sky. I forced myself to calm down, to ignore Demming just for a few seconds and concentrate on those vultures. What did they see? What did they have to tell me . . . if only I could see it?

I watched the circles they were making in the sky.

I had to find the *center* of their flight! That was the answer! Whatever they were interested in, they flew *around* it in a circle. If I wanted to find it, I had to locate the center of those arcs and then follow that centerpoint down to the ground.

So much I had heard from Hawk kept coming back to me now. In the few seconds as I stood there, it seemed the whole last several months came rushing past me.

*Look up, Zack . . . always up. The answers to earth's questions are discovered first in the heavens. It's all about eagle's eyes, son. Learn to understand God and the way things work in his world first. Then bring your eyes down to earth-level, and everything will make sense there too. Upward sight always comes first . . . that's where wisdom begins.*

I wished Hawk were here now to help me with his eyes!

I watched the vultures. One big fellow was flying around and around in what looked to be the tightest circle of the whole group. I locked my eyes on him, trying to keep myself calm, and followed him through two complete circular flights. When I thought I had the middle located exactly, I carefully and slowly lowered my eyes down to the ground.

A small ravine was visible, opening just on the other side of two gigantic boulders. I hadn't been able to see it before because those big rocks were positioned in such a way that they looked to be part of the cliff face behind them. But as my eyes descended down from above, my line of vision somehow came down over and beyond the boulders, and that was when I realized that they were hiding an opening behind them.

It was exactly like Hawk said! I had to look *up* before my eyes could properly focus on what was *down* on the ground.

I looked around quick for someplace to hide the pony in case Demming got back before I got out of there.

I led him up the hill a little further, around a couple turns, then half tied the pony's rope to a shrub and threw down the bow and quiver beside him. Then I ran back down toward the opening between the two boulders.

Demming had said Laughing Waters was in a cave. Had that been to throw the Paiutes off, or had he moved her? This wasn't a cave, but in a way it was even better because the opening was so hard to see when you looked straight at it. If you didn't know you were looking for something more behind it, you'd never know anything was there.

I squeezed through the rocks, inching along sideways.

On the other side, the way opened into a short, narrow gorge. Both sides were of jagged rock and running straight up, with a flat floor between them that was maybe three or four feet wide.

I ran forward into it, then around another big rock.

And there she was!

# CHAPTER 35

## LAUGHING WATERS!

I ran to the girl and knelt down.

She was slumped over sideways, her back leaning against the wall of rock—she was either sleeping or had fainted from the heat or lack of food and drink.

If only I had some water! One look at her parched, cracked, bleeding lips, and I knew she probably hadn't had anything to drink in two days. At least she wasn't gagged, like Demming said.

With that same look I was immediately taken with this young Indian maiden. The exhaustion of her whole body, the dust in her hair, the smears of dirt and the scratches on her arms and face couldn't hide that she could be nothing less than a chief's daughter. I guessed her to be eighteen or nineteen, though her sunken cheeks and closed eyes made it difficult to tell.

I softly spoke a few words to her, but they didn't succeed in waking her. I was getting nervous—I don't know if it was because of Demming or because this was Chief Winnemucca's daughter.

She reminded me somehow of my sister Emily. I guess she looked about the same age and was pretty like Emily, though with darker skin.

I didn't think of it at the time, but later I realized that all three of the things Hawk had spoken about when we had been talking about courage were right then going on inside me.

We talked about what a man *does* and about being brave, which I don't know if I was or not, but I was sure facing danger right then—and his name was Jack Demming!

We'd talked, too, about using your *head* and being a thinking kind of person. I reckon I was doing that, too, trying to remember everything Hawk had taught me and trying to figure where Demming had taken Laughing Waters and how to outsmart him and get her away.

And we'd talked about *feelings* and how that was a part of themselves that most men aren't too well acquainted with. I don't know if that was true about me, but one thing for sure was that I felt things stirring around in my heart right about now that were different than what I felt when I was around Hawk. Maybe they were feelings of compassion or an instinct of protection like I'd feel toward my sisters if they were in danger. Whatever those feelings were, they made me all the more determined to get this girl out of here safely!

I was timid about touching her, but I had to try to get her conscious again.

I touched her cheek softly. A tingle went through my hand. Her skin wasn't soft, but it had a different quality than a man's skin. I touched her again, this time patting at her cheek a couple times.

Still there was no sign of life.

Did I dare *slap* her to try to wake her up?

I laid my hands on her shoulders and jostled her, then shook harder. Finally I did slap her cheek, though gently, then again.

A faint groan sounded. At least she was still alive!

I shook her shoulders again, staring straight at her closed eyelids. Slowly they opened a slit, just as she groaned again. Her head turned toward me.

The moment she saw me her eyes opened wide.

It was a look I will never forget—an awful, terrible expression. The first instant she saw my face, her eyes filled with *fear*. In that instant, maybe more than any other moment of my life, something inside me decided what kind of man I wanted to be—and it wasn't a man like the fella named Jake that Hawk had told me about, or Demming or this girl's half-Paiute tribesman. I couldn't think of anything worse than for another person to be *afraid* of me.

"Please," I said, "you have nothing to fear."

She kept staring at me, as if she was paralyzed. My hands were still on her shoulders. I took them away and leaned away from her.

"Are you Laughing Waters?"

Still she did not move.

"Do you understand me?"

Slowly her head nodded.

"Are you Laughing Waters?"

Again she nodded.

"Don't be afraid," I said. "I have come to take you back to your father."

A look of confusion now replaced the fear.

"The . . . the other man?" she said in a parched voice, but in English.

"We must get away from here before he returns. Can you walk?"

"My feet . . . hands . . . he tied me."

Now I noticed the ropes around her wrists and ankles. I don't know why I didn't see them earlier.

"You have water? . . . so thirsty. . . ."

"No, I'm afraid—"

A feeling of panic shot through me. I heard Demming's horse approaching up the hill!

If he found me here, we'd both be done for.

"He's coming back," I whispered to Laughing Waters. "But don't be afraid. I'll get you away from him somehow."

"No . . . don't leave," she pleaded.

"I have to. Otherwise neither one of us'll have a chance."

I thought for a moment.

"Try to get him to leave again. Ask him for water, tell him you heard somebody coming, tell him you heard a call from one of your people up in the hills behind us. Just try to get him to leave again. I won't be far away."

I stood and left her.

But the moment I started between the two big rocks, I heard Demming coming up the path.

Too late! I couldn't escape now.

I turned and ran back into the ravine, paused a moment where Laughing Waters was watching with fear in her eyes, then kept on further into the little ravine. It was not straight, so I hurried around a bend, and at the end, surrounded by high cliffs, I found a little crevice back under one of the faces of rock.

I crept into the darkness, praying that no hungry snakes were too close by.

Then I crouched down and waited.

# CHAPTER 36

# OUT OF THE HIDDEN RAVINE

I recognized Jack Demming's voice instantly.

At first he thought Laughing Waters was asleep, but the moment he realized she was awake he began growling mean things at her and laughing cruelly. Then I heard a slapping sound followed by a hoarse scream, and I knew he had hit her.

It was all I could do to stay where I was. My natural instinct was to rush out and attack him, but I knew how stupid that would be. Demming was twice as big as me. Even Hawk had nearly had more than he could handle till I'd gotten hold of the rifle when they were fighting. Besides, he had a gun and hated me now as much as he hated any Indian. He wouldn't think twice about killing me.

I waited, hoping Laughing Waters would be able to get the bounty hunter to leave again.

It took a long time, probably an hour, but I heard their voices every once in a while, and eventually I heard Demming's heavy footsteps walking back out between the rocks of the narrow opening. The next second I was rushing back out to Laughing Waters' side.

"Are you all right?" I asked, kneeling down.

"Yes, but hurry. He will be back."

I tried to untie the cords around her hands and feet, but they were too tight and since I'd left the quiver up with the pony, I had nothing sharp.

Finally I picked her up, one arm under her knees, the other

under her shoulders, and carried her to the opening between the rocks. Then I set her down.

"Let me see if the coast is clear," I said.

I snuck through cautiously and peered out. Demming was nowhere in sight.

I hurried back.

"The opening is too narrow for me to carry you," I said. "You'll have to hop through. I'll help you."

Halfway holding her arms and hands, I helped her jostle and jump her way through the narrow opening. As soon as it was wide enough, I scooped her up in my arms again and hurried up the hill toward the waiting pony.

There was no time to lose, no time to stop to try to get the ropes loosened.

"Hang onto me," I said.

With my right hand I reached to take hold of the pony's rope, while she clung tight around my neck and shoulder. Then as best I could I made my way further up the hill, trying to put as much distance as I could between us and Demming's little hideout. We had to move quickly, because if he came back too soon, he was sure to hear the pony's hooves on the rocky ground.

Carrying Laughing Waters as well as the bow and arrows and pulling the pony behind me, I struggled along for four or five minutes before I had to set my burdens down and rest. We had covered a fair distance, I thought, and had wound through several twisting little draws and washes, enough so I thought we would be safe for a few minutes at least.

I set Laughing Waters down as gently as I could, then plopped down beside her.

"Whew!" I sighed.

"You have courage, young man—you risk your life for a Paiute," she said solemnly, "against one of your own kind."

"Demming's not *my* kind," I said. "I've run into him once before, and believe me, there's no love lost between the two of us."

"And yet you are brave to rescue me. Many white men think an Indian girl is not worth the trouble."

I looked over into her face. I hadn't even stopped to think what I was doing until that moment. Suddenly I realized she was right. Once I'd escaped from the Paiute camp, I didn't *have* to rescue her. I could have left the Indians and Demming to fend for themselves. But the moment I looked at her and saw the look of gratefulness that had replaced the fear when she had first seen me, I knew beyond any doubt that she *was* worth whatever it took to see her safely back with her father.

I would even go up against Demming face-to-face for her sake. Why, I couldn't have said, and I didn't stop to analyze it right then. I just knew I would. I knew that here was a girl I would do anything for.

"Well, maybe I'm not like the rest," I said. "But now let's get those bindings off you." I got out one of the arrows and within two or three minutes, being as careful of her wrists and ankles as possible, I had her free from Demming's leather thongs.

"How did you get him to leave?" I asked Laughing Waters.

"I do like you say, tell him I hear a signal from my people. At first he laugh at me. But I keep looking around, moving my head like I hear noise. Finally he gets nervous and goes to look."

"Good for you!" I said. "Lucky for us he went down the hill, or we'd have run right into him."

"What is your name, brave white man?" she asked.

"Oh, yeah—sorry. I'm Zack Hollister."

"Why did you come, Zack Hollister . . . how did you find me?"

"I'm a friend of Hawk Trumbull's," I said. "Your father brought us to your camp and told us Demming had you. Hawk was supposed to find you, but . . . well, I guess I got to you first."

"Hawk is a good man. My father respects him. . . . Oh, I'm so thirsty!" added Laughing Waters with a weary groan.

Recovered from the climb, I now stood up to look around and try to figure out what we should do next. I had to find some water. Laughing Waters was about done in from thirst, and I was mighty parched too!

Then we had to get back to the valley floor without Demming spotting us. And we had to cover the wide distance across it without him seeing us, which, from the vantage point of this ridge of mountains overlooking it, would be difficult.

We had climbed steeply up the hill, zigzagging back and forth along whatever path seemed easiest at the time. But it still seemed that our only clear avenue of escape back to the valley floor led straight back the way we had come, down the draw past Demming's hiding place.

I either had to find some other route down out of the mountains, or else some way to lure Demming a good distance from where he had been keeping Laughing Waters.

I left Laughing Waters and the pony and climbed up the steep face of the cliff on a jagged series of indentations. In a short time I was high up and could see clearly in all directions. Down below us, to my left, I saw the hidden ravine where Laughing Waters had been. Further on down the hill, there was Demming!

He was looking all around and making his way back up the hill. There wasn't a moment to lose!

I scanned about the mountainous terrain in every direction. Then suddenly a plan came into my head. It was probably foolhardy. But against a man like Jack Demming I knew that a face-to-face confrontation would never work.

We would never get out of this alive unless we outsmarted him. That's what I hoped to do.

As quietly as possible, I scurried back down the rocks and rejoined Laughing Waters, then carefully explained to her what we had to do.

# CHAPTER 37

# THE WOUNDED BIRD PLOY

There had been seven arrows in the quiver I'd grabbed, and they were the only weapon I had. Against Demming's gun they didn't seem like much, but they would have to do.

I'd have to use them carefully, hopefully to trick the kidnapper instead of shooting him.

I slung the bow up around my back, took the quiver in my hand, made sure Laughing Waters knew what she was to do, and then crept once more up the rocks above us, this time in a course parallel to the direction of the whole ridge—mostly southward but a little to the east. It was midmorning by now, maybe even getting on toward noon. I headed toward the sun. It was already pretty high in the sky. But by going south, even at midday, I still kept it in front of me. I hoped it would be in Demming's eyes too— enough to keep him from seeing me.

I was trying to work my way in a large circle, both down through the hills toward the south and at the same time closer to Demming. My plan was to lure him away from where he had kept Laughing Waters. If I could get him far enough away on foot, then she could take the pony back the way we had come, past the hiding place, until the mountains began to level off, and then get on the pony and ride back down into the valley. From where we were, the only place safe for the pony's footing was past Demming's position.

I climbed and walked and crawled my way for probably twenty or thirty minutes, then stopped and refigured my position. Demming had returned by now, had found Laughing Waters missing, and even as far away as I was I could hear his swearing plain enough. He was looking frantically around, then finally began to make his way up the hill, just the way we'd gone, toward the east.

I couldn't wait any longer. I didn't dare let him go far enough to pick up our trail. I'd hoped to get a little further away, but this would have to do.

I stood up on a high rock from where I could see him. Then I pulled an arrow from the quiver, slung it into the bow, drew the string back to my ear, took aim, and let it fly.

I waited just long enough to make sure Demming saw which direction the arrow came from, then ducked down out of sight. From this distance I didn't expect to *hit* him, only to attract his attention.

It worked!

He jumped when the arrow struck a rock about ten feet from him, then glanced in my direction. Then he crouched down, still looking toward me. But he saw nothing, because by that time I was out of sight.

I had to keep his attention diverted from where he'd been heading up the hill toward Laughing Waters!

I took off over the rocks as fast as I could, keeping out of sight but making plenty of noise, picking up a few big rocks as I went and tossing them down the hill just to make *sure* he heard me.

I ran for a couple of minutes, then stopped, crouched down, and peered out.

Good! Demming was coming after me.

I glanced around at the sun. If I stood on that big boulder about twenty yards away, I should be in a direct line between it and Demming. I let another arrow fly, this time aiming high over Demming's head to make sure he would see it sailing past him and know the direction it had come from.

Then I scurried to the boulder, climbed to the top, took off my hat, and stood up on top, holding the bow in the air.

"We have girl, white man!" I shouted, making my voice sound as Indian-like as I could. I only hoped the sun behind me blinded his eyes enough to keep him from recognizing that I was white too.

The curses which exploded from Demming's mouth were too awful to think about. The next instant a gunshot rang out, and a slug slammed into the boulder three or four feet from me, sending up dust and splinters of rock.

I jumped down out of sight. That was too close!

"No follow, white man," I called out again in the same voice, "no get girl." But my words were braver than my actions. I was already hurrying to get further away and stay out of sight!

More cursing and two more shots were the only answer to my words. From the sound of Demming's voice, I figured he thought I was an Indian, all right—though he wouldn't have been that fond of me, either.

I picked and ran and climbed my way through and around and over the rugged, mountainous, rocky ground, working my way south, away from Demming's hiding place, but gradually westward, too, down the slope of the hillside toward the valley. Demming continued to chase me, firing a shot now and then, but not really gaining on me. As I moved steadily down the hill, gradually the sun quit being right behind me, and before long I knew that if Demming caught a good look at me without the sun in his eyes he'd recognize me.

I had to get close enough to the valley to make a run for it without getting shot. I also had to get Demming far enough away so that Laughing Waters could get the pony down past the hiding place and make a break for it without getting shot herself.

I picked up a few stones, threw them in Demming's direction, then kept going, mostly staying out of sight, but slowing down a little and letting him see me just often enough to make him think he was catching me. I was getting further and further down the mountainside.

Then behind me I heard the sound of a horse.

I climbed a rock and looked back.

Laughing Waters had led the pony down the way we had come, and was now riding past Demming's hiding place.

I was afraid he would turn and start firing at her!

I jumped up on the highest rock nearby, slung another arrow and let it fly, then called out.

"Demming!" I yelled, this time in my normal voice.

I saw him stop and look up.

"That you, Hollister?"

"Yeah, it's me," I answered. "And I got the best of you this time!"

"Come on down here, Hollister. Give me the girl, and I'll make it worth your while."

"Just like you were gonna make it worth my pa's while? No deal, Demming!"

"The loot's mine, and the girl's mine!" shouted Demming furiously. "Turn her over, Hollister, or I'll leave you out here to rot with the scorpions and rattlers!"

"You're the one who's gonna be left in the desert, Demming!" I yelled back. "You're not getting the girl or me or my pa!"

"I got a gun, Hollister. If that little Indian bow's all you got, I'll find you eventually."

Even as he was saying the words, Demming turned and saw Laughing Waters galloping down the last incline of the hills toward the valley floor. Suddenly he realized the trick I'd played on him to lure him so far from his own mount.

I jumped down out of sight again just in time to hear a rapid round of shots echo out and ricochet around the rocks above me.

"I'll kill you, Hollister!" I heard as the echoes died away.

It was time for me to get out of here!

I ran straight down the hill, through a couple short narrow draws, and around several twisting ravines until finally a straight pathway opened in front of me that led straight down to the expanse of plain. I didn't know the range of Demming's pistol, but I had to keep myself out of sight just in case.

I got to the opening to the valley and stopped, then eased myself out from behind a rock and looked back.

Demming was still following me, but it was slow work. He was still up among the rugged rocks and boulders where I had been, and once I started downhill I'd widened the distance between us considerably.

In the distance, along the valley floor, I saw a dust cloud moving toward me. Now I heard the sound of galloping hooves.

It was Laughing Waters! She was making straight for me!

I ran out from the cover of the rocks to meet her!

Several shots rang out behind me. I knew Demming realized now how badly he'd been duped by following me. If I knew Demming, his anger had reached a white fury by now! But he was too far away for his shots to be close, as long as we kept moving.

Laughing Waters galloped up, slowing the pony only enough for me to jump up on its back behind her.

She reached down with her left arm. I grabbed hold, then gave a leap and landed on the pony's back. I stretched my arms around her waist and hung on while she urged the pony on with hoarse Paiute commands I didn't understand.

Off we galloped, keeping close to the cover of the mountains, her long black hair streaming back into my face, with the faint sounds of Demming's voice ringing in my ears from behind.

"I'll kill you, Hollister . . . I'll kill you."

Several more shots followed, but they were already fading into the distance behind us.

# CHAPTER 38

# WATER . . . WATER . . . BUT WHERE?

We rode for five or six minutes at a full gallop along the edge of the hills.

That was enough to get us well away from Demming for the time being. Even sitting behind her as I was, I could tell Laughing Waters was weakening from the extreme exertion and wouldn't last much longer.

Reaching further around her waist, I took the pony's rope from her hands and eased him to a stop.

I jumped to the ground. The same instant Laughing Waters collapsed and fell unconscious into my arms.

I gently laid her down on the ground. Her face was pale, and despite the strain, not a bead of perspiration shone anywhere.

I had to find water!

We were probably only two hours from the camp of her people. I wasn't exactly sure of the direction by this time, and I certainly didn't want to try to make it without her help.

But she couldn't help me, being unconscious!

Besides, she was just too weak to make it much further. To strike out on one horse, across the desert when I didn't know the way, with Demming bound to pick up our trail sooner or later— it would have been suicide.

I had to have Laughing Waters' eyes to guide us back. To do that, we needed water . . . and soon!

Hawk had taught me how to look for water in the desert. But

I'd always had him with me. Now I was on my own.

One thing Hawk always said was, *If you're really paying attention and learning like you're supposed to, then when the time comes you need it you'll remember all you need, and you'll find out that what you learned was down inside you all the time just waiting to be used.*

I hoped he was right. I guess now I'd find out how good a learner I'd been!

I pulled Laughing Waters to the shade of a large, overhanging rock. I didn't dare leave her alone for more than a few minutes, but maybe I could find something in that time.

Quickly I mounted the pony and loped off along the base of the range. As I rode I scanned the ground for all the signs Hawk had taught me to look for.

I remembered him saying, *Look for the signs . . . the water's there, you just gotta know how to see down below the surface.*

He'd shown me how most of the mountain ranges had underground runoffs as well as the streams you could see, lots of them bubbling up in hot springs, sometimes smelling of sulfur because they come from so deep underground.

*Look for the salt deposits,* he'd say. *Especially if they're yellow or orange, that means something's coming up out of the ground not too far away. Look for steam . . . no way to have steam without water down there someplace.*

I galloped along, searching frantically for any of the signs he'd taught me that indicated water. With Demming not far behind, we didn't have time to stop and coax water from a cactus.

Direct ahead was what looked like a dry creek bed!

I hurried on, then slowed and jumped off the horse.

Water had run through here not long ago, that was for sure, though it was dry now. Hawk had taught me to see in the contour of the sand whether the patterns had been made by wind or water. These signs said "water."

I followed the creek bed with my eyes up in the direction of the hills.

It came from a hollow through a slender ravine. That looked promising!

I jumped back onto the pony and rode in that direction. I

could pick out some of the other signs Hawk'd trained me to look for—slightly more greenery, grass that was finer and more delicate . . . yes, and that was rice grass here and there!

I was sure there was water underneath me here someplace! So much of what Hawk had shown me and told me now came back to me. I could hear his voice speaking to me in my memory, and it all made clear sense.

I reached the edge of the valley floor. Again I jumped down, looking around this way and that. The signs from the plants . . . the look of the sand . . . the shape of the ravine sloping down toward me from the mountains . . . and—yes, partway up there were some salt deposits! Everything looked just like that first place when Hawk had found water in what to me was the middle of nowhere, after telling me about how water disappeared and how the underground streams and sinks behaved out here.

Frantically I looked about.

*Where would Hawk dig?* I questioned in my head. How would he let his eyes *see* what was *under* the ground?

Suddenly a wave of doubt swept over me. It seemed so hopeless! How could there possibly be water here, in the middle of a desert? What was I thinking?

*Learn to see, Zack,* came Hawk's voice once more as a reminder. *There's always more to be seen under the surface of things than most folks realize.*

Then I remembered another of Hawk's constant lessons: *Don't be hasty,* he'd said to me more than once. *More mischief comes from rushing a job that takes time than anything else you'll likely do wrong.*

I paused and closed my eyes.

*God, help me,* I quietly prayed. *Help me see. Show me what I know you can see with your eyes.*

I took another deep breath and then opened my eyes, trying to remain calm.

I looked all around me again. I looked at the sand, the grass, the other plants, the hills, the ravine—everything. I was trying to take in every lesson I had learned, trying to steady my racing brain, all the while knowing that Laughing Waters was in danger . . . and that Demming was probably back to his horse by now.

# CHAPTER 39

## AN EVIL STRIKE

Ten minutes later I was racing back toward where Laughing Waters still lay unconscious.

I only hoped I wasn't too late!

I jumped down and ran to her, kneeling down. My heart sank. Oh, her face was so gray and her poor lips so cracked and dry!

"Laughing Waters . . . Laughing Waters, wake up," I said, gently stroking her face with my hand, then dabbing it with my wet shirt.

At first there was no sign of life. I continued to talk softly to her, moistening her face and forehead as best I could, though already the hot sun had half dried out my shirt.

Then impulsively I bent down and kissed her gently on the cheek. *God . . . God,* I whispered, *wake her up . . . let her live and recover her strength again.*

Almost the same instant I felt her body stir . . . then a faint, high-pitched groan. Her eyes opened and she muttered something in Paiute.

Then she saw me kneeling beside her, and smiled faintly.

"Zack . . . Zack Hollister," she whispered. "How long?. . . Are we still? . . . Why is my face wet?. . . That man—"

"Shh," I said. "Everything will be fine. Yes, we're still out in the desert, and you've been asleep for fifteen or twenty minutes. But we're still safe from Demming. And—guess what? I found a tiny spring of water."

"I felt wetness, and funny tickling here . . ."

She reached up to touch her cheek. I was too embarrassed to tell her she had felt my whiskers. "I doused my shirt in the water," I said. "That's what you feel."

"Feels good," she sighed. "I drink?"

"It's not here. We must go to it. Do you think you can get up and ride again?"

"I will," she replied, the mere thought of water filling her with energy. She struggled to rise. I gave her my hand and lifted her carefully to her feet.

"Can you get on the pony?"

"If you help," she said.

I steadied her. She put one hand on my shoulder, then gave a leap that I could tell taxed her, but she managed to struggle up. I jumped up, scrambled in front of her, and called out behind me.

"Hang on tight," I said.

Her hands clasped themselves around my midsection. I put my left hand over her two and clasped them tight so she wouldn't lose her grip. As soon as I was sure she was safe, I kicked the pony forward, though not as fast as I'd come, and we loped gently southward.

We reached the tiny oasis in six or seven minutes.

"It's not the best," I said. "It tastes like sulfur, but it's wet."

I jumped off, helped Laughing Waters down, and the next instant she was on her knees, scooping tiny handfuls from out of the hole I'd dug. It was probably a foot and a half deep and barely big enough to fit a hand into. In the time I'd been gone, it had filled to five or six inches in the bottom of it. The arrow and sharp rock I'd used to dig in the ground still lay beside the hole.

Her vigor seemed to return almost instantly.

After several handfuls had found their way down her parched throat, she threw the next two on her face and neck, then sat back laughing, water glistening from her skin.

"Oh, so good it feels!" she exclaimed. "I alive again! You save me, Zack Hollister."

She gave me a look of loving gratitude such as I don't think I've ever seen.

The next moment she was down in the hole again, grabbing

at the water with her small hand, bringing up as much as she could without losing it between her fingers.

I stood and walked to the pony, who had to be thirsty too. But one look at him, and I suddenly saw something I hadn't thought of before. His long nose was too big to fit down the hole I had dug!

If only I could find a larger stick with a sharp point to widen the little well with. I glanced around, then walked up a few paces among the rocks and boulders of the hill to see what I could find.

Laughing Waters looked up then and called out to me.

"Zack, do not go up there!"

"I'm just going to find something to dig with," I said, turning around.

"No, Zack," she insisted, "come back. Rocks behind you . . . I don't like—"

"The pony can't drink," I said, backing up the hill as I spoke. "I won't be but a minute or two. I just want to—"

My words were interrupted by a terrible scream.

"Zack, no—stop—!"

But I hadn't heeded her first warning, and this one came too late. Something dreadful seized the back of my thigh, just above the knee.

A sudden chill swept through me. Instinct told me what it was, though I felt no pain for those first seconds.

I tried to run but felt a great weight holding me back.

I struggled a few steps, then looked back.

Terror nearly paralyzed me. A great rattler was stretched out behind me, probably to a length of six feet, its wicked fangs still embedded in the flesh of my leg.

Suddenly the pain from the strike caught up with me, and an awful fear of death at the same time.

I felt myself going faint, then starting to fall, and at the same instant the snake released its grip.

I hit the ground and was conscious the next moment of Laughing Waters running toward me with the full attacking fury of a Paiute warrior. All her previous weakness seemed to have disappeared in an instant. In a single bound she reached me, caught up a great rock from the ground, and pummeled the snake to a quick and gruesome death before it could recoil and strike either of us again.

Almost the next instant she produced a cord of leather from around her neck and tied it tightly about my leg above the bite.

She was running again, back to the watering hole, where the pony was doing his best, with slender nose and long tongue, to lap up a few precious drops from the bottom of it.

Laughing Waters grabbed up the arrow, ran back to me, threw me over onto my front with amazing strength for one so small and in such a weakened state, and began slashing away with the arrowhead at my trousers.

I hardly had time to take stock of what was happening when suddenly a terrific pain exploded in my thigh, far more intense than the bite itself.

By the time I realized she was digging into my leg with the tip of the sharp arrow, I felt her mouth close over the wound and begin sucking frantically. She released me, then spit with revulsion.

Without a pause, she repeated the sucking and spitting process, then did it a third time.

I arched my head around as best I could.

Beside my leg, a small pool of blood, splotched with ugly yellowish venom slowly sank into the sand.

Laughing Waters paused to take a breath, then dug at my leg once more with the arrow. I knew she was probably saving my life, but the pain was almost unbearable, and I could not help screaming.

She paid no attention, but went back to the sucking work with her mouth, squeezing all around the wound with her fingers to coax all the venom she could out through the wound instead of allowing it to flow into my bloodstream.

She kept at it for probably five minutes, until both of us were exhausted and her efforts yielded no further hint of yellow. Then she returned to the hole and rinsed out her mouth.

Following this she scurried around nearby and grabbed at a few weeds that I knew Hawk used, too, crushing them in her hands as she ran back to me. She stuffed some of the dried herbs in her mouth, chewed violently at them, then spit the green mass out onto her hand and slapped it into the wound, packing it down and then holding it in place by tying some of my torn trousers against it.

"Must not delay," she said. "Now it is my turn to ask if *you* can ride."

"And my turn to say, I will," I answered, struggling back to my feet. By this time my leg hurt something awful, and I knew I was weak.

# CHAPTER 40

## RIDING FOR OUR LIVES

I didn't realize how much all the exertion and the snakebite had taken out of me until I went to spring up onto the pony.

All at once I felt a numbness in my leg. I turned faint. It might not have been from the bite yet, but whatever it was, I started to feel very strange. If Laughing Waters had not helped pull me up, I don't know if I could have mounted.

She wasn't very strong yet, but at this point she was stronger than me. The water, or something, seemed to have given her new energy. I didn't question it!

Once on the pony's back, I tried to shake the faintness off. I dug in the heel of my good leg and we galloped away. She pointed in a direction away from the mountains, probably to the northwest, though I had just about entirely lost my bearings by now. I would never have made it back alone.

Feeling Laughing Waters' arms around my waist gave me a surge of energy for a while. It reminded me that we were all alone and depending on each other for our very life. I couldn't get sick or faint now!

We took out across the plain, but by now my head was spinning and I didn't feel good at all. I was kicking the pony to go faster with my one good leg and hanging onto the pony's mane for dear life, afraid every moment that I was going to fall off. That poor pony had been through a lot that day and must have been exhausted!

We weren't even halfway across the plain when suddenly a

crack of gunfire sounded behind us. I felt Laughing Waters' hands grab all the more tightly at my waist.

I glanced around as best I could.

Demming was on his horse and pounding straight toward us!

I saw the explosion from his gun barrel even before the next sharp report caught up to my ears.

We'd left him up in the hills. How had he gotten on our trail so soon?

I turned back around, kicking at the poor pony and yelling at him to go faster.

Another shot sounded!

Laughing Waters gasped. Her restrained terror right in my ears sent chills up and down my back.

I glanced back again.

Already Demming was closer and gaining rapidly! His horse was fresher and had only one rider. Our pony was not only smaller, but was nearing the point of exhaustion.

There was no way we could outrun him!

After his threats there was no doubt what he'd do when he caught us. He'd kill me, and once he had his hands on the half-breed, he'd probably kill Laughing Waters too, just for spite!

For a few seconds more we continued on, but I knew it was no use. He was gaining fast.

Suddenly I pulled on the reins, slowed the pony, reached back and took the bow and quiver from Laughing Waters. Handing her the rope, I jumped to the ground, almost losing my footing from the numbness in my leg.

"Go!" I yelled.

"I won't leave you," she yelled back.

"You have to," I cried. "Get back to your people."

"I didn't suck the poison out of your leg to let that wicked man kill you!"

"Go!" I repeated again, then swatted the pony's rump as hard as I could. He jumped to a gallop again. I turned around to face Demming.

He was riding up fast—luckily so fast that he couldn't get off a good straight shot with his wobbling pistol.

My only hope was to either shoot Demming, or else disable his horse. I only had three arrows left. I would have to make them count.

Hastily I fumbled with the first arrow, got its slot into the bowstring, and pulled back. My head felt twice its size, but I aimed as best I could and let it fly.

In answer, another shot sounded from Demming's gun, the bullet kicking up the dust ten feet away from where I stood. I'd missed badly.

Quickly I restrung another arrow. The result was no better.

I grabbed at my last arrow.

*Slow down, Zack . . . don't be hasty . . . the best things are never rushed. God's never in a hurry, and his purposes are always straight and true.*

Again Hawk's words came into my spinning brain, speaking their wisdom softly and slowly but with a quiet force and power.

*Straight and true.* That's how this arrow had to fly, or else I would be dead inside a minute.

I paused and took in a deep breath. *Don't be hasty . . . the best things are never rushed.*

On came the man who wanted to kill me. I could see Demming doing his best to aim his sights right at my head. I had to wait . . . wait . . . wait until he was so near I could not miss.

He was closing ground rapidly! I could hear the thundering hooves like they were right inside my head.

Why hadn't he shot me! Was he waiting to take aim so that he wouldn't miss, either?

I could see his face now, sweat pouring down it, an evil, angry expression of delight at having me such an easy prey. Maybe he was just going to run me down and save the rest of his shots for Laughing Waters!

Still I waited . . . another second or two . . . now drawing back the string . . .

The arrow released from my fingers.

A great inhuman scream filled the air. I heard what I thought was more gunfire.

My sight began to fade . . .

There was a great commotion all about . . . I heard shouts and could feel dust flying . . . confused sounds of hooves pounding and screaming whinnies flying about in every direction . . .

I could feel consciousness slipping away. I felt no pain, but the last thing I remember was thinking Demming's bullet had found me at last.

I felt bumping and jostling. Hands were on me. I knew I was falling, though everything felt strange and unreal. Voices and sounds I didn't recognize.

Then finally everything went black.

# CHAPTER 41

## BACK IN CAMP

The next thing I knew, I was laying on my back, opening my eyes. My first thought was bewilderment. *Where was I . . . what happened?*

I tried to glance around, but every part of my body felt stiff and sore and heavy. I could barely move my head back and forth.

Slowly I began to remember. *Laughing Waters . . . the ride . . . Demming chasing us . . . gunfire . . . jumping down and trying to stop him with an arrow . . .*

I could remember nothing more. In a way, it seemed like it had all happened an hour ago, but in another way it seemed like a month.

I heard footsteps. I tried to twist my neck around, but a familiar voice spoke before my eyes found its owner.

"You are awake at last, I see," it said.

Even as the words reached my ears, the lovely face bent down over mine. Never have I felt such relief. I must admit that seeing her again, instead of Jack Demming or the desert or a cave filled with snakes, or the inside of a dark grave, for that matter, filled me with such a sudden feeling of happiness that tears came to my eyes.

She saw them and smiled sweetly down at me. Enough time must have passed for her to get back to normal. Her cheeks were full and flushed, her lips no longer cracked, her black hair sparkling, her clothes clean.

And the eyes!

In the two or three seconds that I lay there gazing up into their dark-green depths, I knew why this girl was called Laughing Waters. Though her eyes were nearly black, they had just enough of a hint of green in them that even out there in the middle of the high desert of the Great Basin, they sparkled and danced with a liquid shine that could make you think of an emerald mountain lake or one of the laughing, splashing, tumbling little streams that ran into it. I found myself wondering if she had those same eyes the moment she was born, if the chief had seen the laughing waters in his daughter's face from the very beginning.

I could hardly take my newly-opened eyes off her. But it was not from her beauty alone. Mostly it was because she was so *alive* with a spirit and vitality that poured out of her eyes as if they really had been two tiny dark mountain brooks full of the waters of life.

"What . . . what happened?" I asked. I was surprised to hear my own voice. It sounded like not much more than a whisper.

"You are safe. I am afraid I did not get as much of the snake poison out of your leg as I thought."

"Where am I?"

"The camp of my father."

"How did I get here?"

"I brought you," she laughed. "How else?"

The merry sound of her tinkling laughter was as musical as her eyes were full of life. I think at that moment I would have been content to just lay there and listen to her voice for the rest of the day!

"But . . . but how?" I said.

"You do not think I would leave you out there alone with that bad man, do you?" she said. "I had already turned the pony back around by the time the arrow left your hand."

Now the memory of what had happened began slowly to return to me.

"You have quite an aim with the Indian weapon."

"My best friend taught me," I said.

"His name?"

"Little Wolf . . . but I didn't see anything . . . what happened to Demming?"

"You shot his horse."

Now I remembered.

"I realized at the last instant that I couldn't actually kill a man," I said. "I lowered the arrow toward the horse instead."

"The shot was true."

"A bigger target," I said, trying to smile. "Did . . . did I kill the horse?"

"No. But it stumbled and fell, knocking Demming away and senseless. He lost his gun and lay on the ground just long enough for me to get you away."

"I don't remember anything," I said.

"You fainted," said Laughing Waters, laughing again. "Your face was white as the snow in winter. That's when I knew the snakebite was worse than I thought."

"I fainted? How did I get back here?"

"I pushed you up across the horse's back. You are a heavy load! I was still weak myself. When I rode into camp, they all thought you were dead. You *looked* dead!" she added, laughing again. "Oh, I am so happy you are awake again! I have been so worried! But I knew the whole time that you would not die."

"The whole time—how long have I been here?"

"Ten days."

"Ten days! I've been asleep for ten days?"

"It was a large snake, don't you remember?"

"Vaguely."

"The venom must have gone all through your body. When you should have been lying quiet, you were running and riding and saving my life."

"You saved *my* life," I said.

"Perhaps," she replied. "But all you did to get me away from that terrible bounty hunter, and then getting down to shoot at him and making me go on alone—it was very brave of you. I have told my father everything. You are hero to the Paiute now, for you saved the daughter of Chief Winnemucca."

At that moment someone else entered the small tent, and another familiar voice filled the air.

"So, my young friend, it would appear you are going to live after all!"

"Hawk!" I exclaimed, struggling to rise to a sitting position and turning toward the voice.

"You gave us quite a scare, Zack. I don't know if you'd have pulled through if it hadn't been for this little woman here tending you night and day, making you drink, cooling off your feverish face with a damp cloth. I tell you, she hardly ever left your side."

The flush of Laughing Waters' cheeks deepened at Hawk's words, and she glanced away.

"From what she told me, I owe her plenty just for getting me back here in one piece."

"I reckon you do. But her father's been going around telling everyone that the young friend of Hawk saved his daughter's life and is now a friend of the Paiutes in his own right. From what the girl says, you outfoxed ol' Demming pretty good."

"Where were *you*?" I exclaimed suddenly, remembering more of the details. "I thought you were going to be right on Demming's tail."

Hawk laughed. "A long story."

"I want to hear it," I said. "I kept waiting for you. I could have used your help."

Hawk laughed again. "If it hadn't been for me, you'd have never escaped from this village alive."

"What?"

"A long story, like I said."

"Well, tell me about it."

"We'll have plenty of time when we get back to normal," said Hawk. "You had me thinking I was going to have to get used to living alone again!"

"It'll take more than a snakebite to get you rid of me!"

"In the meantime," said Hawk, "if you *are* going to live, we've got to get some food into you to get your strength back. If you're gonna be my partner, I want you up to full strength!"

# CHAPTER 42

# WHERE HAWK HAD BEEN

Hawk and I stayed another four days with the Paiutes.

I was back on my feet later that day, though I knew right off that I was weak and had lost weight. More than once I heard that I was lucky to be alive.

I ate and drank like a horse, and by the third day I was starting to feel a lot better.

The son of Weeping Feather was still in camp, but after all that had happened he didn't cause me or Hawk any more trouble. He scowled when he saw us, but he kept his knife put away and didn't say anything. On our last day there, I didn't see him around anyplace, and then I learned that he'd left, no one knew in which direction. I wondered if he and Jack Demming would tangle again.

Speaking of Demming, he completely disappeared. Once Laughing Water got me back to camp and told her father all that had happened, Winnemucca sent a small party of braves out to find him. They found his horse wandering about with my arrow in it, but no sign of Demming. The spill that had thrown Demming hadn't broken any of the horse's bones. So they brought it back and nursed it to health. When we left they gave the horse to Hawk.

When I finally got the story from Hawk about where he'd been the whole time, it made me scared all over again. I'd been out there waiting for him to arrive, and he was miles away, clear on the other side of the Paiute camp! If Demming had got the drop on me, I'd have been a goner!

What had happened was this. The Paiutes had let him go early that morning, before I woke up, to position himself somewhere out in the desert and wait for Demming to show up.

As it turned out, he was hiding not far from where I rode past making my escape on the pony, with my hands still tied and hanging on for dear life to the pony and the bow and arrows. Hawk heard the commotion, saw me coming, and saw the Indians chasing me. He knew I was only a minute or two from getting my young life ended with a Paiute arrow in my back. So as soon as I was past, he jumped out of hiding on the back of the horse the Paiutes had given him, and blocked the Indians' way. He knew they might kill him too, but he took the chance for my sake.

He held up his hands, signaling them to stop. They were angry, but he managed to talk them out of chasing me. He said that if they kept going he'd have no choice but to go after them to save me, and then he wouldn't be able to follow Demming and rescue the chief's daughter.

They finally agreed and turned back. But in the meantime, seeing some ruckus on the other side of the camp, Demming had hightailed it away in the other direction. Hawk saw him across the plain. Even though he figured by then that I was safe and he could have taken off after me if he'd wanted to, he'd given his word that he'd help Chief Winnemucca get his daughter back. Hawk wasn't about to go back on his word, even though the Paiute were going to kill me if he failed.

So Hawk rode back through the camp and lit off after Demming. But by then the bounty hunter was out of sight and had begun to circle back around east. Hawk, meanwhile, kept riding west. So the whole time I was involved with Demming and Laughing Waters, Hawk wasn't anywhere close, but was looking for him off in the wrong direction entirely!

"Didn't you know riding in from the west was to throw us off?" I asked.

"To tell you the truth," said Hawk, "I didn't have time to think about it."

"I was pretty sure he'd circle around from where he hid her."

"I didn't figure Demming to be that smart," laughed Hawk.

"You always are telling me to stop and think. You always told me to figure the other person was smart. Well, that's what I did."

"When did I say that?"

"You told me every man has something to teach you, if you only can see it. That's sorta the same thing."

Hawk laughed.

"You proved yourself a cagey young rascal—you out-thought Demming *and* me this time!"

"You taught me good," I said. "I remembered a lot of the things you told me when I was out there."

"Well, you did good, Zack," he said. "You feeling well enough to travel? I don't want to wear out our welcome here."

"Yeah, I think so."

"Tomorrow morning?"

"Good enough by me," I said.

# CHAPTER 43

## GRAYFOX

Our last night in the Paiute camp, I was in for a surprise!

There was a big fire burning, and most of the people in the camp were gathered together. Chief Winnemucca wanted to honor Hawk and me for what we'd done. There was special food and dancing and singing.

I have to admit that most of the time I couldn't keep my eyes off Laughing Waters. She was the only one of the dancers I was interested in watching, and every time she circled around the fire and glanced in my direction, the orange from the flames sparkled in her black-green eyes just like the sunlight did during the daytime. Everything about her fascinated me. She was so full of life. What was it that kept drawing my eyes to her?

When the last dance was over, Chief Winnemucca stood. Everyone became quiet and listened while he talked. At first I wasn't paying much attention because I was still thinking about Laughing Waters. Then slowly it dawned on me that he was speaking in both Paiute and English, repeating everything twice. His English was accented and unclear if you didn't pay attention, so I began listening carefully.

I realized he was telling the legend of the gray fox, just like Hawk had told me earlier. The way he told it was so similar that I knew Hawk must have heard it from him.

When he was finished, again everything got quiet.

Then Chief Winnemucca looked over at where me and Hawk were sitting.

"It no secret that Paiute not friend of white man," he said, still looking at us. "But Paiute able to see good in man, whatever color skin. We know Hawk friend. He treat Paiute with respect, we treat him with respect. He wise man. He know many things. Him see, him understand even what some Indian not see. He give knowledge to Paiute, he help us. He show us many things. We honor him with Paiute name *Hawk*. Him have hawk eyes, see what other white man not see."

Hawk sat listening to the chief talk about him in silence. I wished I could have seen his eyes and face right then. But it was dark, and the brim of his hat kept most of his expression shadowed even from the light of the fire.

"Hawk save life of young friend," the chief went on. "Him teach young man live in desert. We take boy to make Hawk save chief's daughter. But him too smart. We think him only boy. But he man, not boy. He escape. He shrewd, like Hawk. But he no escape just for self. Him risk life to save Laughing Waters. Him have no gun. Him use cunning like fox. He more clever than evil man who take Laughing Waters. Him fool and trick bad man. Him know desert. Him use head to rescue chief's daughter. Him use head to find water. Him cunning and brave. Him risk life to shoot at man with Paiute arrow, save Paiute girl."

All the time the chief was talking, he was looking at me with such a stern expression, it took a while for me to realize he was praising me in front of the whole tribe!

Then came the biggest surprise of all. He asked me to stand up.

But for a moment I just kept sitting there.

"Get up, son," said Hawk, giving me a jab in the side with his elbow. "It's not a good idea to disobey a Paiute chief."

Slowly I got to my feet.

"Come," said the chief.

I approached him, my knees shaking underneath me. What was he about to do!

He stared straight into my face, still without a hint of any expression. "You deserving to be called by Paiute name," he said, "like friend Hawk. Him use eyes and understanding to help Paiute. You use cunning and clever wit to save Laughing Waters. So I give you new Paiute name. Chief now name you . . . Grayfox."

He turned and reached behind him where Laughing Waters was holding a small leather quiver. It had no arrows in it. He took it from her and handed it to me.

It was the same quiver I had stolen the morning I had escaped. I hadn't seen it since I passed out after shooting the last arrow at Demming.

The chief placed it in my hand.

"This now *your* quiver," Chief Winnemucca said. "It empty. Help you remember that man not always able to depend on strength, on arrows, when facing enemy. Sometimes arrows gone. Sometimes quiver empty. Must depend on cunning. Must be shrewd like fox. Must use eyes like hawk. Empty quiver help you remember."

Then the chief reached out and took my hand and clasped it in his with a strong grasp.

"Chief Winnemucca thank you for life of daughter," he said. "You now friend of Paiute. Do not forget your name, young Grayfox."

He gave my hand a final shake, then released it.

I thanked him, then backed up and sat down beside Hawk.

I was so taken by surprise by the whole thing that I hardly remember much of anything else that happened that night. But I *do* remember looking up across the light of the fire a few minutes later.

My eyes met Laughing Waters'.

She was looking straight into my face with a smile on her lips that I knew meant she was happy for what her father had done.

Mostly, though, the smile was in the orange reflection of the fire in her dancing eyes.

# CHAPTER 44

# SAYING GOODBYE

After everything had broken up, I waited a few minutes, then walked toward Laughing Waters where she was still sitting and sat down beside her. The fire was burning low, and most of the tribe had returned to their tents and shelters.

"You must have made me sound braver than I was to your father," I said with an embarrassed laugh.

She smiled over at me, and I thought my heart was going to melt!

"I just told him exactly what happened," she said. "You were *very* brave, very cunning, just like he said. You saved me from that bad man. My father is very pleased with you."

I stared down into the glowing coals.

"Your father will be pleased with you too," she added.

She seemed aware of my silence.

"Where is your father, Zack Hollister? Is he a man like Hawk?" she asked.

"My family is in California," I said.

"Why are you so far away from them? Will you see them soon?"

"I joined the Pony Express. Then I got hurt and Hawk took care of me. That's why I am here."

"My sister and I lived in California for a while, at a mission."

"Hawk told me something about that. I have three sisters."

"Tell me about them."

"Corrie's the oldest—she's, let me see . . . she would be

221

twenty-four now. Then there's Emily, who's two years younger than me, so she's now twenty. But she doesn't live at home anymore—she's married. And Becky would be eighteen. I have a younger brother too, Tad. He's the runt of the family. He'd be, let's see . . . sixteen. How old are you, Laughing Waters?"

"I am nineteen," she answered, a little shyly I thought.

"I wish you could meet my sisters. I would love for you and Corrie to know each other. She's been a lot of places too, just like you."

"Why does she go places?"

"I guess you'd say she's the adventurous sort. Also, she's a writer."

"A writer?" asked Laughing Waters in astonishment.

"Yeah, Corrie's really something," I said, realizing how proud I was of her. "She's been writing in journals of her own for longer than I can remember. Now she writes for a newspaper in San Francisco."

"I would like to know her."

"Maybe you'll meet her one day," I said.

"Tell me about your mother," Laughing Waters said.

"She's dead."

"I am sorry."

"She died probably not far from here, crossing the desert on our way west nine years ago."

"Was it from . . ."

She hesitated.

"No," I assured her. "It had nothing to do with any Indians. It was very hot. She died of a fever."

"It must be very hard for all of you not having a mother."

Briefly I told her what had happened.

She continued to ask questions, and before I knew it I had told her everything about Pa and what had happened since.

By this time the fire had died to a few glowing embers and the camp was quiet. I think we were the only two still awake. I asked about her family, and she told me about her parents, about all her brothers and sisters, and about the time she and her sister Sarah had spent away from their Paiute family.

We talked on for another hour into the night, about so many things I can't even remember them all.

Finally we both fell silent, and I think we both knew that this quiet time neither of us wanted to end had finally come to an end. We sat a long while without a word being spoken. It was Laughing Waters who finally broke the still night hush.

"Will I ever see you again, Zack Hollister?" she asked.

It was not a question I expected. Neither was the answer one I planned.

"Yes . . . yes, you will see me again, Laughing Waters."

"When?"

"I don't know, but I will find a way."

That was the end of our conversation. A minute or two later, we both rose and softly made our way to our tents in opposite directions.

The following morning, at sunrise, Hawk and I left the camp of the People.

# CHAPTER 45

## WHY DID GOD MAKE FATHERS?

It's funny how things change.

When the Paiutes brought us into their camp all tied up, I'd never been so scared in all my life, and I figured we were both about to die.

Now, only a week and a half or two later, I almost didn't want to leave.

I'm not sure what Hawk was thinking. He was real quiet as we rode along. So was I, but I *knew* why I was quiet. I couldn't stop thinking about Laughing Waters and wondering if I'd ever see her again.

It wouldn't be for a while that I *would* find out what was on Hawk's mind that day. As it was, *my* mind was filled with a dusky face and lithe form and especially the black-green laughing eyes. So the question he asked me seemed like it didn't have much to do with anything. But it got us talking again, almost like we were picking up the conversation we'd had riding into the Paiute camp, and we talked steadily for an hour. And it had more to do with what Hawk was thinking about than I realized when he said it.

"Let me ask you a question, Zack," said Hawk as we rode along. "Why do you figure God made fathers?"

Like everything Hawk said or did, by now I'd learned he likely had more in mind than what it might seem like right off. I was learning not to give hasty answers to things he'd say, but to think about his words.

"I don't know—what do you mean?" I answered.

"I mean, why did God make fathers? Just so they can have sons and daughters and keep the race of men and women alive? Or do they have some other purpose?"

"I guess to provide for them and to teach their sons and daughters," I said.

"Provide for them and train them?"

"I reckon."

"Your pa do a good job of providing for and training you, Zack?" Hawk asked, looking at me out of the corner of his eye. Over the course of our months together, gradually I'd told him everything about Pa's past and how he'd left years ago, so Hawk knew the answer well enough. But he just kept looking at me, waiting for an answer.

"What do you want me to say?" I said finally, I suppose with a little irritation. "You know what happened." The reminder of Pa was such an unpleasant subject to be thrown at me right in the middle of happy thoughts about the last few days.

"I just want an honest answer," said Hawk. "What do you think, did your pa do a good job of it with you?"

"Well, if you want me to be honest about it, then I reckon I'd say no, he didn't. He was gone most of the time I was growing up, so how could he train me like he ought to? Ma had to do most of the providing, not him."

"Still sticks in your craw some, doesn't it?"

"Yeah. Why shouldn't it?"

Hawk was poking me in a touchy spot. I could feel the edge come in my voice and that I was getting hot under the collar. Thinking about Pa wasn't pleasant, though just being around Hawk made it nearly impossible not to think about Pa. He was the kind of fellow that made you think about things whether or not you wanted to, and whether you were trying to or not.

"I'm not saying anything about what you should or shouldn't feel, son. I'm only trying to get at why God made fathers."

"Yeah, well, whyever it was, I don't figure my pa did such a good job of it," I said.

"He should have done a better job of it?" asked Hawk. I knew that probing sound in his voice, but today I wasn't in the mood for it.

"Yeah, I guess that's how it looks to me," I snapped.

"So maybe that's the answer to my question, huh, Zack? God made fathers to do a *good* job of providing for and training their children. You figure that's it?"

"If he made them at all, seems he would have wanted them to do a good job, to do it right."

"Yep, that's the way I see it," said Hawk.

He stopped and we rode on quiet for a spell.

"'Course, most of 'em don't do a good job," he said after a bit. "Fathers, I mean. You figure your own pa's the only father that's made a mess of it, Zack?" he asked.

"No, I don't reckon so," I answered.

"Fact is," Hawk went on, "in all likelihood, every pa that ever lived has made a mess of fathering in one way or another. Your pa's not the only one."

I didn't say anything.

"Matter of fact, you might even say Chief Winnemucca back there didn't do right by his daughter—letting Demming kidnap her and all. If she wanted to, she could probably be pretty riled at him, you reckon?"

Still I said nothing.

"Seems a mite peculiar, doesn't it, Zack, that God would make fathers to raise their kids, even though he knew they *weren't* going to do it all right and that some would be downright bad fathers? That's puzzled me for a lot of years, Zack."

We rode on for another five minutes or so. I knew Hawk had said all he was intending to say for the moment and was leaving it to me to think it over now. And I was thinking, but not exactly over what he'd said.

"Can I ask you a question?" I said after a while.

Hawk nodded.

"Why did you bring all this up now? You know all about the trouble I've had with my pa. Why'd you ask me all that about fathers now?"

"I reckon I figured that after all that happened back there, it was finally about time for you to think about facing what drove you away from home. No one can run away forever. There comes a time when a man's got to stand up and look some things in the eye. I guess I figured your time had just about come."

I didn't say nothing more. Neither did Hawk.

He wasn't going to say nothing until I wanted him to. If I didn't care enough to think about it and try to figure it out on my own, he wasn't going to push it on me.

That wasn't Hawk's way.

# CHAPTER 46

# BACK UP TO THE WINTER CAVE

We rode in near silence the rest of the way back to the camp where the Indians had nabbed us. In fact, except for general conversation about what we were going to eat and where we were going to go next, we didn't talk too much for a couple of days after that.

But Hawk's words had a way of getting inside you.

So I thought about our conversation all during the week that we were breaking up one camp and getting ready to go to another one. And as I pondered his question about why God made fathers, I couldn't help thinking about Pa a lot.

I was kinda surprised to find out I wasn't mad at him anymore. I'd just been in the habit of forcing my mind not to think about my family, or when I did to keep acting like I was mad. Sometimes you just get into a habit of thinking a certain way, even when you don't really even want to.

But now I could see that my anger was more or less gone, and I found myself wondering about Pa. In fact, the more I thought about things and I tried to pray to God about it all, the more I realized I really did want to understand what happened with Pa. Deep down, I think I wanted to find a way to forgive him and make it right with him inside myself. I just didn't know how to do anything about it.

Hawk figured all this, of course, and that's why he brought up that talk about fathers. But the subject didn't come up again till, like I said, a week or so later. And that was when I found myself asking *him* a question, even though I hadn't exactly planned it.

We'd broken camp that morning and had begun the climb back up into the high country. We were on our way back to the cave, in fact, where I first woke up with Hawk after my accident. Even though Hawk lived there mainly in winter, it still needed tending to occasionally during the summer, to make sure a family of coyotes or some other varmints wouldn't decide to make it their permanent home, or to get water from the snow if one of the other springs ran dry.

"So if fathers ain't gonna do a good job of fathering," I blurted out as we rode, "why do *you* figure God made fathers?"

Hawk looked over at me with a thoughtful expression. "You asking what I think?" he said.

"I am. You said it puzzled you a long time. So you must have got it figured out eventually."

"I don't know about *all* figured out," he said, "but I did figure a few things out about that mystery."

"Mystery?"

"Doesn't it seem like a mystery to you? It sure does to me."

"How do you mean?" I said.

"Well, the first thing I gradually figured out," Hawk said, "was why I think God made fathers. He did it to make a picture of what *He's* like. God's called the Father, isn't he? So earthly fathers must have been made to show us what God's heavenly fatherhood is like."

"Makes sense, I guess."

"Well, you see, everything else is that way. Everything God made is a picture of Him somehow. The sky, eggs, plants, animals—everything! So it must be the same with fathers."

I just nodded and waited to see what he would say next.

"But fathers don't do a very good job of showing us what God is like," Hawk went on thoughtfully. "That's the mystery. Why did God make something that is supposed to show us himself but that doesn't work, that's broken? It's a mystery, I tell you, Zack! A downright mystery."

By this time we'd arrived at the mouth of the winter cave.

Hawk motioned to me to stay where I was, sniffing at the air as he dismounted with a look of concern on his face.

"What is it?" I asked.

"Got a feeling we might have company," he said, walking slowly toward the cave.

He inched his way toward the opening and disappeared inside. Then a moment later he came running back out, grabbed his rifle from behind his saddle, shot a few rounds into the air, and started yelling wildly. I just stared at him, wondering what was going on.

A few seconds later a brownish-colored bear came lumbering out, stopped to sniff at the wind, looked at us mildly, then headed off down the hill.

"That critter's a long way from where his kind usually go," said Hawk with a sigh. "How'd he ever get this far up in the desert?"

Slowly we walked in, and Hawk inspected the place. The bear hadn't done too much damage, and the best thing of all was that the bear seemed to be a bachelor.

As we were looking about, Hawk took down a cracked, blackened looking glass that was sitting on a rock shelf and held it up to my face.

"What do you think, Grayfox?" he said with a smile.

"Is that me?" I exclaimed, peering into the wavy, blackened glass. I could tell I looked different from when I started out—my beard, for one thing—but it was really hard to tell much of anything in that cracked, wavy glass.

He laughed.

"It's you, all right."

"But I can't hardly tell in that thing!"

"Well, this mirror may not give the best reflection in the world, but it's you, there's no denying that. How 'bout some coffee?"

"You bet."

"Let's get some water from down below."

We made a fire, then Hawk lit a torch and we walked deeper into the cave to get some of the snow water he stored, still looking about to make sure we were the only creatures in that cave.

Thirty minutes later we had water boiling on the fire and coffee brewing.

"So," I asked while we were enjoying our coffee in the coolness of the cave, "tell me how you figured out the mystery about fathers."

"Well, I finally started thinking that God knew all along that the father system was broken. He never figured it would work perfectly."

"That doesn't seem like an altogether smart way of doing it."

"I admit it didn't make a whole lot of sense to me, either. But then nothing in the world shows us what God's like *perfectly*. Everything God made only shows a little, incomplete piece of him. So why should it be any different with fathers?

"Fathers, I think, weren't ever supposed to be perfect pictures, just partial ones. They reflect God like that little looking glass over there reflected you. You said you could barely make out your image, but it still looked a little like you! Looking in it, I could get a basic picture of what you're like."

I thought a minute about what Hawk said. But he didn't give me much chance to get it lodged into my brain before he threw out a new idea that was even harder to get to the bottom of.

"You know what my greatest realization was?" Hawk asked.

"What?" I asked him back.

"Let me ask you another question," he went on. "Whose job is it to see what's in the mirror?"

I looked at him kinda funny.

"Who's supposed to figure out what the image in the mirror's reflecting?" he explained. "Is that the mirror's job, or is it up to the person looking into the mirror?"

"It's the person's job, I reckon," I said.

"Sure it's the person's. How can a broken old mirror have anything to do with it? You could have closed your eyes and refused to look when I held it up to that scruffy face of yours. Or you could have said, 'I don't believe that's my face I see in there!' So it's *your* job to look and make sense of what you see, not the mirror's."

"I guess I still don't exactly see what this all has to do with God and fathers," I said.

Hawk laughed.

"All right, son, let me try to make it plain for you. Leastways, this has helped me understand a lot of things better. I picture it like this. Our pas are standing there, and they might not even know they're supposed to be showing us what God's like. But all faulty and imperfect as they are, God still says that we're supposed to learn about him from them. All right, you got the picture of a mirror in your head?"

"I guess so," I said.

"So God reaches down and holds a mirror right in front of our fathers and then says to *us*, 'Now look into that mirror, and you'll see a reflection of me.' We're standing alongside our fathers, and they might not even know the mirror's there. God's talking to *us*, not them. But while he's talking, he's still sticking that mirror in front of our *fathers* and saying that if we want to learn what *he's* like as a heavenly father, then we've got to start by looking in that mirror at our *own* pa. 'Cause even if he doesn't know it, he's reflecting God just because he's a father, even if for no other reason."

I was trying hard to follow him, but it was all pretty confusing.

"You see, it's *our* job to find out what that reflection looks like, not our pa's. It's the person's responsibility, looking into the mirror, to see what can be gotten from the mirror, however warped and broken it might be."

"That seems backwards," I said.

"Yep, it does," replied Hawk. "Like I told you before, just about everything is backwards from how it looks."

Hawk turned quiet and thoughtful for a moment.

"It's us who oughta be looking to see what's in our mirrors," he went on, "cracked though they may be. We'd be pretty foolish to ignore what's supposed to be going on and say we're not going to look at God's reflection just because it's a broken mirror. That ought to make us look all the harder, knowing that the image isn't perfect. That ought to make us try all the harder to see what God is like. Wouldn't you have been a mite foolish if you'd have shut your eyes and refused to look when I held up the mirror to your face?"

"Yeah, I reckon you're right," I said, laughing. "But there's still something about it I don't understand."

"Go on," said Hawk, pouring us each some more coffee.

"You're making it sound like no matter how bad a boy or girl might think things are, there's still good in their fathers for them to see God in, if they look hard enough for it."

"That's something like it."

"But what if there just ain't nothing good there? What if the mirror's turned black or all broken to bits? What if a man's just downright bad through and through? What about orphans that ain't got no pa? What about folks that don't know who their pa is? And that half-breed Tranter? How does he find good in *his* pa, who hated him? Don't look to me like there's any good for him to find."

Hawk sighed.

"You ask mighty hard questions, Zack," he said. "I ain't sure I got the answer to all of 'em. Lots of questions don't have easy answers."

"Tell me what you think, then," I said.

"Well, the way I figure it is that most folks—maybe ninety-five percent of 'em—have fathers with a lot more good in them than they realize. So they're the ones who've got to learn to see even though the mirror's broken. But the others, the five percent, where the mirrors are just piles of dust or the men are just plain varmints and don't reflect God at all, and orphans or kids who don't know their pa, I figure that God still has to use the image of a father as the doorway to himself."

"I don't see how he can if there ain't nothing good there."

"For them maybe it won't be in the way of learning to see good in their own fathers, since maybe they don't even know their fathers. Maybe it'll be just in thinking about their fathers or learning from somebody that isn't their father, or even in thinking what bad men their fathers are, in a way that'll make them look up and find God's fatherhood."

"So that's what folks like Demming and Tranter could do?"

"Right. Even people with bad fathers can look up and seek God, can't they?"

I nodded.

"Tranter and Demming could have said to themselves, 'My father was a bad man. Therefore I better look up and find what true manhood and true fatherhood is. I don't have an example in my own pa, so I got to seek all the harder to find the truth.'"

"They didn't do that."

"No. They chose a different pathway. Every man and woman's story in life is different, Zack. Most folks have to learn to see God's reflection in their fathers. A few have to take something that maybe *doesn't* reflect God at all and use it to learn to look up to find God. Your story won't be like mine, Demming's won't be like Tranter's."

"Like we're different books?"

He nodded. "Different, yet in *every* man and woman's story— yours, mine, Demming's, Tranter's, Laughing Waters'—God will use earthly fatherhood kinda like a tool, even though he uses it to accomplish different purposes in each of our cases."

I thought a minute or two about everything he'd said.

"I think I get what you mean. So what you're saying is that God will use earthly fatherhood even in the life of an orphan?"

"Even an orphan can say to himself, 'I don't know anything about earthly fatherhood. I don't have a broken mirror. I don't have any mirror at all! Therefore, I have to look all the more carefully to find out what it means that God is my father.'"

"It must be hard for orphans."

"There's lots of broken mirrors around, Zack—lots of orphans, lots of young'uns with rascals for fathers, or whose fathers don't live with them, lots of different kinds of stories people's lives have to tell. But we still all gotta learn to look up and find our heavenly Father somehow."

Neither of us said anything for a bit.

"Trouble is," Hawk went on, "most folks, seeing that the mirror of their own pa is either broken or blacked out or gone, they turn their backs and walk away, and then they never find out what God's fatherhood is like at all."

Hawk paused a minute, a look of sadness coming over his face.

"That's the way I was for a long time, Zack," he added, "till I finally figured out what that broken mirror had been reflecting back to me all my life, but I'd never seen."

"You mean your own pa?" I asked.

"Yep, my own pa."

"What was he like?" I asked.

Hawk got real quiet and thoughtful, and didn't say anything for quite a spell.

"I didn't mean to pry," I added, feeling suddenly awkward about what I'd asked.

"It's okay, son," he answered slowly. "It's only that I haven't told a soul all these years . . ."

He put down his coffee, reached over to stir up the fire, then sat back and continued.

"Up to now, I never met anybody I could tell."

# CHAPTER 47

## TWO MEN

It was a long time before Hawk spoke up again.

When he did, his voice sounded a whole lot different than I'd ever heard it before. I knew his words were coming out of a different place down inside him, and something about his voice made me pay closer attention than to almost anything I'd ever heard him say before.

"You recollect me telling you about two men when we was talking about courage?" he said finally.

"Yeah," I answered. "One was called Jake—the tough, fighting fella. But I forgot the other name."

"I called him Mr. Fenwick," said Hawk in an even quieter tone.

I waited for him to say more, but it was a long wait.

He was staring down at the ground, but his eyes looked like they were boring right through the dirt and seeing a mile underneath it. It was the same kind of look that comes over somebody's face when they are seeing back into the past.

"'Course, Fenwick wasn't his real name," Hawk finally said, then paused again.

"You mean he's a real man?"

"Yep."

"What is his real name?"

"Trumbull," answered Hawk. "Mr. Fenwick's name was Trumbull."

"But . . . but why'd you call him Fenwick then?" I asked.

238

"'Cause making it seem like he's somebody different keeps the pain of remembering a little further away," replied Hawk. "You see, son, the fellow I was talking about was my pa."

"Mr. Fenwick—I mean Mr. Trumbull?" I said in astonishment.

Hawk nodded slowly. "That was my pa—glasses, music, reading, thinking—just like I described him to you."

"Where is—I mean, is he still—"

"No, Zack," said Hawk quietly. "He's dead now. Been gone a lot of years."

"I'm . . . I'm sorry, Hawk," I said, fumbling for words. I'd never seen Hawk like this, so quiet and emotional, and it suddenly made me feel different inside—like he wasn't so much older than me, like we were more on the same level.

"That's all right . . . thanks, Zack."

"What . . . what about the other fella?" I asked.

"Jake?"

"Yeah. You just make him up?"

Hawk smiled, but in a melancholy way.

"No, he's real too."

"Who is he?"

"Jake's my brother," said Hawk. "He's just like I told you too—a tough customer, like Demming, who's killed more men than I can count. Makes me shudder just to think of what's waiting for him some day."

"What do you mean?"

"I mean when he dies and finally meets his Maker."

"He's still alive?"

"Yeah," Hawk answered with a sigh. "Though I can't say as I'd exactly call it living. But you're right, he's still alive—far as I know, anyway."

"You don't know for sure?"

"No, I haven't seen him in more than fifteen years. He and I didn't exactly part on the best of terms."

By now I was so curious I was dying to know more, but I was almost afraid to ask. So I just waited, hoping Hawk would want to tell me.

"You see, son," he said at length, "I grew up with both those two men—my pa and my brother, Jake. Jake was four years older'n me, so all my life, when I was a little fellow, I just figured he was mostly a man too. Our ma died when I was eight, and after that it was just the three of us."

"And . . . and what happened?"

Still that far-off gaze was in Hawk's eye.

"You remember, when I told you about them, I was talking about courage?"

I nodded.

"Well, I reckon the long and the short of it is that I spent the next ten or fifteen years watching the two of them, my tough brother and my meek, soft-spoken pa, looking back and forth between them, watching how they did things, trying to figure out which one of them was a *real* man. They were about as different as two men could be. So I reckon I figured one of them must know what being a man was all about, and the other didn't."

"And . . . did you get it figured out?" I said.

Hawk nodded, slowly and thoughtfully.

"Yep . . . yeah, I did." He sighed. "Though by the time I did, it was too late."

"Too late . . . too late for what?" I said.

"You really want to know, Zack?"

"Yeah, 'course I do."

Hawk paused a minute, then suddenly got up.

"You feel like going for a walk?"

"I guess," I said.

"Let's walk out across the hills. I'll tell you as we go."

We set down our cups of coffee and walked out of the cave into the bright sunlight and the hot afternoon sun.

# CHAPTER 48

## THE REST OF HAWK'S STORY

That day, the whole desert seemed full of memories.

Hawk was thinking about his past, and I was thinking about my first months with him. Maybe the tightness in my thigh as we walked made me remember my broken leg.

We walked up past the spot where Hawk had first talked to me about the sky and the importance of learning to see. I realized what a treasure it was that he spoke to me as he did about such important things rather than just always talking about surface matters.

I reckon a lot of folks would have considered Hawk a strange bird, always trying to find meaning in things, always looking at everything spiritual-like, always making things so personal.

Yet I realized how fortunate I was to have time with him. A man like Hawk doesn't come into a person's life every day. It was a time, which I reckon comes for lots of kids like me, when I wasn't able to see maybe some of the things I should have from my own pa. But God gave me the gift of another person to help me learn during that time. Hawk wouldn't have wanted to be a substitute for my own pa, but he was there to be kinda like a pa for a while, all the time helping me to gently look at the things I might not have otherwise.

We walked a good ways before Hawk said any more.

When he did, I could tell right off from the sound that he had drifted a long way back in time, through the years, to when he was a lot younger even than I was right then.

"My pa was a soft-spoken man," he began, "like I told you. I reckon there's things in everybody's fathers they wish was different. For me, I always wished my pa'd talk more. You never knew what he was thinking. He was a decent man and pleasant enough, just quiet. He wasn't what you'd call a *man's man* either. Like I told you, he was a music teacher. He was small and wore glasses, and most of the time when he was home he'd spend his time reading or playing on the piano we had or writing out some music for his students. My ma loved him and loved music right along with him. She taught me to play the piano some, but—"

"You can play the piano?" I interrupted.

"I haven't even laid eyes on a piano in years," Hawk answered. "I don't know what would happen if my fingers found themselves on one again.

"At any rate," he went on, "when my brother Jake started growing up, it was clear right off that he was about as different from my pa as any kid could be. He sure wasn't interested in music or the quiet kind of life we had. I remember overhearing my mother and father talking once, wondering to themselves where he'd got his loud, tough, rebellious streak. He was a lad to give any parents fits, especially ones like ours. By the time he was five he was getting into fights with other boys twice his age. I think he first hit Pa when he was seven. I don't remember, but he bragged to me about it later.

"By the time our ma died several years after that, Jake was twelve and might as well have been running the whole place. I think Pa kinda gave up trying, what with his grief over ma's dying and figuring it was impossible to control Jake."

"What happened?" I said.

"The next few years must have been hell for my pa, though I couldn't see it much then. He went on with his teaching and kind of left me and my brother to fend for ourselves. It wasn't from not caring, I don't think, but just because he didn't know what to do about Jake.

"Jake just did whatever he pleased. He'd started stealing when he was ten, stole a gun right after Ma died and kept it hidden from pa, and the next year he ran away, left home, hired on with a riverboat, and by age fifteen or sixteen he was already getting a reputation as a feller to stay away from.

"I knew it broke Pa's heart. A little bit more of him died every time we'd get some kind of word about something else Jake had done. I remember one time when Jake came home, he was bragging about the first time he'd killed a man. The brokenhearted look on Pa's face—"

Hawk stopped and looked away. I could see him blinking back tears. I looked away too. I didn't want him to be embarrassed from me seeing him cry.

The rest of our walk was pretty quiet.

There didn't seem much more for Hawk to say. And I didn't want to ask any more questions. I knew the memories hurt him deep inside.

By the time we got back to the cave, I had to sit down. My leg still got sore from the snakebite when I walked on it too much at one time. So I just had to sit down and rest it a spell.

"Feel like some more coffee?" Hawk asked.

"Yeah . . . thanks."

"And now that we're up here, how about I start us a pot of beans for tomorrow? We got some dried pintos left, and a little bacon. I'll be heading down for supplies next week."

"Sounds right good," I said.

There was a long pause. Hawk just kept sitting there.

"You know, Zack," he added finally in a far-off voice—and for once he didn't look at me, but kept staring straight into the fire—"having you here . . . I've enjoyed myself more than I have for years. It's been good for me to have someone to share life with. You been a good companion."

Again he stopped, still just looking into the fire.

"I wish you could stay here with me," he went on. "Not that I got any regrets. I was at peace with my life alone. But I could get real used to having you around."

Finally he looked over to me, then added, "What I'm trying to tell you, son, is that you've been a good friend."

I tried to reply, but no words would come out.

# CHAPTER 49

## LOOKING INSIDE MYSELF

Laying there in the mountain cave that night, with the fire slowly burning itself out, I didn't fall asleep for a couple of hours. I looked around, and my mind kept going back to my first days with Hawk, and that couldn't help but remind me why I was out there in the first place.

But it wasn't only from being in the cave again.

I couldn't listen to all Hawk said about his own pa without doing some mighty hard thinking of my own about leaving Miracle Springs like I had. I'd said some pretty awful things, and now I was sorry about what I'd said. After being with Hawk all this time, I was looking at a lot of things in a whole new light.

Hawk knew what I was going through and what I was thinking about. I knew he knew. He gave me lots of room and didn't push.

But then a day came, after we'd been up at the mountain cave about a week, when I reckon he knew I needed prodding to take the next step where I needed to go.

It was mid-summer and really hot. He'd mentioned a couple of times that he had to go down to the Desert Springs trading post in the valley to pick up a few supplies. At first I figured I might stay up in the hills alone. The mood I was in was a quiet one, and I wasn't all that anxious to see other people right then.

Hawk had told me all along that I ought to get in touch with the Pony Express people, to let them know I was still alive, and my family too. But up to now I still hadn't done that. Though I always intended to get word back home, somehow the time passed

245

faster than I realized, and I just never did anything about it.

At any rate, on this particular afternoon we were out in front of the cave, tending to one of the mules, which had picked up a stone in its hoof. That ornery critter always hated to have its foot messed with. Hawk had to hold its head while I dug out the rock.

We were standing out there, working hard under that hot sun, when Hawk made a statement right out of the blue.

"It's time, son," he said.

I thought at first he was talking about his trip down to the valley.

"Time for what?" I said. "You going after your supplies?"

"No, I ain't talking about me," he answered. "It's time for you to show what you're really made of."

"Huh?"

"You proved you got the one kind of courage. Now what about the other?"

"I don't get what you mean," I said. "You afraid that bear'll come back while you're gone? I'll be careful."

"I'm not talking about that."

"What then? I'm not facing anything dangerous."

"For what you *got* to face."

"I still don't get your meaning."

"Zack, you're not facing a war or a band of Indians or a charging bounty hunter trying to shoot you down . . . or even a bear. But you're sure enough facing a challenge—and it's something that takes a different kind of bravery. What you got ahead of you takes more courage than most men have."

"How's that?"

"It's easier to be brave when you're up against something outside yourself, no matter how fearsome it is, than when you're facing something inside yourself. That's where you need the real courage. That's why real manhood comes from courage *inside*."

"How do you mean?"

"Facing what's on the inside's a long sight harder than facing what's only on the outside. Nothing's harder than facing your own fears, your own past. That's where the greatest courage comes— when the thing you're up against is yourself."

Neither one of us spoke for a few minutes.

"I reckon I kinda figured, after what happened with Demming and Laughing Waters, that maybe I'd taken a couple more steps toward being a man than I was before," I said finally.

"You did," replied Hawk. "Several big steps."

"But that's not enough to make me a man—that what you're saying?"

Hawk's smile was kinda sad and thoughtful.

"Most folks think it is," he said finally. "That's what the Indians think. That's why they honored you by giving you a name that means courage and cunning. Their main purpose in life is to survive. Their whole way of living, their whole outlook is based on that tough, warrior approach. But no, Zack, my boy—no, that's not all of what manhood is."

"So does what I did matter at all?" I asked.

"Sure it matters. You saved the girl's life, and you proved you got some guts. Those are good things."

"But not enough to make a man of me?"

"I'm afraid you got that right. No, what you did won't make a man of you. Any fool can go out and get his head blown off. Any fool can be brave or courageous if he's determined enough to prove that he's tougher than the next feller—or if he doesn't think he's got anything to lose. Tell you the truth, Zack, any fool could have done what you did by standing there and shooting that last arrow at Demming. Now, I'm not saying you're a fool, and I don't mean to take anything away from what you did, because it was still a mighty brave thing. I gotta tell you, I was right proud of how you handled yourself."

"I'm glad to hear that," I said.

"It was selfless too," Hawk went on. "That takes guts, putting yourself in danger for the sake of someone else. And you used your brain to do it so that you wouldn't shoot too soon and get yourself killed! So you did good, don't get me wrong. You showed yourself a pretty brave rascal. But that still can't make a man of you all by itself. Jake could have done the same."

"So what will make me a man, then?"

"That you gotta discover for yourself, young Grayfox. If you're gonna live up to your name, which means cunning and courage, then you're gonna have to apply that cunning to finding the answer."

Now it was my turn to be quiet again.

# CHAPTER 50

## A DESERT RAIN

While Hawk and I stood there talking and holding onto that mule, a clump of black clouds was drifting in from the west. Now they were directly overhead, blocking the sun. And suddenly a downpour erupted, threatening to drench us.

We ran to take cover in the mouth of the cave and then stood watching the rain come down in sheets. The way it cooled the hot air and the ground sure felt good.

"I sure wouldn't have expected that," I laughed as we stood watching the rain from under the overhanging ledge.

"If it doesn't rain once in a while, the plants won't grow," replied Hawk.

"Aw, nothing much grows out here, anyway," I said, not really thinking what I was saying.

"Come on, Zack—how can you say such a thing after all this time?"

"You're right. It was a dumb thing for me to say. But still, it doesn't seem like one thunderstorm would do much good after days and days of baking sun."

"Out here it doesn't take much to do what it needs to do. You've seen what it's like after a rain—whether it's a ten-minute shower or a two-day storm. It might be messy for a while—with the flash floods and the high winds. But afterward the land is refreshed."

Hawk was quiet a minute, and I could tell from the look on

his face that he wasn't thinking of the rain anymore.

"You know, Zack," he said after a while, "before you left home, you might have been a little like the desert—dry, tense, knowing that something needed changing. You joined the Pony Express, and you finally wound up out here with me. This is your time of storm, your time to get refreshed, your time to grow, your time to let the rain clean out some places inside you. You see what I mean?"

"I think so," I said.

"Anger's like a storm. It can spill out just like the rain out of those clouds a minute ago. But things always calm down afterward. In people, just like on the desert, a storm can bring refreshing, and even new kinds of life."

"You saying anger's a good thing?" I asked.

"No. It's not exactly like a rainstorm, just sorta like it. I doubt anger's ever too good a thing between folks. But sometimes it can have the effect of a rainstorm, and maybe some new growth can come because of it."

And then suddenly Hawk was back to what he was talking about before the rain interrupted us.

"Tell me, Zack," said Hawk after a bit, "which do you figure would be harder to do—get on the back of a wild stallion and try to tame it, or look another man in the eye and tell him you were wrong about something—tell him you acted selfishly and then apologize to him for it?"

I thought a while but didn't say anything.

"Is it harder to talk tough or to swallow your pride and eat crow?" he asked.

"Well, swallowing your pride's never easy," I said.

"My point is, what most men figure is being manly and tough doesn't really take much. That's one of the lessons my pa could've taught me if I'd been able to see him for who he really was. By the time I learned it, he wasn't there for me to share it with."

Again his mind seemed to drift off into the past for a minute, but then he went on.

"It's a sight harder to face up to your own shortcomings," Hawk went on, "and even admit them. That takes a different kind of courage! A courage that looks inside, where the *real* fearsome things are! Most men never learn to look inside themselves. So they go through their lives trying to earn their manhood by showing how brave and self-reliant they are toward the outside things.

"That's easy. Lots of men can do that. All it takes is being tough. But it takes a real man to face the stuff inside, to grow into all that a feller is supposed to be, to lay down those pieces of yourself that are not what they ought to be."

"So what did you mean, a while back," I asked, "when you said it was time?"

"I meant, are you ready to *really* look down inside yourself, Grayfox?" Hawk asked. "Down deep . . . down where you never looked before . . . down where maybe nobody's ever seen except the God that made you?"

I shrugged, but didn't answer him. In my own way I'd already been trying to make my peace with the past. That kind of thing's never easy. Even when you want to grow and change, there can still be pain that goes along with it. And when the growing requires cutting on your own self, and you're holding the knife in your own hand, there's a part of you that always shies away from sticking it in too deep.

Hawk kept waiting. He wouldn't say more unless I gave him leave.

"Yeah, I reckon," I said finally.

He looked at me a minute longer, seriously, but with eyes that were full of love. I knew he cared about me, and so I trusted him to say anything he wanted to me.

"What have I been teaching you all this time we been together?" he asked me finally.

"To look inside things," I said.

"You're a good learner, Zack. You got a good head on your shoulders. You know how to use it. The Paiutes knew what they were doing when they called you Grayfox. But there's lots of smart folks in the world that don't know the first thing about using their brains for the most important thing those brains were given to us for. Learning how to see inside things ain't much good if you don't use it to see inside the one thing we gotta look inside of the most.

You know what that is, don't you, Grayfox?"

"I reckon so."

"Yep, it's looking inside your own self—*that's* why we gotta train our inner eyes. So now, young Grayfox, it's time to see if you're really ready to be a man."

My eyes had wandered down to the ground as I'd been listening to Hawk. But with the words about being a man, I glanced up.

Hawk was staring straight through me. I think he wanted to make sure I had really heard what he'd said. But his next words changed the subject entirely.

The clouds had passed by already, and the rain was over. The bright sun sparkled over the whole landscape. Everything looked fresh and clean and wet.

"I'm hungry," Hawk said. "I got a hankering for a rabbit stew. What do you say, Grayfox? Feel like seeing if we can scare us up a coupla rabbits?"

"You bet," I said.

"Then let's go."

# CHAPTER 51

## DON'T BE HALF A MAN

The desert was so clean-smelling from the rain. The plants almost looked pretty, with wet drops hanging from every branch and blade and thorn. But the desert had been so thirsty that in ten or fifteen minutes the sand and dirt and rocks were drying and almost back to their normal arid glare.

I found myself remembering how Hawk had first taught me about how plants grew in the desert without much water or soil, and how he'd learned from the desert how to get what he needed out of what looks like nothing. People are like that too, he said. If you send your roots deep enough, there's nourishment to be found anywhere.

"Life is everywhere, Zack," I remembered him saying, "even in the middle of the desert. No matter what things look like, there is life in all these growing things around us. God puts his life in everything."

For the next hour we used every trick we could think of, but in the end we only managed to bag one measly sized little animal that didn't look like he would make much of a stew. But Hawk said it would be tasty enough by the time he got finished with it. As we made our way back to the cave, he started talking again as if we'd never stopped the previous conversation.

"That's what it's all about, Zack," he said, like he was just finishing up a sentence he'd started earlier, "being a man. And now I figure you're about ready to step up into your own manhood. You brave enough for me to keep on talking?"

"If I can do what I did three weeks back, I reckon I'd be a coward if I couldn't hear what you have to say."

"That's the way I see it, and hearing you say so proves to me that you're ready. So here it is then. You remember when we talked about anger, Zack?"

I nodded.

"Well, you'll never be all the way a man until you learn what to do with it, how to get rid of it, and then how to swallow your pride and learn to live with the people closest to you."

We were just getting back to the cave, so we stopped talking long enough to put down our rifles and get a fire started. I got working on the fire while he brought snow water up from what he called his cellar to start boiling in the pot. Then he pulled out his knife, took the rabbit outside, and began to skin and clean it.

"Who knows where anger comes from, Zack?" he went on as he worked. "But everybody's got it. I'd have to say most folks have got anger down inside them toward either their ma or pa, maybe both. It's a mystery that the people who gave us life would be the people we'd have the hardest time not being angry with, but that still seems to be where most anger gets its start, toward our own folks. Why do you think that is?"

"I don't know," I said.

"I got a feeling it's on account of independence."

"How do you mean?" I asked, throwing on some more wood, now that the fire was going pretty good.

"From the minute we're born we want to be independent. Most of us figure we got a right to be that way. Since our folks are there so close by, and since we need 'em so much when we're little, they're the ones we're always trying to be independent from. But I learned something after I got old enough to see a few things more clearly. You want to know what I learned?"

I nodded.

"I learned that a fellow will never be complete until he learns not to swagger around like he's the head honcho of the world, but to be comfortable with other folks being honcho over him. Anyone can act tough. But it takes a *real* man, or woman, too, for that matter, to know how to let somebody else be the boss. That's a lot harder."

"It's the same for women?" I asked.

"Different . . . but the same," Hawk answered. "Women want to be independent just like men. They just have a different way of showing it."

I thought about Almeda and how she ran for mayor. Afterward, she'd said almost that very same thing.

"Until we learn that lesson," Hawk went on, "especially with our own folks, but with everybody else we have to do with too, we're bound to keep having little pockets of anger deep down inside us. I never learned it with my pa, and I'm a poorer man for it. I'll regret till my dying day that I was so slow to learn it. You see what I'm getting at, Zack?"

I nodded again.

"As long as we're thinking we gotta be independent, and as long as we don't want anybody telling us what to do, then we're gonna be angry. The world ain't set up in such a way that independence makes things work right."

"Yeah. But, Hawk, ain't you your own boss?"

"I reckon on the outside it looks that way. But inside, I know I ain't all that independent. I know how much I depend on the rain and snow and the birds and the plants out here. I depend on the mules and the trading post. I need someone to talk to at least now and then, and I sure need the Paiute's tolerance to stay alive.

"You see, Zack," he went on, "independence has to do with how you think about things and what you want, more than if there's somebody actually telling you what to do or not. It's the *attitude* of independence that causes folks so much trouble and breeds anger down inside."

Hawk took the skinned rabbit in by the fire, cut it up, and threw the pieces of rabbit into the iron stewpot, then burrowed into his food sacks for salt and herbs and some jerky and a little rice. He had just a spoonful of cooked beans from last night, so he tossed them in too.

"Independence is a sure road to misery and disaster," he went on, stirring up the mixture and then putting on the lid, "'cause we're *dependent* on the God that made us for every tiny breath we breathe. We're just fooling ourselves if we're bent on being independent.

"Folks that never face that and come to terms with it are gonna go through their lives being angry and out of sorts with everything and everybody. Men like my brother Jake, and Demming and Tranter, men that never want anybody telling them anything and that flare up at anyone who dares cross them, they just haven't got it figured out yet what life's all about.

"Independence, Zack—it's the root of anger, and it's standing in the way of most folks' being able to find any happiness in life. It all boils down to accepting that you can't be your own boss, no matter how hard you try. You might as well try to fly. It ain't the way the world is. You remember when we talked about courage?"

"Yeah."

"You want to know what the most courageous thing is that a person can do?"

"Yeah, I'd like to know that."

"Facing yourself. Facing your own independence and anger and selfishness for the enemies they are. Standing up to those kinds of attitudes face-to-face, being brave enough to take them on and battle against them, and fight them until you defeat them.

"There's a fight most men aren't man enough for. When it comes to that fight, most men turn out to be cowards. You asked about women, well, there ain't too many women can do that either. There's cowardly women as well as cowardly men, just like there's courageous women as well as courageous men. That's why I told you that nearly anyone can be brave when facing some danger coming at them from the outside. But to fight their own anger and independence and selfishness takes a higher level of courage altogether. That's where you need real bravery and humility. Takes a real man to forgive, Grayfox."

Hawk stopped, and the two of us were quiet a long time, watching the fire shoot its flames up around the sides of the black stewpot. Both of us in our own way were thinking about all he'd said. When he spoke again, his words were real personal.

"You and I've talked some about your pa," he went on. "If I read you right, my young friend, you've probably begun to realize some things about your pa you didn't know before. You're probably starting to see some things in that broken mirror, aren't you?"

I nodded, poking at the fire with a stick.

"But there's much more to see. So I'm going to tell you one more thing about that mirror. As cracked as it might be, the biggest problem we have in seeing it is usually our own blindness—our own stubbornness about not wanting anyone telling us what to do. Our biggest problems with our fathers have nothing to do with our fathers at all! And those problems are the things that are so hard for most folks to lay down, and most never do at all.

"That's what it takes to be a real man, Zack—humbling yourself, laying down that independent spirit, laying down your anger so you can forgive anyone you got something against—father, mother, brother, sister, whoever it is.

"You'll never be altogether who God made you to be until you become a thorough child, with the kind of humility it takes to not think you have to be independent. And here's what's funny: To be a child like that—with the kind of childlikeness our Lord spoke of, you have to be a thorough man. Only a man can be a child, and only a childlike man can be *fully* a man. That's something my brother Jake never understood and probably never will until he meets his Maker someday face-to-face.

"Only takes half a man to be able to live out in nature all by yourself, Zack. Everything you and I have done out here together, it's something anybody with half an ounce of sense could learn to do. I don't doubt that I've done a pretty fair job of teaching you how to take care of yourself out here and how to see some things.

"But now, Zack, my friend, it's time you learned to be a whole man. What you've learned with me and what you did out there with them Indians was just getting you prepared to do it. Now you got to take the half of yourself you put together out here and put it to use growing into the other half.

"Zack," he said—and now there was a look of pain on his face like I'd never seen before—"Zack, don't make the mistake I did of never going back! I've learned a lot of things. I know how to live in the wilds. But in a way I'm still only half a man because I didn't learn to see what the broken mirror had to show me about both my fathers until the earthly one was dead and gone. And now it's too late for me to make it complete. In a sense, I'll only be half a man till the next life, when I hope I can look my pa in the face and shake his hand. That'll be when I can tell him how grateful I am that the Father chose him to be my pa . . . and tell him how much I love him.

"Being able to say and do that, with all your anger gone and buried forever in the past, that's what makes you a full-grown human being, or at least that goes a long way toward it. It's too late for me now. I drifted too far from my pa before I realized all this. Now most of my own people are gone."

He paused and looked away. For one of the first times since I'd known him, I saw a look of regret in Hawk's face. Then he looked straight at me.

"But it's not too late for you, young Grayfox," he said, with an expression that made me realize how lucky he thought I was. "It's not too late for you to be brave."

He rose and walked out of the cave to let me reflect on what he'd said . . . or maybe to reflect on his own regrets. Probably both.

When he returned it was with a handful of desert roots to put into the pot in place of vegetables like carrots and potatoes.

The stew bubbled for another hour or so. It was mighty tasty by the time Hawk was done with it.

# CHAPTER 52

## DOWN TO THE VALLEY

Hawk saddled up his old mule the next morning, put a pack-saddle on the other to haul the supplies, and got ready to go down to the valley. He'd gone down before a few times while we were together, but I'd always stayed behind. Maybe part of me was at peace there and didn't want to be reminded of the rest of the world. In so many ways I'd become a new person during the months out there with Hawk—breathing the high desert air, knowing that even as desolate as the countryside was, it was a land I could call my own.

But things were changing inside me.

After all that Hawk and I had talked about the day before—actually, after everything that had happened that year—somehow I knew it was time I sucked in a deep breath and faced the world again. Or, like Hawk would say, maybe it was time I faced myself.

"I ain't so sure I like the idea of leaving you alone up here," Hawk said, strapping the last of his empty bags to the mule. "I don't think Tranter will bother us, with the chief keeping an eye on him, but Demming still worries me."

"You think he's still around?"

"Doubt it, but a tough customer like that's got plenty of guts to keep himself alive when he's looking for revenge. Now he's got two beefs against you—one for you, one for your pa. If he's still alive, you can bet he's trying to figure a way to get even. Why don't you come with me, Grayfox?"

It didn't take me long to think about it.

"I reckon you're right," I said. "I'll go."

My reason didn't have anything to do with Demming, though. I just figured it was way past time that I let the Pony Express people know I was alive.

I grabbed up a few things, including the quiver the chief had given me, which I took with me everywhere, and was ready in a couple of minutes.

We rode down, and the first place we stopped on the way to the trading post was the next Express station west from Flat Bluff. What a surprise it was to walk in and see Hammerhead Jackson there instead of at his own station!

He stared at me for several seconds, squinted hard like he was trying to remember something. Then gradually his scarred-up face spread out, not exactly in a smile, but as close to it as Hammerhead was likely to come.

"Tarnation, if it ain't the Hollister kid!" he said in something between a sigh of disbelief and an exclamation. "Alive and kicking after all!"

He walked toward me and shook my hand, looking me over up and down from my boots to my hat.

"Not exactly kicking," I said, "but it's me all right."

"It's them whiskers what threw me. Why, you look ten years older. You look like a man, not that little kid I sent off last summer."

I laughed kind of sheepishly.

"Blamed if we didn't all think you was done in long ago."

"Nope," I said. "I would have been, but Hawk here kept me alive."

The stationman acknowledged Hawk for the first time.

"How you doing, Jackson?" asked Hawk as the two men shook hands.

"All right, Trumbull. Why didn't you tell us you had the boy?"

"Figured that was his business."

"But what're *you* doing here?" I asked. "Here at this station, I mean?"

"Feller in charge here quit a few months back. Things at this station had got kinda sloppy, so they moved me here for a spell."

"What about Flat Bluff?"

"Smith's in charge?"

"And Billy?"

"Barnes?"

I nodded.

"Ornery as ever. Still riding both directions outta Flat Bluff. You'll see him later today."

"We ain't gonna be here that long."

"You ain't coming back on the line, Hollister!"

"Not planning to just yet."

"What in tarnation for! You can't be telling me life out in the desert's better'n a good-paying job like you had?"

I shrugged.

"Hey, that reminds me, Hollister. I still got your last paycheck around here someplace. The two of you sit down and have something to eat while I find it. You're just in time for some grub."

I sat down at the table, which was already laid out. I quickly recognized the food from Hammerhead's kitchen.

"Might wanna look at them papers too," Hammerhead called out from across the room. "Blame country's at war—you probably didn't know that. Fool southerners!" he added to himself.

A minute or two later he brought over an envelope with my name on it and handed it to me. I opened it and my mouth dropped open. There were two tens and a five-dollar bill—a whole week's pay from last fall!

I dug into the pot of beans, and a minute later I was scooping them up with a fork in my right hand while reading the newspaper I held in my left. Hawk had walked over to the other side of the room and was talking to Hammerhead about buying a few supplies from him before heading on to the trading post.

The paper was from Sacramento. I scanned over the front page, which was all about the war between the states that had just broken out. As huge as the news was, though, I think I might have been wondering if I'd run across something my sister Corrie had written.

I was scanning through the paper more or less casually, paying more attention to the beans on my plate than what I was reading.

I never thought I'd consider Hammerhead's cooking wonderful, but after months of eating only what you could cook over an open fire, whatever it was that Hammerhead put in his pot made those about the best beans I'd ever tasted in my life! Even better than Hawk's rice and rabbit stew!

The paper was from sometime back in May, and it was now July. But as long as I'd been out of touch with the rest of the world, it hardly mattered that the news wasn't current.

I was turning the pages, glancing up and down and reading bits and pieces of the whole paper, when a line caught my eye. I don't know why I happened to see it, but it said something about a resolution being passed by the California legislature to support the Union cause. To tell you the truth, I don't know why I started reading that piece, because I hardly knew anything about the argument over which side to support.

Then all of a sudden my eyes shot open and stopped dead on the page. I couldn't believe the words I'd just read!

*According to Assemblyman Drummond Hollister, who was interviewed briefly after the vote . . .*"

*What!* I shouted to myself inside. It couldn't be!

But I kept reading.

*The new legislator from the mining town of Miracle Springs, where he has served as mayor for the past four years, has been an outspoken pro-Union voice in the Assembly . . .* I didn't need to read another word!

I threw down my fork and jumped up from the table. I ran over to Hawk and shoved the paper in his face. He didn't have a notion what I was talking about. All I could say was, "Look! Look . . . right here. That's my pa! He's an assemblyman!"

I didn't even wait for him or Hammerhead to say anything. I was so overcome with so many thoughts and feelings that I suddenly had to be alone.

# CHAPTER 53

# WHAT KIND OF MAN DO I
# WANT TO BE?

Still clutching the paper in my hand, I stumbled out the door and toward the stables and barn where all the equipment was.

I wandered inside and sat down on a bale of hay.

Even here, so far from home, suddenly everything I saw and felt—every leather strap, every smell from hay to manure to wood to horseflesh—reminded me of home. In those few moments, all the things that Hawk had been saying to me over the last couple of months about courage and manhood and seeing the hidden things came into my mind—especially what he said about looking inside yourself . . . and about fathers.

In those few minutes, sitting there in that barn on the bale of hay, I saw it all so clearly—what I had done, how closed off I had been to all the love Pa had tried to give me ever since that day since my sisters and brother and I first laid eyes on him in California outside the Gold Nugget Saloon.

Suddenly I was so ashamed of everything I'd said to Pa, ashamed of the way I'd left home.

What a fool I'd been—all wrapped up in nobody but myself, completely blind to how things really were!

I opened up the paper again and looked down there toward the bottom where the article was.

Over and over I read those words . . . *Assemblyman Drummond Hollister*.

All I could think was what a good man that "new legislator"

was, a better man and a better father than any of those people in Sacramento could possibly realize.

Better than I'd realized till right then!

The one thing I knew more than anything else was that I *had* to see him again. I didn't want to wait! I had to see him now.

I had to go home!

I was crying by then. I'd have been embarrassed if Hawk or Hammerhead had walked in and seen me. But I'm not ashamed to tell it now 'cause I know how important and cleansing it was to let the whole past year of pain and frustration and anger and confusion out once and for all like that. It was just like Hawk said about the rain. As unpleasant as crying can be in one way, in another way I felt like I was taking a bath in an icy mountain stream or standing in that desert downpour and looking straight up into the sky. There were tears falling all over that newspaper page, but I couldn't take my eyes off the words.

I was so proud of Pa . . . so proud of the man he was!

I sat there for probably five or ten minutes. In that time, several of the men I had met since leaving home passed through my mind. I saw their faces, heard their voices, remembered conversations with each one. There had been Hammerhead Jackson and Billy Barnes, then Jack Demming and Tranter.

And of course, Hawk.

They were all so different. Yet all except Hawk and maybe the chief, they all had a similar streak too. I thought about the kind of men they were, about the choices and decisions they'd each made that had got them where they were, that had made their lives turn out the way they had. They were all loners, all living only for themselves. Independent in the wrong way, that's what Hawk would say about them.

Did I want to be like any of them?

What kind of man did I want to be? Suddenly I realized it was time I gave some honest attention to that question. How did I want to turn out? What kind of person did I want to become?

Did I want to be like any of those men?

They had all left their pasts, their families, their friends. They had struck out alone and were now living lonely lives with no one to keep them company but themselves. Men like that never seemed to look back.

What set such men apart from men like Pa and Uncle Nick? They'd run away too. They'd gone off on their own. But now they had turned around and were living again with people, with family. They'd chosen to lay aside that independent life where they were thinking of no one but themselves. Now I could see that Pa was living not just for himself, but for other people—for Almeda, for Tad and my sisters, even for the people of Miracle Springs and California. What he did didn't have to do with just him.

Was that the difference between Pa and men like Hammerhead and Billy and Demming and the half-breed—just who you're living for, yourself or other folks? There weren't really any other options. It was either yourself or other people that you put first. Whichever path you chose made a difference like night and day in what kind of character you're going to turn out to have.

When I thought about Pa alongside Demming or Hammerhead Jackson, there was no comparison. Pa had been like them once, I suppose you might say. Now he was a California congressman!

It all depended on what kind of choices a man made.

Now suddenly I saw Pa's character for what it was. It had been in front of me all the time, but I hadn't had eyes to see it. I'd been too busy looking only at myself. Now I saw that a lot of what had bothered me before had to do with small, insignificant things when placed alongside the kind of man he was.

Pa had been making good choices for years—unselfish choices that showed he had the kind of manhood Hawk was always talking about. One of the reasons he'd gotten into trouble in the first place was that he was trying to help Uncle Nick!

As I sat there, I remembered how he'd been willing to sacrifice everything, the mine and all he'd worked for, to save Becky from Buck Krebbs and Grissly Hatch. He was ready to give it all to Royce in an instant, just to save Becky.

Other things came into my mind too.

It had taken me all this time to see that all the things that had built up in my mind to the point where I exploded that day a little over a year before—I saw how small they all were alongside the kind of man Pa was and what kind of man he'd been trying to train me to be.

And then I thought about Hawk.

Hawk was completely different than all the other men I'd met out here.

He was a loner too, I reckon you'd say, but in a whole different way. He wasn't selfish like the others, not independent in the same way. He thought about his past, though he'd lost his chance to go back and make things right with the people he now realized he loved. Even Hawk, in a sense, was living in his own world, by himself.

He'd been like a second father to me during this year. But did I even want to spend the rest of my life like Hawk, as much as I admired and loved him?

What kind of choices did I have to make now to determine what kind of man I was going to become and determine the way the rest of my life went?

I looked down at the paper again. The words were still there: *Drummond Hollister*.

I just wanted the whole world to know that he was *my* pa!

And I had to tell him! I had to tell him how much I loved him! It was too late to go back and undo what I'd done and said, but it was not to late to go back and patch it up with Pa!

I remembered Rev. Rutledge saying that asking for forgiveness always clears the air. Hawk had said the same thing, more or less. So it was suddenly clear what I had to do next.

I don't know how much longer I sat there, not too long, but long enough to get myself looking halfway normal again. Finally I went outside, doused my face with some water from the horse's trough, then went back inside the station house.

# CHAPTER 54

## GOODBYE TO A FRIEND

"You got a horse I can buy for this $25?" I asked Hammer-head. "I could give you this money up front and send the rest later."

"What you want with a horse?"

"Gotta get home," I answered.

Hawk moved closer.

"You figure it's time, son?" he asked softly, with deep feeling in his voice.

"Yeah. I think I finally figured out what you been trying to get me to see all this time."

"About your pa?"

I nodded. "And about some things inside *me*," I said.

"Your eyes are seeing what's inside, huh?"

"Yep. You're the best teacher a fella could have, Hawk."

"Anybody can teach. It takes someone special to be a learner. Growing doesn't come from teaching, son. Growing comes from learning. Only someone that *wants* to see can learn the best kinds of things. I knew you *wanted* to see—that's why I kept pointing, and kept asking you questions. You're a learner, Zack. That's why you're growing."

I took in a deep breath. As anxious as I was to see my family again, it sure wasn't going to be easy to leave this man!

"So," I said, turning again to Hammerhead, "you got a horse a fella could buy?"

"I still got your own horse," he answered.

"Gray Thunder!" I exclaimed. "You kept him all this time?"

"I had a feeling maybe I hadn't seen the last of you," he answered with just a hint of a grin.

"Where is he?"

"Well, that's the part you ain't gonna like. He's still back at Flat Bluff."

"That's fifty miles east."

"Yep. It'd set you back a couple of days to go fetch him. But he's in good shape. Rode him around myself to give him some exercise, but I ain't let nobody ride him out on the line."

"I appreciate it. But I don't have the two days it'd take to go get him."

"You been out in the desert around eight months, and you're worrying about two more days!"

I glanced over at Hawk briefly, then turned back to the stationman.

"When the time comes for a boy to see if he's got the courage to be a man," I said, "you can't delay it. You gotta go up and face what's in front of you squarely. My time's come. So . . . you got a horse I can buy?"

"I reckon, seeing as how it's you, and considering what you been through, I don't figure Russell, Majors, and Waddell ought to mind too much. Yeah, Hollister, I'll sell you a horse."

I turned toward Hawk.

"Hawk," I said, "I'd like you to have my horse. Gray Thunder's his name. He's the best horse I ever had. I want to leave you something that's really part of me."

Hawk nodded. He understood.

"I'll take good care of him, Grayfox," he said softly.

I gave the money Hammerhead had given me back to him. Then he took me outside and we picked out a horse that he figured would get me back to California. It took the best part of an hour to get it saddled and for Hammerhead to get me fixed up with grub and water . . . and for me to say my goodbyes.

That last part was hardest of all.

How could I say goodbye to someone like Hawk, who'd changed my way of looking at everything and my whole way of thinking—how could I say goodbye, knowing I might not see him again?

Especially so sudden-like.

I hadn't had the chance to prepare for it, and all of a sudden there we were standing face-to-face, me ready to jump up on the horse Hammerhead was holding and ride away west, and him ready to go back up in the hills . . . alone.

Maybe it was best that way. How do you prepare for a moment like that, anyway?

I stuck out my hand.

Hawk took it and grasped it firmly. He didn't shake it, he just held it firmly and strongly while his eyes looked straight into mine.

We held each other's gaze for a long time. There weren't any words to say. I knew now more than ever why the Paiutes had called him Hawk. His eyes were piercing straight into mine, and I knew he knew everything without me having to say a word.

His eyes were looking *inside*, just like he always taught me to do. Maybe I was learning, because I think I saw deeper into *him*, too, than I ever had before.

His eyes got bright and grew thick with tears, just like the tears that were swimming around in my eyes. I reckon what I saw in that moment, as much as it humbles me to say it, was that Hawk loved me and was gonna miss me as much as I would miss him.

"Well, Grayfox," he finally said, in a husky voice, "looks to me like you're about to finish earning your name."

I nodded and blinked a few times. If I tried to say anything, I knew I'd break out crying again. And though I knew Hawk wouldn't think less of me for it, it just didn't seem like the right time.

"Do what you got to do, and then you'll be a man, Zack Hollister," he said. "I'm right proud of you."

"Thanks, Hawk," I said, finally choking the words out. "Thanks for everything."

"God go with you, son."

He shook my hand, then let it go.

For another second our eyes held their final embrace. Then I turned and mounted the horse.

"Miracle Springs," I said down to him. "You can always get in touch with me there . . . or find me, if you get a hankering to see California."

Hawk laughed. "I just may take you up on that, Grayfox," he said.

I took the reins in my hands, spun around, dug in my heels, and galloped away. I glanced back for one final wave, then turned again and didn't look back until I was out of sight over the next ridge heading west.

I couldn't have seen him then if I had. My eyes were full of tears again, and I just clung tight with my knees and hoped the horse knew the way well enough to stay on the trail.

# CHAPTER 55

# THE RIDE BACK

The ride back across the desert of the Great Basin was miserably hot and dry, and after the first day or two, I found my pace slowing. 'Course I'd have killed the horse if I hadn't. But also, once my sights were set on home, I became less anxious about hurrying.

There were a lot of things I needed to think about first.

Most of the time I was hardly aware of the country I was riding through. It was hardly boring anymore, now that I knew its secrets, but my mind was so full of different kinds of thoughts that I didn't notice much. It seemed like everything Hawk had told me over the past year made sense in a whole new light. The inner eyes he was always talking about had opened and suddenly a lot of things came clear.

That was another thing he said—that once you make up your mind to *do* something and then follow through and do it, your understanding would follow, but you can't *understand* until you *do*. Now I remembered him saying that, and I was seeing it happen right inside my own brain. The second I set my sights on home, everything started to make sense.

I thought about how Hawk had drawn out Jack Demming that night around the campfire, got him to talking about his father. I saw it all so clearly now, how he wanted me to see that *everyone* has things they can hold against their folks, if that's what they're determined to do. Everybody's got the choice whether to turn grudges into hate, like Demming had, or to turn them the other

271

way, into forgiveness and strength of character . . . like Hawk had.

One of the things I saw had to do with Hawk himself. I saw that a lesser man would probably have tried to get me to stay with him. It was obvious he enjoyed having me there with him. He'd said so more than once. He could have tried to make me even more dissatisfied with home and tried to talk me out of going back and kept me to himself.

But instead of taking advantage of my problems with Pa, Hawk tried to help me work them out. He never tried to make himself look good in my eyes, but he always tried to make me look at Pa and myself more honestly.

I saw what a sacrificing thing Hawk had done, even when it meant him having to be alone again, by forcing me to face up to my situation and then sending me—almost forcing me in one way of looking at it—to go back home and make it right. When we said goodbye, he didn't even say he'd miss me. He didn't want to do anything to make it harder for me to leave.

One night as I lay down on the hard desert ground by myself, and then as I drifted off to sleep beside the fire I'd made, I dreamed about Hawk. I saw his face smiling at me, almost like he was looking down on me as I lay there.

Remembering it the next day, I realized that Hawk really was one of the best friends I'd ever had *because* of how he made me look at myself and then, when he figured the time was right, pushed me back toward home. He was a real friend because he cared more about me than himself.

I realized a lot of things about Pa too. And probably the strongest realization was the simplest of all—that *I was the son of Drummond Hollister*, and that in a bunch of ways I was who I was because of *him*.

I'd been so quick to criticize him and to think he'd done me wrong in a lot of ways. But I now saw that much of what I valued about myself had come straight from him. I was more like him than I'd ever realized. He'd taught me more than I'd ever been aware.

I'd been so quick to credit Hawk for teaching me so many

things—and he had. Yet for years Pa had been quietly building into me too. I'd just been so confused by the brokenness of his mirror that I hadn't let myself see how many good ways he shaped my life and who I was.

For instance, I'd saved Hawk's life—and probably my own too—because I knew how to handle a rifle. When I shot the pistol out of Demming's hand, that was Pa's training coming through. He gave me my first rifle and taught me how to use it.

Here's another thing—I'd gone off to try to find Laughing Waters even after I was safely away from the Paiute camp. I didn't have to do that. I could have just tried to save my own skin instead of risking my life for an Indian girl I'd never seen. And *why* had I gone riding into danger without even thinking twice about it? I'd seen Pa make sacrifices for the rest of us dozens of times without ever thinking about it. Now I saw that by watching him, some of that same quality had got into me . . . without me even knowing it.

Then I thought about Pa leaving Ma and us kids so many years before, when we still lived in New York. That was something I reckon I was angry with him about all this time. But now I began to realize that maybe Pa had done it *in order to keep the danger away from us*.

If he'd been around men like Buck Krebbs and Jack Demming, it made sense that he'd been trying to protect us from harm by getting as far away as he could. They both tried to follow his trail—and maybe he knew they would. Maybe he knew we would never be safe with him. So he left, as hard as it must've been . . . *for our good*.

It was just exactly what I did to lure Demming away from Laughing Waters—getting him to follow me so the danger wouldn't be so close to her. And all that time, without knowing it, I was following the example of just what Pa had done!

In so many ways, I was just like Pa!

Hawk taught me how to look for things in the desert, how to see what the birds and weather and terrain out there were saying, how to find water. But it was Pa that helped shape me into the person I was. It was Pa who made me the kind of person that *wanted* to look and see and always find more.

Suddenly talk after talk with Pa came back to me, times we'd be together in the mine, and he'd be teaching me things just like Hawk.

"You see there, Zack," I remembered him saying, "you see where that line of quartz runs out?"

He pointed with his finger down along the wall of the mine, and I followed with my eyes.

"That tells me there's likely more quartz back there behind this wall someplace. Usually when it runs out so sudden like that, it pops back up again. Only trick is knowing where it's gonna do it!"

Then Pa's laugh came back to me, as I remembered him and me leaving the mine that day, his arm slung over my shoulder as we talked back and forth all the way down to the house.

I heard him laughing more and more these days in my memory, and it made me sad to think I'd forgotten how much fun we used to have together. He *had* been a fun pa to be with, to work with, to sweat with . . . until I'd let myself believe the lies and let the anger and independence get hold of me.

I regretted all that now.

Then I remembered something else Pa'd told me, not only that day but lots of times.

*"What you gotta realize, son,"* he said, *"is that there's always more gold back inside this hill. We can't see it . . . but it's there. The trick is learning to see what most folks can't—learning to see into the middle of the mountain . . . learning to sense where the vein is, even though your eyes can't see it."*

I couldn't believe it! Pa had been teaching me to look *inside* things long before I'd ever met Hawk!

And then I started to realize one more thing about Pa and about how much like him I was. I'd been angry with Pa all this time for leaving his family to go off alone. But what about me? What had I done but *that very thing*? I'd run off too . . . and I didn't have any reason for it other than feeling sorry for myself!

And Pa had eventually taken responsibility back on his shoulders. He faced up to his past mistakes and had admitted everything to Sheriff Rafferty. He was even willing to face going to jail if it came to that. He didn't try to run away from his past and hide from what he'd done. He'd owned up to it all . . . like a man.

He'd shown that greater and deeper kind of bravery, just as Hawk talked about—the willingness to face what was inside himself.

Pa *had* that kind of courage!

Did I have as much courage as my own pa? Like Hawk had forced me to ask: Did I have the guts to take responsibility for what I had done and be fully the man I now saw Pa was?

I was riding west toward California, on my way to find out the answer to that question.

# CHAPTER 56

## HOME AGAIN

It was a hot, muggy day toward the end of August 1861, when I rode back into Miracle Springs, California.

There wasn't a breath of wind.

My poor horse was tuckered out, both from the heat and the days of riding. And as anxious as I had been to get home, I was tuckered out too—plus a mite jittery inside. So I was content to sit on his back and ride along slowly.

I rode through town with my hat pulled down over my eyes. I didn't want to see anyone I knew. There were too many thoughts and emotions going through me in too many directions. I only glanced about now and then from under the brim of my hat just in case Pa might be in town. I looked in at the Mine and Freight, but didn't see Pa or Corrie or Almeda anywhere around.

Then I headed out of town and up toward the house and our claim.

I was nervous by then!

What would Pa say? He'd have every right to give me a real tongue-lashing for what I'd done. He'd even have the right to deck me with his fist for what I said to Almeda. If he did, I wouldn't argue.

No matter what Pa did, it was still going to be hard to face him again. I knew that's exactly what I had to do. I'd done wrong, and it was time to own up to it. But that didn't mean it was going to be easy.

The closer I got to home, without even thinking about it, I

must've let the horse move slower and slower. By the time I rounded the last bend and saw the house again, his hooves were clomping down that dusty road in a slow cadence that seemed as sleepy as the hot afternoon.

The first thing I saw was Corrie, standing on the porch with her hand over her eyes, shielding them from the sun. She was looking in my direction, but then I saw her turn and look up toward the mine.

There was Pa, walking slowly down toward the house!

I heard a voice call out something inside. But I wasn't paying attention to the house anymore. My eyes were fixed on Pa.

And now he'd seen me . . . he was running toward me!

More noises came from the house . . . shouts . . . people were running outside! People were calling out my name!

I reined my horse to a stop and slipped out of the saddle. I tried to walk forward, but I'd only taken a step or two when Pa reached me. He threw his big arms around me and squeezed me tight, holding me to his damp, sweaty chest.

I stretched my arms around his waist and closed my eyes.

I couldn't believe it—Pa was weeping.

So was I.

# CHAPTER 57

# WHOLE AGAIN

Pa and I stood there silently holding each other for a long minute.

When we finally let go and stepped back, Pa looked into my face, and then said, "Welcome home, son!"

It was like a spell was suddenly broke.

All at once everyone else rushed forward and swarmed around me with hugs and kisses and a thousand questions, laughing and talking and grabbing at me. I couldn't say a thing! At first I forgot that they must have all thought I was dead.

"Nice beard, Zack!" said Tad.

"You little runt," I said back, giving him a friendly little shove with my hand, "you went and grew up while I was gone!"

I was turning all around, trying to take everybody in.

The next person my eyes lit on was Becky.

"And you, Becky!" I hollered. "When did you get to be such a beautiful, grown-up woman!"

Then I spotted Corrie.

At first I couldn't find any words to say to her. Corrie and me were the oldest of the five, and I think the older we got the more special she was to me. She was just about the best sister a fellow could ever have, and in those first seconds, seeing her again, I realized how much I loved her.

Finally all I could do was give her a long hug.

I could tell she was trying to say something, but it took a while for her to get the words out of her throat.

"Oh, Zack," she finally said. "I . . . I was afraid . . . I'm just so glad to see you!"

Then I hugged my stepma. "Almeda," I said.

"Oh, Zack . . . we love you so much!" she said, still crying. I didn't hardly have any breath left in me after she got done hugging me!

All this time Pa had been standing back, wiping his eyes. Now he stepped toward me again. I wondered what he was going to say, if he was going to mention anything about the day I left so angrily. The nervousness I felt riding home came back. But Pa wasn't thinking anything about that awful day—at least not right then.

"How about a handshake of welcome, Zack?" was all he said. "A handshake between men . . . *man to man!*"

Pa stuck out his hand toward me.

I couldn't reply. I knew if I tried to say anything, I would lose my voice altogether.

I reached out and took his hand.

It was just like the final handshake with Hawk. We just stood there grasping each other firmly, gazing deep into each other's eyes. There wasn't nothing neither of us needed to say.

I think at that moment both Pa and me knew well enough what the other was saying *inside*. The look we gave each other meant that everything was forgiven—on both sides.

This time it was Becky who spoke up first.

"Why did you grow the beard, Zack?" she asked.

"It's a long story," I answered as I released Pa's hand.

"Where you been?" asked Tad.

"Another long story!" I laughed.

"What's that hanging from your saddle, Zack?" asked Tad.

I turned around and looked.

"That's a quiver . . . for arrows."

"Why's it empty?"

"That one's real long," I said, only this time I didn't laugh when I said it.

"How did you get—" asked Corrie, then she interrupted herself. "Wait, I know—it's a long story, right?"

I nodded. "Right," I said, "but the *why* of it isn't so long."

I paused and thought for a minute. It was another one of those times when everything you've been through runs past your mind in a few seconds.

"Are you going to tell us the *why*, then?" Corrie prompted.

"I'll tell you everything," I answered, "when the time is right."

"Give the man a chance to get the dust off his feet, Corrie," said Pa.

Probably none of the others noticed. But my heart practically leapt out of my chest. It suddenly dawned on me that Pa was calling me a man. I don't know that he ever had before, or if he had maybe and I hadn't noticed. But it sure sounded good. Maybe for the first time in my life, I was ready to believe it!

"Come on, Zack, son," Pa went on, "let's get that horse of yours put up. Then what do you say me and you go up and give a *howdy* to your uncle . . . and Alkali up at the mine!"

"Sure, Pa," I said. "Yeah, I'd like to see them too!"

We turned and headed toward the barn. I reckon by now I was an inch or two taller than Pa. But that didn't matter. Pa threw his arm up around my shoulder as we walked. With the leather reins in my free hand I pulled the horse along behind us as we walked.

When we were about halfway to the barn, Pa stopped and turned back around.

"Almeda!" he called back. "You start figuring on how to fix up the best vittles we ever had! Corrie, you make up a heap of those biscuits of yours. We'll invite the Reverend and his wife, and Nick and Katie—I know they'll all be anxious to see Zack. We'll have us a great time!"

He turned back, and he and I continued on to the barn.

"It's mighty good to have you home, Zack," said Pa softly.

"It's good to be home, Pa."

# CHAPTER 58

## WORDS BETWEEN MEN

We got the horse put up, then puttered around in the barn a while, making small talk.

Finally we both wound up standing side by side, leaning against the rails of one of the stalls, looking inside at the horse that brought me all this way back from the desert.

It was quiet for a long time.

"Pa," I said finally. "I want you to know how sorry I am."

"Don't think nothing of it, Zack."

"I had no right to say the things I did. I'm sorry, and I apologize. I hope you'll forgive me, Pa."

"I appreciate it, son. 'Course I forgive you. You got my apologies too. Some of what you said was right—I ain't been the best pa to you. So I need you to forgive me too."

Everything Hawk said about broken mirrors flooded through me.

"You're my pa, anyhow," I said. "So I don't reckon you gotta do it all perfect. Nobody can do that. I'm just grateful to God that I got to be your son."

"Thank you, Zack," said Pa. "Those words mean more to me than you can ever know."

We stared straight ahead for several more minutes, not saying any more. I knew both of us had tears in our eyes. And then I told him just briefly about the accident and how I'd managed to stay alive.

"I hope you can meet Hawk someday, Pa," I said.

"I'd be honored to," said Pa. "Can't think of anything I'd rather do than shake the man's hand and tell him thank you for taking such good care of my son."

"You and he'd like each other, Pa."

"I like him already, son."

Again it was quiet a minute.

"Well, let's go see Nick," said Pa at length, slapping his arm around me again.

We left the barn and walked up the creek. On the way, he told me everything he'd been doing at the mine.

We spent the whole rest of the day together, him telling me about the mine and Sacramento, me telling him about Hawk and Nevada. We both got a lot of things said that we ought to have said years before. Most of all, when the day was over, we'd both apologized for a dozen more misunderstandings, and I don't think either of us had any more doubts that we loved each other. It was sure a day I'll never forget as long as I live.

By the time evening came, it felt almost like I'd never been gone.

# CHAPTER 59

## FAMILY REUNION

Dinner that night was something special!

Pa treated me like a guest of honor. I had a hard time not thinking that I didn't deserve it. But everybody was so happy about me being home that I couldn't keep them from making over me. It was embarrassing, but it felt good too.

Everybody was there, like Pa had told Almeda and Corrie. There was food and laughing and singing and more of Alkali Jones's tall tales than any of us could have swallowed in two weeks.

I was having a great time. But I'd catch myself every once in a while remembering something Hawk had said or something that had happened, and it would make me thoughtful for a few seconds right in the midst of all the celebration.

Everybody kept coaxing me to tell everything that had happened since they'd last heard from me. I wasn't especially anxious to relive the bitterness of what I'd been feeling when I left home, as wrong as I now saw it had been. But then when Pa and Corrie told how they'd come looking for me and what a narrow escape they'd had with the Paiutes themselves,* well, that perked me up enough to start up my story right from there without having to dwell on the past.

So I told them about my first months riding for the Express and then what had happened the day when I suddenly found myself face-to-face with the band of unfriendly Paiutes. Everybody laughed so hard they cried when I told them about how I'd

*See *Sea to Shining Sea*, JOURNALS OF CORRIE BELLE HOLLISTER, Book 5.

285

remembered Rev. Rutledge's sermon. Alkali Jones's *hee, hee, hee!* was nearly one continuous cackle!

"I even tried what you said you couldn't do, Reverend," I said. "I stopped laughing long enough to close my eyes and count to ten. I thought that just maybe they *would* go away, that it was just a bad dream. But when I opened my eyes again, they were still there. And I still had to do what you said in your sermon— either go through them or around them. But I gotta tell you, Rev. Rutledge, I found myself wishing I'd paid better attention that day at church, because I thought maybe you *had* said something else that I just couldn't remember!"

"No, that was it, Zack, my boy," said Rev. Rutledge, wiping his eyes. "Through them or around them, that's all I said." He was still chuckling as he spoke.

Then I continued on, telling them about the accident, then about waking up in one of Hawk's caves, then about Hawk himself.

I told them a lot of what had happened during the months— things I'd learned, how I'd grown up. Tad was most interested of all in the caves. He always had liked those places, even after our own mine had fallen in on him.

"How many caves does Hawk have?" he asked in astonishment.

"I don't know, Tad," I said. "I don't suppose I ever stopped to count. Eight or ten maybe. We'd store different things in different places, use them at different times—that is, if a bear wasn't occupying one."

"Zack!" exclaimed Almeda.

"It only happened once," I said, laughing.

"What did you do, shoot it?" asked Rev. Rutledge's wife.

"No, Hawk doesn't like to kill unless he has to, unless it's life or death. No, that time we took sort of a backwards approach to your husband's advice. We stood out of the way and let the problem go down the hill past us!"

"Sounds like you owe the man your life, Zack," said Pa.

"I owe Hawk more than my life."

"How do you mean?" asked Rev. Rutledge.

"He taught me how to live, how to survive, how to see things most people never have a chance to see, and never would see if it was stuck right in front of their noses."

I told them the way Hawk would teach me to see. But it was just stirring up too many other emotions to say anything about Demming and the Paiute trouble and Laughing Waters. So I didn't bring that up.

The house fell real quiet after I was all through.

"A remarkable-sounding man, your Hawk," said Almeda.

"Best friend I ever had," I admitted.

And again it was silent.

"Actually, I reckon that ain't quite true," I said. "He's the one who helped me see I had an even better friend than him and had for a long time."

"Who, Zack?" asked Becky.

I didn't answer her directly, but kept talking about Hawk.

"Once he began to find out about my background, and I began to tell him about all of you and about Miracle Springs—what my life had been before he picked me off the mountainside—he started trying to make me use my extra set of eyes to see inside myself. He helped me see a lot of things I never saw before, things about all of us, this family of ours, and . . ."

I hesitated.

I'd been speaking real soft, and suddenly I was afraid I was about to start crying. It wasn't easy saying these things with so many people listening. It would have been a lot easier *not* to say any of it. But I reckon this was the moment Hawk had told me about, when you found out whether or not you had the courage of true manhood.

I took in a deep breath and continued on.

"Mostly he helped me to see," I said, "a lot of things I'd never seen or understood about me and Pa. Once Hawk realized how it had been when I left, he asked lots of questions. He probably knows you about as good as any man alive, Pa, even though the two of you have never met. He told me some things about myself that weren't too pleasant to hear, even though I knew they were true. He's a straightforward, honest man, and I knew I could trust him. So I had no choice but to believe him. I had to look at myself, at some of the foolish things I'd done, like running off half-cocked and blaming things on Pa that I had no right to blame on anyone."

Again I stopped and took in a deep breath.

This wasn't easy! No wonder men didn't usually dig around down inside and let folks see what was inside them. Hawk was right. This *did* take more guts than facing someone trying to shoot you!

"He made me look down inside myself," I went on, "just like he'd all along been making me look at things in nature. He made me look at my anger. He told me that I'd never be a man until I learned what anger was supposed to be for. He said I'd never be a man until I learned to swallow my pride and come back and say I was sorry. 'Only takes half a man to be able to live out in nature all by yourself, Zack,' Hawk told me just before I left. 'So now,' he said, 'it's time you learned to be a whole man. It's time to take the half you learned out here and put it to use being the other half.

" 'Don't make the mistake I did of never going back. I learned a lot of things. I know how to live in the wilds. But in a way I'm still only half a man. It's too late for me now. I drifted too long and too far. Now my own people are gone. But it's not too late for you, young Grayfox.' "

"*Grayfox* . . . who did he mean? Was that you, Zack?" asked Tad.

I smiled.

"Yeah, Tad, it was me."

"Why'd he call you that?"

"For a while, that was my name up there."

"It sounds like an Indian name, Zack," said Almeda.

I smiled again.

"Yep," I said, slowly nodding my head. "That it was. Given to me by the Paiutes."

"Why? What does the name mean?"

The long silence that followed was all full of memories for me. How could I possibly tell them all that had happened with Demming and the Paiutes and Laughing Waters and being given my new name? That would take another whole evening. It was all I could do to tell Hawk's part of it!

Besides, whenever I thought of Laughing Waters, which I did every day, I felt strangely quiet inside. I didn't know if that was part of the story I *wanted* to tell just yet . . . or keep to myself.

At last I sighed deeply.

"It's part of the long story about the quiver," I said. "Maybe even longer than this one."

"Please tell us, Zack," implored both Tad and Becky at once.

"Someday I'll tell you all about it," I answered with a smile.

"Why not tonight?"

"I can't tell you now."

"Why?"

"I'm not sure it's finished yet . . . and I gotta get to the end *myself* before I can tell you about it."

# CHAPTER 60

## PA'S EYES TO SEE

The next morning I was up early.

Pa came upon me outside where I was standing with a wash-basin beside the creek and holding up a mirror to my face with one hand—a broken one at that!

"What in tarnation you doing?" he exclaimed.

"Shaving off my beard, Pa," I said.

"What in thunder for?"

"I figured if I'm going to come back to civilization, I ought to look civilized. Besides, I figured you'd want it off."

"Well, you figured wrong. I like it!"

"You do?"

"Sure I do. Makes you look like me when I was your age."

"You want me to keep it?"

"Well, it's up to you, son. But I sure think a man's beard looks good on you."

"Okay, Pa," I said with a smile. "I'll keep it."

Pa turned and walked a few steps away, then stopped and glanced back around at me. His eyes had a twinkle in them. If I didn't know better I'd think *he* was the fox.

"Hey, Grayfox," he said, "who's the young lady you didn't tell us about last night?"

"What?" I exclaimed

"You heard me plain enough."

"How'd you know?" Right then I was mighty glad for that beard! I could feel red crawling all over my cheeks.

"What do you think, son, that I don't know that look in a young man's eyes? I been in love a coupla times myself, you know. So . . . what's her name?"

Pa had eyes to see too!

"Laughing Waters," I admitted sheepishly, staring down at the ground.

"Indian?"

"Yeah . . . the Paiute chief's daughter."

"I can't believe it!" exclaimed Pa. "My son smitten over an Indian princess. She pretty?"

I didn't answer immediately. I had to stop to think, even though Laughing Waters' face was hardly ever out of my mind.

"I . . . I don't know, Pa," I said. "Her eyes are as pretty as I've ever seen. But I don't know if she's what other folks would call pretty."

"You gonna see her again?"

"I plan to, Pa . . . I sure plan to."

He grinned at me, and then we turned and walked back toward the house.

# A PERSONAL WORD FROM THE AUTHOR

It is considered somewhat unusual for a writer, especially a novelist, to intrude himself personally into his work. But this is a very personal book for me. Therefore, I hope you will forgive a few intimate words from an author to his readers.

This is not a book only about growing into manhood. I hope many girls, young women, and grown women have enjoyed it, too. For this is a story for boys *and* girls, women *and* men. It is about discovering *personhood*, discovering who we are. *All* of us— male and female—have to discover our unique identity and personhood within the context of our own masculinity or femininity.

Zack, and the men who read his words, have to discover what being a *man* means in their lives. We men are notoriously noncommunicative, and we have an extremely difficult time becoming comfortable with the inner worlds of thoughts and emotions— especially within ourselves, as Zack discovered. We tend to make what we call *independence* an idol, thinking there is no greater goal in life. How wrong we are!

So we men have much to learn about the nature of the true manhood God intended for us.

Women, likewise, have different points where *inner eyesight* will help them see the pockets of independence within them. Corrie and the women who read her words have to discover what being a complete *woman* means in their lives.

The principles of personhood, however, are universal. What

Corrie has learned about herself in the other books of this series applies equally to men and women. So does what Zack has learned about himself.

There is one aspect about the discovering of personhood which is uniquely masculine.

God is our *Father*.

All of us must, therefore, at some time in our lives, come to terms with that Fatherhood in order to be whole and integrated sons and daughters of God. As we strive to do that, however, our own earthly fathers stand directly in the middle of the path.

That's why Zack's story and his struggle are so important and so universal. Men *and* women must all experience something of that same struggle, for earthly fatherhood is indeed a "broken mirror" in its reflection of heavenly Fatherhood.

The whole range of human family relationships—fathers and sons, fathers and daughters, mothers and daughters, mothers and sons—come into and are contained within the all-encompassing Fatherhood of God. Wholeness in *all* such relationships is the destination we journey toward on the road that also leads to fruitful, contented, integrated personhood in one's relationship with our heavenly Father.

Zack's story, I hope you see, is but one small window into a much larger story—a story in which each one of us, you and me, are the main characters, the real-life adventure of learning to see and hear what God has to tell us about himself.

The mirrors of example we all look to are broken. Never forget that. But just the fact that mothers and fathers exist means that God's Fatherhood cannot help but be built into the relationships they have with their sons and daughters—if only we allow God to develop our inner eyesight to see it, whichever side of those relational fences we may be standing on.

If you are interested in reading more that I have written along these lines, may I suggest two novels, *Robbie Taggart, Highland Sailor* and *The Eleventh Hour*. Both are listed along with my other books at the back of this book.

I hope and pray you enjoyed the story of Zack "Grayfox" Hollister and that you will continue reading in the JOURNALS OF CORRIE BELLE HOLLISTER series. If you know a young man or woman whom you feel would benefit from Zack's story, but who is unable to afford it, please write us. We will do what we can to see that he or she obtains a copy.

God bless you!
Michael Phillips
1707 E Street
Eureka, CA 95501

# ABOUT THE AUTHOR

 Bestselling author, bookseller, historian, and publisher Michael Phillips has produced more than sixty books on a wide range of topics. Known chiefly for his historical fiction, Phillips is also the redactor primarily responsible, through his edited editions of MacDonald's books, for the current worldwide resurgence of interest in the nineteenth-century Scottish novelist George MacDonald.

In his own right, Phillips has written more than twenty books and co-written (with Judith Pella) another dozen. Fifteen of his books have been nominated for Gold Medallion awards and a dozen have appeared on bestseller lists, and nearly all have appeared as book club selections and been translated into several foreign languages.

For a complete list of Michael Phillips titles available, please contact your favorite Christian bookstore, or write to Bethany House Publishers.

If you liked *Grayfox*, you may also enjoy these other books and series by Michael Phillips

THE JOURNALS OF CORRIE BELLE HOLLISTER (Bethany House Publishers)

These companion volumes to Zack's story are told in the voice of his sister, Corrie Hollister. They trace the Hollister family's story from the time of their arrival by wagon train in California in 1852. If you enjoyed *Grayfox*, you will not want to miss any of these titles:

*My Father's World* (with Judith Pella)
*Daughter of Grace* (with Judith Pella)
*On the Trail of the Truth*
*A Place in the Sun*
*Sea to Shining Sea*
*Into the Long Dark Night*
*Land of the Brave and the Free*
*A Home for the Heart* (Available June, 1994)


*Good Things to Remember:*
*333 Wise Maxims You Don't Want to Forget*

The practical wisdom and spiritual perspectives that Michael Phillips' readers have come to associate with his uniquely insightful fiction are available now in this thought-provoking collection of maxims and quotable quotes from Phillips and other sources. Get to know Michael Phillips, the man behind the bestselling books!

TALES FROM SCOTLAND AND RUSSIA (Bethany House Publishers)

Adventuresome, dramatic, and mysterious stories from the romantic worlds of nineteenth-century Scotland and Russia. Coauthored with Judith Pella, these books are packed with abiding spiritual truths and memorable relationships. If you haven't yet discovered the worlds of adventure and intrigue opened up by these series, a wonderful treat awaits you!

Scotland:
> *Heather Hills of Stonewycke*
> *Flight From Stonewycke*
> *The Lady of Stonewycke*
> *Stranger at Stonewycke*
> *Shadows Over Stonewycke*
> *Treasure of Stonewycke*
>
> *Jamie MacLeod, Highland Lass*
> *Robbie Taggart, Highland Sailor*

Russia:
> *The Crown and the Crucible*
> *A House Divided*
> *Travail and Triumph*

THE SECRET OF THE ROSE (Tyndale House Publishers)

This is the newest series from the pen of Michael Phillips, set in Germany before World War II—a page-turner with spiritual content and rich relationships you won't soon forget!

> *The Eleventh Hour*
> *A Rose Remembered* (1994)

THE WORKS OF GEORGE MACDONALD (Bethany House Publishers—selected, compiled, and edited by Michael Phillips)

Twenty-eight books in all, both fiction *and* nonfiction, that will delight and edify both adult and young readers. Please consult your bookstore or write for a full list of availability. Especially recommended titles include:

Fiction by George MacDonald Edited for Today's Reader:
*The Fisherman's Lady*
*The Baronet's Song*
*The Curate's Awakening*
*The Highlander's Last Song*
*The Laird's Inheritance*

Nonfiction from the Writings of George MacDonald:
*Discovering the Character of God*
*Knowing the Heart of God*
*George MacDonald, Scotland's Beloved Storyteller*
(a biography of MacDonald by Michael Phillips)